What Happens in Piccadilly

Piccadilly

The Hellion Club, Book Three

by Chasity Bowlin

DRAGONBLADE PUBLISHING, INC.

Dragonblade Publishing, Inc. is an imprint of Kathryn Le Veque Novels, Inc.
P.O. Box 7968
La Verne CA 91750
ceo@dragonbladepublishing.com

Produced in the United States of America

First Edition May 2020
Print Edition

ARE YOU SIGNED UP FOR DRAGONBLADE'S BLOG?

You'll get the latest news and information on exclusive giveaways, exclusive excerpts, coming releases, sales, free books, cover reveals and more.

Check out our complete list of authors, too!

No spam, no junk. That's a promise!

Sign Up Here

www.dragonbladepublishing.com

Dearest Reader;

Thank you for your support of a small press. At Dragonblade Publishing, we strive to bring you the highest quality Historical Romance from the some of the best authors in the business. Without your support, there is no 'us', so we sincerely hope you adore these stories and find some new favorite authors along the way.

Happy Reading!

CEO, Dragonblade Publishing

Additional Dragonblade books by Author Chasity Bowlin

Prologue

NUMBER 114 PICCADILLY was in a state of uproar. Servants ran to and fro, frantically shouting at one another while managing to get no work done at all. A child sat in the corridor and wept. Another sat dejectedly on the front steps and yet one more appeared to be hanging precariously from an upper floor window. Calliope St. James eyed the chaos before her for just a moment and battled the overwhelming desire to flee from whence she'd come. But the sad-faced little boy on the steps looked up at her then, and all thoughts of running were eradicated. He had the face of an angel. A fallen one, to be sure, but a dirty-faced angel nonetheless.

"There appears to be a bit of a commotion occurring. Would you like to tell me what happened?" she asked as she stopped in front of him.

"Who are you?" the boy asked.

"I was sent here by my employer to interview for the position of governess. I'm fairly certain I won't do that now, but I can't help but be curious as to what," she waved a hand about, encompassing the child who now leaned even further out the window, "this is all about."

"I don't really want to talk about it," the little boy said. "We'll all be punished."

"Likely. I'll tell you what... I'll walk inside with you, and then you'll get your sister in from that window, and I think you have another sister somewhere in the madhouse beyond... the three of you will meet me in the drawing room and I will tell you all a story and we'll try to stay out of the way while all this resolves," Calliope offered. Looking up once more at the child whom a stiff breeze would knock to the ground from above, she tried to suppress a shiver of fear.

"You won't punish us?"

"Why would I do that?" Calliope asked.

"Well, you're a governess... that's what they do," the boy said.

"Oh, well, some governesses. Not me. And I'm not your governess, not yet, and likely not ever. But I've come all this way and it seems a bit of a waste not to even meet you all," she said, as if the conversation and the situation were perfectly normal. The whole while, she was watching the little girl dangling above, preparing to throw herself bodily beneath the child should she actually fall.

He looked at her skeptically. "You promise?"

Calliope made an "X" over her heart with the tip of one finger. "Cross my heart. Now, run along inside, get your sisters... get the one off the window ledge first, though. I think perhaps that warrants a bit of urgency, don't you?"

The little boy looked up, saw his sister and uttered a curse that stunned them both. He looked back at her. "Sorry."

"I'm not your governess," she said, and lifted her hands while shrugging elegantly. "Go get your sister and I'll have the butler show me to the drawing room."

"He won't... no butler here no more. He run off with the last governess," the boy said. "That's why the whole house is arse over tits."

Calliope's mouth formed a slight "O" of surprise. "You really shouldn't say those words to ladies," she said softly.

"Arse or tits?" he asked.

"Either," she replied evenly, softening the admonishment with a smile. "But under the circumstances, I can see where it's an apt description. Run along, and I'll let myself into the drawing room."

The little boy nodded. "I like you. I hope you are our new governess. You're not all missish and you don't seem like a crier. Not like the last one. She cried all the bloody time."

Calliope blinked as a child's shoe landed in the flower bed just left of the steps. "No. No, I'm not much of one for tears. Your sister, sir. It's growing increasingly more urgent I think."

He glanced up once more, cursed again, and then loped into the house, leaving the door open wide. After a moment, the dangling child vanished from sight, back into the house, and Calliope followed at a more sedate pace. Entering the house, she found that there was, indeed, no butler. The footmen all appeared to be in a complete uproar, none of them knowing what to do as they no longer had a butler to direct them. Well, all but two of them. Those two seemed ready to come to blows over who was better suited to step into the position of butler now that their predecessor had apparently fled into the night, or in this case, the early afternoon, with the runaway governess.

From her vantage point inside the front door, she could see the drawing room. Without further ado, she moved toward it. Once there, she settled into a chair near the fireplace, though it was dark and no fires were necessary given the warmth of the day. In fact, she even removed her pelisse. Since no servants seemed to be willing to make the effort to take it for her, or were in fact even aware of her presence, she simply draped it over the back of her chair and waited. After a few minutes, the little boy reappeared. His sister, much smaller than she'd appeared from the ground, and also much dirtier, stood next to him. She clutched a doll in the crook of her arm. As she looked at Calliope with pure malicious challenge in her eyes, she shoved a thumb into her mouth.

Right on their heels came the third sibling, the oldest, a girl who had also clearly been weeping. She appeared to be around eleven or so, and was wearing a dress suited to a much younger girl. It was inches too short and also impossibly tight, stretched at the seams to the point it couldn't possibly be comfortable.

"Hello. I'm Miss Calliope," she offered. "I thought, if you'd like, I could tell you a story. Won't you sit down?"

"Is this a trick?"

The word came out "twick" as the little girl had asked it around her thumb. Calliope bit back a smile. "No, it isn't a trick. It seems to me that your house is in a bit of disorder and disorder is not very good for children, I find. So I will sit with you here and we will stay out of the way of all that's happening out there and I will tell you a story until your father returns home."

"He's not our father. He's our uncle. Our father is dead. So is our mother," the little boy from the porch said.

It was said so matter of factly that it took Callie aback. "Oh. I'm very sorry."

"Are your parents alive?" the oldest girl asked, a challenge in her voice.

"I don't know," Calliope replied with complete honesty. "I never knew my parents."

The little girl popped her thumb out of her mouth. "That's the story I want to hear."

Calliope considered the request for a moment. It would need to be a somewhat edited version, but she saw no harm in it. "Very well. That is the story you shall have." After taking a moment to collect her thoughts, Calliope began, "Once upon a time—"

"I thought we were getting your story. Not some blimey fairy tale," the boy said, clearly disgusted.

"You shouldn't use that word either... the one that began with a b," she corrected him.

"Can't spell, can I?"

"You can't spell?" Calliope asked. "Can any of you? Spell, read,

4

write?"

"I can a little," the oldest girl said.

"But you all should have been reading and writing years ago! Why not?"

"Well, our first governess was more interested in Papa than in us. Of course, Papa was more interested in her than he was us, too," the littlest one replied. "Mama and Papa fought about it all the time, then Mama sacked her. What's that mean? To sack someone?"

"It means that you end that person's employment and they do not get to work for you anymore," Calliope said. "But go on, you were saying?"

"After that, Papa yelled and Mama cried and he said he was bringing the lot of us back to England. So we got on a ship. Then Papa died and then Mama, and we came here," the little girl explained, then promptly popped her thumb right back into her mouth.

The oldest one spoke up, "And our last governess, the one our uncle hired, was only interested in the butler. I don't think we've had a single lesson since we've arrived."

Oh, dear heavens. She'd wandered into bedlam. "I see. Well, enough about your governesses and their apparently numerous failings. I am telling you the story of why I don't know who my parents are, but I am telling it as a fairy tale. So, no more interruptions. All right?"

All the children nodded their agreement and Calliope began again. "Once upon a time, there was a place called the St. James Workhouse, which still stands today. And in eighteen hundred and four, a little girl was left on the doorstep there. Her name was Calliope. But Calliope was too small to work, and too small to care for herself, and the workhouse was only for people who could do so. But the vicar of a nearby church arranged for a childless couple to take in the little girl and care for her. And they did so, until the little girl was eight years old. In eighteen hundred and twelve, the little girl's foster father went away to war. He was very brave but, alas, he died in battle. Then her foster mother became very sick and died. The vicar, now a widower, couldn't take her in himself as it would not have been seemly to do so... instead, he sent her back to the workhouse where first he'd found her. And that is where her true guardian angel found her... Miss Euphemia Darrow."

"Sounds like a governess' name," the oldest girl said.

Calliope bit the inside of her cheek to keep from smiling. "It is a governess' name, but not simply any governess. Miss Euphemia Darrow is the ultimate governess. She trains young girls who have no other way to make their way in the world in how to be excellent governesses so that they might be able to fend for themselves in life."

"Is that what she did for you?" the smallest child asked.

Calliope did smile then. "Indeed, Miss Euphemia Darrow plucked my young self from the workhouse and took me to her school which is not very from here. And there, she taught me to read and write, speak multiple languages, do arithmetic, sew, paint, play the pianoforte and comport myself with all the dignity and propriety that is deemed necessary by society. She taught me those things, among others, so that I might be able to pass them on to my charges."

"It sounds boring," the boy scoffed.

"Some of it can be," Calliope admitted. "So, to make it less of a burden, Miss Darrow gave us prizes. We would earn sweets or get to stay up late or get to sleep later in the morning. There were all sorts of little things and freedoms that we were given if we did what was asked of us all and did it well."

"Our old governesses didn't do that," the oldest girl said. "They'd tell us to do something and if we didn't, they'd wallop us."

Calliope blinked at that pronouncement. Certainly, she was not unfamiliar with such practices. But it never failed to leave her stunned when a child spoke so matter of factly about being beaten. "Well, walloping did not occur at Miss Darrow's school."

"Would you wallop us if you was our governess?" the boy asked with narrowed eyes.

"I don't believe so. You'd have to do something very terrible indeed to warrant any real punishment, I think. Even then, I would likely not do so myself but speak to your uncle about whatever infraction had been committed and let him determine a suitable consequence," Calliope answered. *But it would never be walloping.*

"You'll be our governess," the little girl said firmly. "We've decided."

Calliope grinned at the small child's dirty face and tangled hair, all of it outshone by her beatific smile. "But I haven't decided yet, my dear. And I must have a say, as well."

"Well, what sort of say?" the boy demanded of her.

"I must speak with your uncle first. We must see if we can come to agreeable terms before I can commit to anything... and perhaps he will not like me and then he would not wish for me to be your governess!"

"He don't care," the boy scoffed once more. "Don't care one whit. Wants to be shed of us all, I think."

"I think that's quite enough from you, William."

Calliope looked up to see a man standing in the doorway. He wore a simple but elegantly fitted coat and a pair of snug riding breeches. His boots were dusty, his gold-streaked, brown hair disheveled and wind-blown. And he was, quite possibly, the most handsome man she'd ever seen. From his broad, high forehead, patrician nose and perfectly sculpted jaw line and cleft chin, he was simply perfection. His undeniable masculine beauty was coupled with a tall and imposing frame, broad shoulders and lean hips. If this man was the Earl of Montgomery, she could never work for him. Not in a million years.

Chapter One

THE SCENE SPREAD out before Lord Winn Hamilton, Earl of Montgomery, was unlike anything he'd witnessed in all of the madness that had become his life since the children first appeared on his doorstep. Ignoring the chaos in the hall and the servants who ran willy-nilly in hysterics, his gaze was glued to the dirty, bedraggled and yet shockingly well-behaved children seated in a circle at the feet of a woman who could only be an angel. Her nut brown hair was swept back into a low chignon, her simple morning dress of a rather faded lavender hugged a lush and generous figure that reminded him very keenly that his own needs had been ignored since his brother's children had been unceremoniously deposited in his care. Her features were soft and pretty, her eyes framed by long lashes, and her lips were a perfect bow, the bottom lip turning out ever so slightly in a soft, provocative and perpetual pout. In short, she was the least governess-like governess he'd ever seen. *Excepting, of course, the one who'd just fled his house with his butler and a large quantity of the silver.*

"You are Miss St. James, I presume," he said, peeling off his dirty gloves and tossing them into his hat before placing both on a side table. He needed a moment to compose his thoughts.

She rose to her feet. "Indeed, my lord. I am Miss St. James."

Defaulting to caustic humor to mask the rather surprising effect the girl was having on him, Winn said, "I apologize for the disorder of my house. I have not yet replaced my housekeeper—whom these three ran off last week and my butler, just this morning, eloped with their former worthless governess. You haven't by chance taken a fancy to one of the footmen, the stable lads, or the chimney sweep, have you, Miss St. James? Frankly, another elopement will bring this house down around my ears."

Her lips quirked but she did not smile. "I have not met the footmen, nor the stable lads, and charming as chimney sweeps can be, I feel that I am safe in saying that my marital prospects and aspirations are all equally absent at the moment."

"Good, good," he said. Then he turned his gaze toward the three children who sat like dirty-faced cherubs at her feet. She was like a snake charmer he'd seen once in India. "The three of you, get your coats, go into the garden. Do not go beyond the garden. Do not invite any passersby into the garden and do not come back into the house until you have been fetched by a maid. While you are in the garden, do not climb anything in it that would require you to go higher from the ground than the top of your own head when standing flat-footed next to it. Is that clear?"

All three of them nodded and shuffled out and, no doubt, all three of them would disobey. More hedonistic, obstinate and willful creatures he had never encountered. And yet he loved them so fiercely it made his chest ache. He hadn't even known them until a little more than a month ago. His brother and sister-in-law had been sailing back from Spain with them when they'd all taken a fever aboard ship. The children, miraculously, had survived. Most of the adults on board had perished. The captain of the ship, one of the survivors who had been hastily promoted from the ranks, had delivered them to his doorstep per his brother's dying instructions. What had occurred in their young lives prior to the deaths of their parents was really anyone's guess. His brother had never been the most responsible of men, he'd also certainly never been the most faithful of men. And while Winn had no proof of it, and there was no one left alive he could ask, he strongly suspected that his brother hadn't planned to stay in England with his wife and children. Rather, he'd thought to foist them off on family and go on his merry way. It seemed the most likely of scenarios.

"You are rather deep in thought, my lord," the would-be governess mused, drawing him from his reverie. She was reaching for her discarded pelisse, clearly intent on escaping his unfortunate version of Bedlam.

"Contemplating what manner of mayhem they shall wreak next," he answered and crossed the room to the chair opposite hers. "Please sit, Miss St. James, so that I may as well. I've never been more tired in my life."

She paused, pelisse in hand, as if weighing her options. Finally, after a lengthy pause, she replaced it and faced him, then seated herself once more. "I assume you have been in pursuit of your runaway servants?"

He grimaced. "More accurately, I was in pursuit of the family silver they lined their pockets with before they fled. I should have known from the second that governess—if ever she'd been one in her life, I will eat my hat—showed up here that she would be nothing but trouble. Governesses don't look like that!"

Miss St. James blinked at him. "And how do governesses look, my lord?"

Realizing that he might have offended her, Winn backed off from that. "Rest easy. Governesses can be very attractive women. They simply tend to be a bit more... buttoned up, as it were. And less painted. Miss Guinn looked rather like she'd stepped fresh off the boards at Drury Lane."

"Then why in heaven's name did you employ her, my lord?"

That was a very good question. "Desperation, Miss St. James. I mistakenly thought any governess would be better than no governess, at least in the short term. Especially for little girls who'd just lost their mother. Having been a boy myself, albeit a hundred years ago it seems, I felt I could get on well enough with William. But Charlotte and Claudia are a different matter. I know nothing of little girls." The very idea of seeing such creatures to adulthood was terrifying to him. It was tears and sobs one minute, screams and flying crockery the next, then they'd sit and braid one another's hair. Though to be fair, Claudia did more of the braiding than Charlotte. She simply tied knots that resulted in a repeat of the tears and sobs.

"Well, my lord, I'm afraid you'll have to learn. A governess is no substitute for family. They need you, and they need to feel that their place here with you is a permanent one. You cannot give them that by dragging in one disreputable woman after another to care for them." Her words might have been harsh, but they were uttered in a mild tone. Still, the reproach was gentle but present nonetheless.

"I don't mean to drag in any more disreputable women, Miss St. James. I mean to drag you in, metaphorically speaking, of course," he said. From what he'd seen of her brief interactions with the children, she was well worth her weight in gold if not more. "I'll pay you double your last position. Triple, if need be."

"That is a very generous offer, my lord."

He grinned. "It isn't. It's a desperate offer and we both know it. I don't know what to do with them, Miss St. James. Not a clue. But clearly, you do and that is invaluable to me at this time."

She eyed him like he was a specimen on display, as if she were picking apart every flaw and cataloguing every detail to determine how he functioned and worked. It was decidedly uncomfortable. Her perusal continued as he fought the urge to squirm beneath her steady gaze.

At last, she said, "It isn't only about the money, my lord. I was led to believe that this household was headed by a much older man... as it stands, it would be very inappropriate for me to reside here with a single man of your age and no hint of a chaperone, not even a housekeeper. While I might be a governess by position, I have been gently reared enough, at least in the last years, to be aware of how that might appear to others."

"Then I'll buy you the house next door," he said. "You can staff it to your heart's content. Just do not leave me alone with those bloodthirsty, hell-spawned, and utterly precious children."

"I cannot do that and I cannot allow you to do that," she said, and there was a note in her voice that might have been regret. Then her eyes widened and she added, "But perhaps there is a way forward if we are a bit creative. I could be their governess, if not a governess in residence. I would continue to live at the Darrow School and would take a carriage daily to and from this house. I would work eight hours daily, except for Sundays which I will have off and I would take a half-day on Saturday that will usually be comprised of an outing for the children. And I will teach the children, but I will also teach you."

"Teach me?" he asked, somewhat shocked at the suggestion. "I assure you, Miss St. James, despite my current state of readiness for a lunatic's asylum, I can read. In four languages, no less."

"That is an excellent achievement, my lord, but your literacy was never in question. Your education will be on how to conduct yourself with the children so that they do not get the upper hand... again. Assuming we can wrest it back from them to start," she explained pertly.

"I told them to go in the garden and they did. Does that not signify that I have the upper hand?"

She clucked her tongue at him like he was some poor, misguided fool. Though he supposed in some way that was true. What did he know of children, after all? His father had been so disinterested in both him and his brother that the man had been little better than a stranger to him. "Because it served their purposes to do so, my lord. Not because you demanded it. You really do understand nothing about them!"

There was a ring of truth to the statement that he could not deny. "Very well. Ten hours a day. Two hours instruction for me in the evenings and eight hours instructional time with the children because, I daresay, they need that much. After a while, those hours can be revisited, but their education has been terribly neglected and I cannot even fathom why."

"I think perhaps they have never had a very good governess," Miss St. James posited.

"And are you?"

"I am not a good governess, my lord. I am one of the best governesses," she said. "Isn't that why you sent to the Darrow School, after all?"

"So it is, Miss St. James. So it is. Do we have a bargain?"

She considered it, her expression thoughtful and cautious. At last, she stuck out her hand to shake as one would with a business partner.

Bemused, Winn accepted it. But nothing could have prepared him for the jolt of it, for the pure sensation of heat and light and want that swamped him like a wave. And she felt it, too. It was obvious in the way she quickly drew back her hand and looked at him with a new kind of caution.

Almost immediately, she rose and reached for her pelisse. There was no hesitation this time, only determination. She took several steps away from him before shrugging into it. With one last glance in his direction, she said matter of factly, "We have a bargain, my lord. I will send you a bill for my services, to be paid one month in advance and I will begin on Monday."

Winn had risen himself by this point, finally recovered from the moment where a simple touch of her hand had rendered him utterly dumb. "Good day, Miss St. James. I shall endeavor to keep myself and all three of the children alive and in one piece until you return."

She smirked. "I'm certain you shall prevail. Good day, my lord."

When she had gone, Winn considered what had just transpired. It was not such a bad thing for her not to reside in his home. In truth, Miss Calliope St. James was far too beautiful, far too tempting, and far too innocent. Women like her were a kind of trouble he hadn't the time or inclination for at the moment. There was more than enough disorder in his life already.

But she did certainly make a pretty picture, he thought. With her nut brown hair and her sparkling eyes, she was just the sort of girl who might have caught his eye across a ballroom. If he'd been in the market for a bride, which he certainly was not. Heaven knew she was more tempting by half than any of the wretched, giggling misses that all the matchmaking mamas put in his path. Their shrill voices and silliness set his teeth on edge.

Getting to his feet once more, Winn stepped out into the corridor. "Who is the most senior footman here?"

"I am, my lord," one of the men said. "I've been here for seven years."

Winn nodded. "And your experience prior?"

"I worked in my father's shop."

"You can read?" Winn asked.

"Aye, my lord. Read, write and do sums," the man said proudly.

"Your name?"

"John, my lord."

"Your last name, John," Winn said and pinched the bridge of his nose.

"It's Foster, my lord."

"Well, John Foster, you've been promoted to butler, temporarily of course. I'll send round to one of my estates to have someone sent up who can show you the butlerly ropes, so to speak, and we'll progress from there. I don't suppose you have any female relatives who are qualified to be a housekeeper, do you?"

"My aunt, my lord. Recently widowed and eager for the job. She's worked as a housemaid for many years, and then as a housekeeper in a smaller household."

"While married?" Winn asked. It wasn't entirely unheard of, but it was unusual.

"Her husband was in the army, my lord, and they had no children," the footman-turned-butler explained. "He died nigh on ten years past."

"Right. Send for her. I'll meet her tomorrow morning promptly at ten and we'll decide from there whether or not she will suit."

John Foster nodded vigorously. "Certainly, my lord. I'll send her a note round now... then I'll find the master list of the silver and compare it to what's left behind so we can let the proper authorities know precisely what's been taken."

"I'm the proper authority, Foster. I may hire a runner but, for now, I just want to know what that bastard absconded with."

"Yes, my lord."

With that, Winn walked away, feeling marginally more in charge of his household. Or at least he did until he heard the shouting from the garden. Cursing under his breath, he took the shortest route outside and found the children hanging from tree limbs like monkeys. All of them so high up it made his heart leap straight to his throat and then drop back down into his stomach.

Rather than tell them to get down, he walked over, placed his hands on little Charlotte's waist and lifted her down. Once her small feet were firmly on the ground, he went to Claudia and handed her down as well. William had already begun to climb down but was still high enough that he and Winn were eye to eye. "Your job, William, is to protect your sisters. If they are engaging in a behavior where they could be injured, you should try to stop them, not indulge in it yourself."

"Claudia is the oldest!" he protested.

"So she is, and she should have known better, as well. But little Charlotte is only three years old," he said.

"I'm six," the little girl protested.

"You're four," Claudia corrected. "You're four, William is seven and I'm ten. If you really cared for us, you'd be able to remember that!"

Winn sighed heavily. "It isn't about caring, Claudia. It's about walking into this garden and seeing the lot of you risking life and limb by doing the very thing you'd been expressly warned against. All of you are to go to your rooms and remain there until the dinner hour."

"Fine," Claudia said, and spun around, her skirts swishing about her shins as she marched into the house. It seemed females of every age had mastered the trick of making an exit.

Turning to little Charlotte, he saw her eyes welling with tears. Then her thumb popped out of her mouth and she began to wail. Loudly and enthusiastically. After only a moment, she turned and ran after her sister. William followed suit, stomping after them until Winn was alone in the garden.

Alone. It seemed that he was forever winding up alone to clean up the messes left by others. The fewer people he allowed in his world, the fewer people he would have to clean up after. Unsettled by the maudlin turn of his thoughts, Winn shook his head to clear it. He was tired. More than simply tired, in fact.

Exhausted beyond measure, infuriated by his brother, his former butler, his former governess, his housekeeper and even the children who were now upstairs plotting his downfall, he sank onto a nearby bench and put his head in his hands. He wanted to drink enough brandy that he wouldn't be able to speak coherently for three days. But he wouldn't. Because he couldn't. Because like always, it was on his shoulders to be the responsible one, to be the one who cleaned up his brother's messes. Damn, damn and double damn.

Chapter Two

"THAT IS A very unorthodox solution. Typically speaking, we provide governesses in residence," Miss Euphemia Darrow said. "Though, I daresay that under the circumstances, it is the best option for everyone involved."

Calliope recalled the moment in the drawing room when the Earl of Montgomery had shaken her hand. It wasn't the best option. Not in the least, but she couldn't say that. Admitting to such wayward thoughts and feelings for a man she'd just met, a man who'd been interviewing her as a prospective employee as much as she'd been interviewing him as a prospective employer, well—it was hardly the sort of thing one admitted to their mentor and idol. What on earth would Effie think of her? "I do hope you're right. The children are a bit incorrigible, but very sweet. I think they are a little lost right now. So much in their lives has changed, after all." Not just theirs, but his as well... Lord Winn Hamilton, Earl of Montgomery. He'd lost his father recently enough that it hadn't even been known to Effie. And now, he'd lost his brother and sister-in-law. Yet he didn't strike her as a man terribly bereaved. He struck her more as a man at the end of his tether, as if he were simply waiting for one more thing to go wrong so that he might snap. Of course, Callie knew well just how deeply grief could be buried. She'd had years of experience doing just that.

"Indeed," Effie said. Her gaze shifted to one of sympathy and she patted Callie's hand. "And if anyone understands loss, upheaval and change, Callie, it would be you. I can't imagine that there is another girl in this school who would be a better fit for that position and those poor children."

Callie considered it. "They were very sweet, but they do not recognize boundaries. Nor, I daresay, do they recognize anyone's right to place boundaries upon them. But they aren't bad. And I do believe that he cares deeply for them. He's just muddling through, however, and they know it."

Effie laughed at that. "There is no danger greater than having a child in your presence that knows you haven't a clue what you are doing. When I first brought Willa and Lilly here, why, it is a wonder the whole place didn't simply collapse under the weight of chaos and upheaval. But we muddled through eventually. I daresay he will, as well. But I am very confused as to why we didn't know he was a young and single man."

"His father passed away very recently, I understand," Callie answered.

"He told you that?"

Callie blushed. "No. He did not. I asked our servants and they are clearly more keen on current affairs and current gossip than we are. His father passed away only a few weeks before the children were deposited on his doorstep, which I believe has been a matter of weeks, as well. So he's only been the Earl of Montgomery for a very short time. I imagine that is where our misinformation arose from."

"It must be terribly difficult to face such upheaval in the midst of such bereavement," Effie reflected.

"I believe that his relationship with his father might have been strained. I know he had not seen his brother in some time as he'd been residing in Spain for many years."

"Is this more gossip from our servants?" Effie asked.

"Please don't be cross with them. I did ask them, after all," Callie stated.

"Given the sort of trouble you girls have been finding lately," Effie asserted with a smirk, "I might need to raise their wages for being such accomplished spies. Regardless, I find it somewhat unusual that he had such a small number of relations and seems to have suffered some estrangement from them both."

"We can hardly hold him responsible for his brother's situation. Given the rather unorthodox manner in which the children have been brought up thus far," Callie pointed out, "we must assume that he was living in a fashion that was not compatible with that of our society. And as for his father... well, Effie, we both know that many men father children when they are quite unsuited to the raising of them."

Effie nodded. "You're quite right. And I imagine that regardless of the nature of their relationships, he must be grieving, even if in his own quiet way."

"I would certainly say that is true," Callie agreed.

Effie eyed her suspiciously for a moment. "You aren't worried about his intentions at all, are you, Callie?"

Callie's blush deepened further and she could feel the all-knowing, all-seeing gaze of her friend and mentor penetrating through to the very heart of the matter as always. "He is a very attractive man and one to whom it would be unwise for me to develop any sort of attachment or feeling. He is my employer, after all."

"Yes, but you feel something for him?"

"I barely know him! Why, we've only just met!" Callie protested.

"Wasn't it Marlowe who said, 'Whoever loved that loved not at first sight'?" Effie reminded her. "I'm not suggesting that you've fallen in love with him. That would be utterly preposterous. But I am suggesting that if you find him attractive, and given your obvious and immediate affection for those children, it puts you in a particularly vulnerable position, Calliope St. James... one that is cause for great concern to me."

"I'll be quite all right. He is the Earl of Montgomery, after all, and I know very well my own place in society is quite different from his."

"As if that means anything!" Effie scoffed.

"It means everything," Callie insisted. "I do not think he is the sort of man who would thumb his nose at propriety and all that society mandates for him when choosing a bride. And as we both know, I would never consent to be anything else. Yes, I find him handsome and witty, and I think he's a very good man. But that doesn't make me love him, nor does it make me suddenly forgetful of our very disparate situations in life."

Effie nodded after a moment. "You will be cautious, won't you? I've never heard anything untoward about him but that doesn't mean anything. I have my own sources that I can suss out information about him through. And I fully intend to do so before you go to that house on Monday."

Callie rose. "And I won't even try to stop you. I do believe he's an honorable man, but if women were capable of truly determining a man's character based on such short acquaintance, there would be no need of a school such as this one to tend all the resulting births of that dishonor!"

"True enough. I must go out. I have errands to run and you, my dearest Callie, have lessons to plan. Lots and lots of them it would seem."

To that end, Callie went upstairs to her small room and began looking at her materials. She had some primers and some simple mathematics books. They would do for a start, but she'd provide a list to the earl on Monday of all that they'd need to truly begin the children's instruction. She fervently hoped that providing daily instruction would be enough for them. There was a loneliness, a sadness in those children. As if despite having had their mother and father, they'd never truly had anyone, that they'd been alone for most of their lives. It was a feeling that Callie understood all too well.

⫸⫷

EFFIE HAD TAKEN a hack to her destination. Dressed in a heavy cloak, the hood pulled up to shield her face from any passersby, there was little fear of anyone recognizing her. Climbing the steps to the rather imposing edifice of the townhouse that was twice as wide as any other on the street and an entire story taller, she lifted the ornate knocker and let it bang heavily against the brass plate beneath.

The butler answered almost immediately. His raised eyebrows were his only indication of shock. "May I help you?"

"I'm here to see Lord Highcliff. He's expecting me."

"No, Madam, he most assuredly is not," the butler replied.

"We are old friends. He is always expecting me," she stated firmly, in a tone far haughtier than she would typically use with anyone. "Now, let me inside and you may tell him that Effie is here."

Apparently, the tactic worked. The butler stepped back and allowed her to pass. As she stepped into the hall, Highcliff appeared from the doorway of a room down the hall. He looked at her sharply, clearly recognizing her in spite of her disguise.

"Come," he said rather sharply and gestured for her to join him there.

Effie closed the distance, walking along the corridor. The house felt empty. And as she looked about, she could see a fine film of dust on everything.

"Have you no servants beyond your butler?" she asked.

"I have a housekeeper and a maid who comes in a few times a week."

Her own eyebrows arched upward at that. "Really?"

He shrugged. "I never said they were particularly good at their jobs, did I?"

"No," she agreed. "And if you did, I would have to call you a liar or a fool. Why are you living this way, Nicholas? You're not a pauper, you're not a man who has never lived with luxury. You could have an entire battalion of servants to see to your comfort!"

"Because the fewer people who are in this house, Effie, the more I get to be me. Not the me that I have to be out there," he said softly. "All the pretending grows tiresome. And here, with only my butler and a cook who remains in the kitchen, I need not do so."

There was something in his tone that created a sharp, biting fear in her. She'd never heard him sound unhappy. Bored, sardonic, angry, sarcastic and biting—but never unhappy, never lonely. And tired, she thought. He sounded utterly exhausted. "Then give it up," she urged him. "Let someone else do it for a change! I worry about you. For the toll it takes on you."

"And what should I do instead?" he asked simply, ushering her into his study. "Manage my estates? They are all in good hands. Entertain? Go about in society as the man I truly am and not the mask I've worn for years? I'd soon be a pariah, as well you know. No one, Effie, likes to be played for a fool, and save for those gentleman who have worked with me and for me and you, I have played them all for such. It's not something that would be easily forgiven."

"You could marry. Have a family. You wouldn't have to be alone, then." Even as she said it, it cut her to the quick. The very idea of him loving someone else pricked her soul, but she'd paste a glad smile on her face if it meant he'd have even a moment's happiness.

He looked at her for a moment. There was something in his gaze she could not identify. Then he smiled at her rather patronizingly. "That is not for me, Euphemia Darrow, as well we both know. And you should not be here."

"I need information," she said. "I made assumptions when I received a letter requesting the services of a governess for the Earl of Montgomery. I didn't realize that the title had been passed down to the son."

Highcliff frowned. "Winn? I honestly don't know much about him.

But that's a good thing, really. The less I know, the less likely he is to associate with those he should not. He's a good sort, as far as I know. He's never been heavily into gaming or... ladies."

"Prostitutes, you mean."

He donned an expression of mock outrage. "Such language, Miss Darrow! What would your charges think?"

"That I'd learned it from listening to them. Contrary to what people might think, it isn't just the castoff bastards of gentlemen I instruct. I've taken some special cases from the workhouses and even debtor's prison. Will Calliope be safe going to and from his home? Will she be safe in his home?"

He ushered her deeper into the room and showed her to a small sitting area near the window. "You cannot protect them from everything, Effie. You know that, don't you? These girls are not girls at all! They are women fully grown and the world, as we both know, can be a vicious place."

"Which is all the more reason that I should do what I can to mitigate the risks," she pointed out. "I only want to know that I haven't put her in harm's way by not doing my own due diligence."

He leaned back in his chair and sighed heavily. "I will look into it. I'm certain he's fine. I've never heard a single word about him that was unfavorable. In truth, people rarely talk about him at all. That can only be a good thing. His brother, on the other hand, he was another matter. Wild, reckless, faithless. But he took off for Spain amidst a scandal and eloped with the youngest daughter of a nobleman whom he'd compromised quite thoroughly. I am assuming it's their children the Earl of Montgomery is employing a governess for?"

"Yes," Effie admitted. "Calliope says the children are very troubled. I hope she can help them."

"For what it's worth, so do I," he said. There was a long moment of silence then, not uncomfortable but certainly filled with a kind of tension that had been growing more noticeable and more persistent with every meeting between them. "This is no place for you. Don't come here again, Effie."

"Why not?" she asked. There were a dozen reasons. He was a man. She was a woman. They were both unmarried. Her career depended upon her sterling reputation. His reputation was anything but. They were in Mayfair where nothing went unnoticed. The list continued. She was waiting for him to utter something irrevocable. That he was done with her. That he despised her. That she was as unwanted by him as she was by her father.

He looked at her, that one dark brow lifted in challenge. "You know why. I am an unmarried man and you are an unmarried woman. I don't even have enough servants in this house to keep it together, much less provide even the barest hint of respectability."

She shook her head. "I was careful to keep my identity concealed... and I have nothing to fear from you, Nicholas. You are my friend."

"No. I am not," he said. "I was once. But that was a long time ago. Men and women of our age, unmarried and unfettered as it were, cannot be friends. Besides, being your friend, now or in the past, does not make me any less of a threat to you."

She rolled her eyes at that. "You would never harm me."

Those were the last words she uttered. He lunged forward in his seat, one of his arms closing about her waist to pull her forward while the other one wound through the loose chignon of her hair, scattering pins as he gripped it tightly. Their faces were less than a single breath apart. "There are many ways to harm a woman."

Effie's chin notched upward and she met his gaze boldly. "Then go ahead. Do whatever it is that you mean to do. Teach me your lesson. Because that's what this is about, isn't it? You don't desire me. You don't want me. You never have. But you're damned determined to make me a slave to my fear, so go ahead!"

His eyes darkened, the pupils dilating until they were pools of black ringed by pale silver. Then they narrowed, dropping to the curve of her lips. And before she could even think that he actually meant to do it, his lips touched hers. As fierce as his hold was, the strength of his arm like a steel band about her and his other hand tightly wound in her hair, his lips were gentle. It was the merest whisper of contact at first. His mouth brushed against hers once, twice, and on the third pass settled more firmly, mapping the curves of contours found there.

Effie let out a soft sigh, a sound that was half-pleasure and half-dismay. It was a moment she'd been waiting for, as if now that it had occurred, she could finally release that little bit of breath she'd been holding for more than half her life. Then he deepened the kiss, the press of his lips more firm over hers, the sweep of his tongue as it invaded was insistent but also seductive. And she was lost. She'd longed for that moment for many so years, for him to kiss her or acknowledge that there was something between them. And now that he'd done so, she regretted it instantly. She could feel it changing her, altering the very fabric of who she was. Wondering what it would feel like was so much easier than knowing it and wishing fervently for it to happen again.

It might have been only a moment or it might have been an eternity. Either was both not enough and entirely too much. But he drew back abruptly and rose, crossing the room to the window, keeping his back to her, and leaving her alone there, bereft and rejected.

"You need to leave," he said. "And do not come back. I'll send word when I have it, or if there's simply none to be had."

"Why did you do it?" she asked, hating that her voice trembled and tears stung her eyes.

"Why did I kiss you?" he asked without ever turning to face her.

"Yes. We've known each other for nearly two decades and you have never touched me in such a manner."

He didn't turn around. His voice echoed, bouncing off the glass in front of him as he replied, "Because I can. Because you need to know that you are vulnerable, Effie. That there are men in this world who would take advantage of you, and God help us both, but I am one of them."

Chapter Three

I T WAS EXACTLY eight in the morning when Callie knocked upon the door at the Earl of Montgomery's elegant Palladian home. The butler, a dour-faced man who was being shadowed by a youngish and nervous-looking man that had worn footman's livery on her last visit, met her there and frowned. "As a servant, Miss St. James, you should not be making free with the front entrance. From this point forward, you will utilize the servants' entrance below stairs."

Callie laughed. Recalling Effie's often stated motto, *begin as you mean to end*, she said, "Oh, no. I will not. I'm not a servant. I'm a governess. A sought after, highly respected graduate of the Darrow School. You might be able to bully girls from other agencies, but I'm not one of them. I'll come and go through the front entrance as is my right as a young woman of quality and I will not skulk about in any manner that suggests my presence here is anything other than entirely appropriate. But thank you for this little talk. It's certainly nice to know where one stands in the household."

With that, Callie breezed past the man, approached a maid who was standing there agape in the corridor, and asked, "And are the children awake yet?"

"Certainly, Miss St. James. They are in the breakfast room with his lordship. Do you wish to join them?" the maid asked as she looked past Callie to the disapproving butler.

Callie smiled warmly at the girl, as if her power struggle at the door with the butler was nothing of note. "I've already broken my fast, but I would certainly love to go in. It will be beneficial to me to see how their table manners are at present and to know what we might need to work on."

"This way, Miss," the maid offered and led Callie down the corridor, past the grand staircase and toward a small room that overlooked the garden. The Hepplewhite sideboard was laden with dishes but the matching table was a scene of chaos. Claudia and William were throwing bread at one another. Little Charlotte was blowing bubbles in her teacup and the earl had his nose buried in his news sheet, ignoring the lot of it.

Callie made a great production of clearing her throat. The news sheet folded down and the Earl of Montgomery met her gaze across the top of it. "Would you care to explain all of this?" she asked.

"I think it rather self-explanatory, Miss St. James," he said. "They are savages."

Her lips pursed, as much in actual disapproval as to keep from laughing at his rather flat delivery of such a statement, Callie countered, "My lord, as the only adult in the room, if the children are behaving savagely, it is a result of the direction you have given them, or in this case, I would rather guess it is the direction you have not given them." To illustrate her point, she called each of the children down in turn. "Charlotte, we do not blow bubbles in our teacup. Tea is for drinking and not for playing. Claudia and William, we do not throw food. It is for eating and not to be used as some sort of weapon. Now, I want all three of you to sit down, face the table as intended, and eat your breakfast. If you do so, then we will go out for a walk in the park before we begin our lessons."

Lord Montgomery lowered his news sheet then, folding it and placing it just so next to his plate. "And that, Miss St. James, is how you take control of the situation? By resorting to bribery?"

Callie seated herself next to Charlotte and took the little girl's serviette which was tucked into the front of her dress and draped it over the small child's lap. "We don't tuck our serviettes into our clothes like we're field hands. They are draped across our laps just so. It's much more convenient for wiping sticky fingers," she said and then gave the child a little pat on her head. Turning her attention back to the earl, she said, "It is only bribery if I'm offering incentive for them to do things they should not. Offering incentive to do things they should is simply a reward. We all like to be rewarded for our work. I wish to be paid for being a governess, after all."

"And what, precisely, is their work?" the earl demanded. "They are children, after all!"

"The work of children is to play and to learn by doing so. It is also to learn how to emulate the adults around them and function in the world when they are grown," Callie replied simply. "For that to happen, we must interact with them and teach them by example rather than ignoring them in favor of our news sheets." The last statement was rather pointedly directed at him and his arched eyebrows and tightened jaw indicated that he was well aware of it.

"Then they should attempt to be as entertaining as my news sheets," he replied with a snap to his voice.

"I was blowing bubbles," Charlotte offered helpfully.

He smirked at Callie then. "So you were. I shall endeavor to pay more attention."

"Finish your breakfast, children. Then we shall walk," Callie instructed.

"What if we don't wish to walk?" Claudia asked.

"Then you may remain here with the servants while I take William and Charlotte. Or if they do not wish to go, then I shall go alone, I suppose."

"But you're our governess! You're supposed to spend time with us!" Claudia stated, all but stamping her feet.

"I think the real issue here, Claudia, is not that you don't wish to go for a walk… it's that you don't wish to do what another person has suggested. You may stay here if that's what you wish, but I'd rather hate to see you cut off your nose to spite your face, dear. I think being outdoors would be good for all of us. We're having rather fine weather at the moment. Certainly more fine than we'll likely see again for some time. So if you wish to remain in the house, you are certainly welcome to do so. But I, for one, mean to take advantage of the little bit of sunshine we have and walk in the park. I thought we might gather some leaves and some flowers and attempt to identify plants. It's important for you to know the native flora and fauna of England, since you've been abroad so very much."

"I thought you were going to teach us to read and to write our names," William protested.

"And I shall. You're bright capable children. I daresay you can learn more than one thing in a day, can't you?" Callie challenged.

William puffed his skinny chest out with pride. "I can learn anything. I'm very smart."

"I'm certain you are and you will have ample opportunity to prove it. But if you're done eating, you should go upstairs and get your coats. The sun is shining but it is still chilly," she admonished lightly.

The children filed out of the room, even Claudia, and went to do as they'd been bid. She could feel the earl looking at her.

"How do you do that?"

"Do what, my lord?" she questioned.

"Make them do what you've asked them to do. Even when they challenge you, you simply roll right along as if it bothers you not at all!"

"Well, it doesn't," she said with a smile. "Those children do not know me well enough for me to be offended at all by anything they might say or do. They are looking for boundaries. Children need structure and rules in order to flourish, with just enough room to figure a few things out for themselves. I provide that. And I talk to them like they understand the language and aren't wild, feral creatures whom one must fear."

He grinned. "Is that what I do? Do I act like I'm afraid of them?"

"No. But you don't act like you're very interested in them either. These are children who have lost everything. Surely given you're own recent losses, you can empathize with their difficult position?"

He grimaced. "My father had been ill for some time. His death was not unexpected in the least. I daresay, given his failing health, it could almost be looked at as a relief for him... an end to his suffering. It's hardly the same!"

"No. It isn't the same at all. They've lost both their parents and all that they knew. But you've lost your father and your brother and had your life turned upside down. Perhaps, my lord, if you could use that common ground of having your life altered so drastically as a way of bonding with the children—"

"Miss St. James, I will spend time with the children. I will endeavor to be more interested and attentive to them. I will not throw myself prostrate on the floor and weep with grief while inviting them to do the same!"

Callie's lips firmed into a thin, disapproving line. "You are intentionally misconstruing my words, my lord, in order to avoid having to discuss something so very bourgeois as one's feelings. These children need to feel safe with you and that can only happen if they know their tender feelings will not be mocked or met with derision!"

"I would never do that!" he snapped. "They are children, after all. One could hardly expect them to be in control of their emotions as an adult would."

"Then you must provide an opening for them to express themselves! They have lost everything. They don't even have the comfort of familiar surroundings, my lord. And I know that you care for them, but I think it more important that they know it. You show them that by taking an interest in them, talking to them, by hugging and kissing them, letting them know that their presence isn't just welcome here but desired," Callie stated. "I realize it isn't fashionable, but you do not strike me as one who is a slave to such things."

"What you describe is unheard of except among the serving class!"

Callie shrugged. "And do they often not look happier for it? I've no doubt that you often slipped down to the kitchens as a boy to wheedle some treat from the cook, did you not?"

He grinned. "Of course, I did!"

"And did those treats often come with an embrace or some sign of affection?"

His grin faded and he regarded her thoughtfully for a moment. "Always."

"Which of those things—the treats or those simple demonstrations of affection—do you recall most fondly now?" she demanded.

WINN STARED AT the girl before him. She wasn't a girl, precisely, but it was better for both of them if he could think of her as one. Calliope St. James was ridiculously beautiful, ridiculously appealing and was currently in the process of reducing him to a sentimental, calf-eyed fool. She was demanding, far more assertive than he would have ever imagined given her appearance, and was pushing him into dangerous territory, toward things he wasn't ready to address. But it was quite obvious to him that, ready or not, for the sake of the children, he might have to forgo his own comfort to some degree. "Your point is well taken, Miss St. James. I shall endeavor to be more openly affectionate with them. But I'm not entirely certain it will be well received. The children seem to be resistant to such things... or anything that hints at civility and domestication. They are lovely but quite feral, I'm afraid."

She smiled, that sort of knowing half-smile, half-smirk that all females seemed to have perfected from the cradle. It was maddening and alluring all at once. "Of course, they are. All children are feral, my lord. Some are just domesticated earlier in life than others. As for their hesitation over matters of affection, well, children are always resistant to things that are good for them... eating their vegetables, washing behind their ears, going to sleep at reasonable hours. Why, if we were to allow children to refuse everything they are resistant to, the world would descend into chaos."

Winn looked about his house. Dusty floors, dusty furnishings, fireplaces that had not been cleared of ash, a footman turned butler and no housekeeper in sight yet—they'd already descended into chaos. "We wouldn't want that, would we?" he posed caustically.

"It could be worse."

"How?" he demanded.

A slight smirk played about her perfectly formed lips. "Bed wetting, bodily injury, one of the children could have an affection for amphibious creatures found out of doors and best to remain outdoors. Really, the possibilities for how that could occur are endless, my lord. Best not to tempt fate anymore by discussing it. And I have children to take for a walk."

"What's the real reason you're taking them for a walk before beginning lessons? And don't tell me that it's to reward them. We're both smarter than that," he observed. Miss St. James—seductive, beautiful, innocent, forbidden—was also a master tactician.

That half-smile transformed into a full-blown grin, satisfied, a bit smug, and blindingly beautiful. "Children, by nature, are active creatures. They long to run and play. In order to properly engage their minds, all that energy must be expended first so that they might sit quietly and take in what is being taught. Is it terrible to let them think it's a reward?"

"No. And I don't see any reason why it can't be both," he replied.

It was a perfectly sensible approach and he frankly couldn't understand why no one had thought to employ it with them before. "There is much to be admired in your approach, Miss St. James. There is much to be admired about you entirely."

Her lips parted in surprise at the compliment. But if it had taken her aback, it had rocked him to his core. It was an inappropriate thing to have said to her. She was the children's governess, not some pretty miss he would flirt with at a ball. Giving voice to his rather complicated appreciation of her many attributes would only strain the bounds of what had to be—what could only be—a very proper relationship between employer and employee.

"Forgive me. I spoke out of turn," he said. "It won't happen again."

"I hope not, my lord. As pretty a compliment as it was, the nature of our arrangement precludes such things."

"I am aware, Miss St. James. Despite my lapse in judgment, I can assure you that you are safe here."

"If I didn't believe that, my lord, I would not have taken the position." There was a moment of silence that stretched between them then before she spoke again. "I think you are not just alone. I think you are lonely. The loss of your family and the arrival of the children into your life has left you on uncertain footing."

"Careful, Miss St. James. I am not the only person speaking in a manner that would indicate forgetfulness of our positions," he warned her.

"I am out of line. I know that. But that doesn't make it any less true. For what it is worth, I hope you find the direction you so desperately need and that you allow these children to become something much more important to you than simply the obligation and duty they represent to you now."

"And what is that, Miss St. James?"

"Family, my lord. If you let them, they will become your family.

And that is what you need most of all."

"You are very free with your opinions on the matter."

She smiled then, but it was an expression of bitterness and quite possibly the saddest thing he'd ever seen.

"I am somewhat of an expert on the matter, my lord... having no family at all, I speak from a wealth of experience when I state that their value is immeasurable."

"I will take that under advisement, Miss St. James," he replied stiffly.

She nodded, looking away from him as a pretty blush stained her cheeks. With quick, and slightly less than graceful movements, she tidied the items on the table before her. It was an unnecessary task and one obviously undertaken to calm her jangled nerves. "Let me see what's keeping them."

"At some point, Miss St. James, we need some sort of accounting of what the children need. It's been such chaos since they've arrived and I've little doubt that their wardrobes, intended for mild Spanish winters, will be ill-suited to one in London."

"I'll see to it, my lord. Now, let me go upstairs and circumvent their mischief."

As she rose, Winn did as well, watching her exit the room in a swish of skirts. Yes, Miss Calliope St. James was trouble. The worst kind of trouble. The kind that, for the sake of her honor and his own, was entirely off limits. He'd need to remind himself of that by the hour. Of course, considering just how alarmingly attractive she was, he might need reminders by the minute.

"Why couldn't she be homely? Or old? Or a shrew?" he asked aloud, but there was no one in the breakfast room to answer and they were questions that didn't bear answering at any rate. She was as she was for the same reason everything else had occurred in such a fashion in his life. The good Lord was punishing him for some unknown sin and he'd simply have to grit his teeth and bear it.

No longer interested in the remnants of his breakfast, Winn left the small breakfast room and bypassed his study to head out via the front doors. He would go to his club and take solace in a space where no females, regardless of their age, were permitted.

Chapter Four

C ALLIE HAD BUNDLED the children into their coats and ushered them out of the house and to the park. It wouldn't be long before the days were too chilly for such outings and she wanted them to take advantage of it while they could. While the children certainly possessed an abundance of energy, they were not disobedient. It seemed to Callie that what the children had experienced in their lives was a lack of guidance. They weren't breaking rules because they were bad or wanted to misbehave but because no one had bothered to tell them what the rules were.

They'd been in the park for almost an hour when Claudia fell in step beside her. The other two children were playing still, with no signs of slowing down, but at Claudia's age, play was becoming a thing of the past for her. Glancing over at the child, Callie could see the promise of beauty. But she could also see that her hair had not been brushed well and her clothes were not only inappropriate for the coming weather and far too small, they were threadbare as well. That pretty young girl was dressed like a pauper. What sort of living had their father managed to obtain for them in Spain? Had they gone by choice or had he been banished there for his sins, his children paying the price?

Glancing over at the other two, she considered their garments as well. While their clothing was adequate for the moment, if terribly worn, she knew that the earl had been correct in his assessment that they did not have all that they needed for the coming winter. Further, it showed just how lax their previous governess had been. She should have inventoried what they had and what they needed and presented a list to their guardian upon her arrival. And if the governess could not have done so, then the housekeeper certainly should have. It seemed as if every moment spent in the company of those children was simply another opportunity to discover how the adults in their lives had failed them.

"What do you think of your uncle, Claudia? The earl?" Callie asked her.

"He doesn't like us very much," Claudia said softly. "He says we've turned his world upside down."

Callie smiled at that. "I suppose you have, but that doesn't mean he doesn't like you. I think it rather means he isn't quite sure what to do with you or what to make of you. He is a bachelor, after all, and children have, for him, always been the province of other people."

"I suppose so. But he's always telling us not to do this, not to do that, not to get in trouble. I'd just like for once, for people to tell us what we can do," she said rather forlornly. "What we're supposed to do!"

Callie placed her arm about the young girl's shoulders. "I shall endeavor to do that. Every morning, when we begin lessons, I will try to give you a list of all the things we can do during the day."

"Like what?"

Callie grinned, "Like we can race to that tree at the end of the lane, if you want. Or we can sit on that bench just over there. Or we can play in the dirt with your sister."

"We can get dirty?" Claudia demanded.

"Of course we can! People can be cleaned and so can clothes. A little bit of mud or dust never hurt anyone," Callie answered. "Is that what you want? To get dirty? To have mud under your fingernails and streaked on your face?"

"No," Claudia answered. "I don't really like it. But I like knowing that I could if I wanted to."

Curious, Callie found herself asking, "And what sorts of things did you do when you were with your mother in Spain?"

They walked on in silence for a long moment, circling the small grassy area where the other children played. Finally, Claudia answered, "We tried to be quiet. Our mother didn't much like us either. She was always taking to her bed to escape us, especially William. She always said her head ached and we made it worse with our noise."

The very words seemed to pierce Callie's heart. She glanced up, her gaze landing unerringly on the boy who was currently having a sword fight with a mighty oak tree. He was sweet, feral, precious and completely incorrigible. It was a combination that she wasn't certain anyone who actually liked children would be able to resist. "That must have hurt your feelings terribly... and William's."

Claudia looked at her in a way that belied her years. In that moment, she looked impossibly grown up despite her braids and her pinafore. She wasn't really a little girl, at all, Callie realized. Oh, certainly she was a child still, but she hovered on that terrible precipice between being a girl and being a young lady. Dolls no longer held her interest, but neither did embroidery, watercolors and all the things that would make her an accomplished young woman when she entered the marriage mart. So while William climbed trees and Charlotte spun in circles until she was dizzy and laughing, Claudia walked beside her and confided to her as she would have done if they were friends rather governess and charge.

"She had her reasons, I suppose," Claudia murmured.

Realizing that simply denying the girl's claim was an insult to her intelligence and also to the pain she had clearly experienced, Callie asked, "And what do you think those were... her reasons?"

The little girl sighed heavily. "I think it's because he reminded her of our father who was always gone, or going away, or just coming back from being away. And whenever he was there, he was always in a foul mood because he'd lost money gaming… money we didn't really have. He and Mother would argue terribly, about his gambling and about other women that he spent time with… it would go on for days until he got tired of it and went away once more. But William is not like him. Not really. He only looks like him a little."

Callie nodded. Claudia needed to talk. She needed to let out all the awful things she'd been holding inside and it seemed very much as if no one, in all the time she'd been there, had bothered to offer her the opportunity. "I see. And in what ways is he different?"

"Father was selfish. He only ever worried about how being poor affected him. He couldn't go to the places he wanted and do the things he wanted… meanwhile, we had landlords threatening to throw us out into the streets. There was no money for clothes and no money for food, and he didn't really care. But that's not William. William loves us. He wants to protect us. He looks out for us, after all, as much as a little boy can. Father wasn't mean. He didn't hit us or yell at us, not very much anyway. But he just didn't want to be bothered, not with us and not really with Mother… and during his long absences, Mother would take to her bed and wail about it and she didn't want to be bothered with us either. Anytime William went to her, wanting to hug her or get a kiss from her, she'd just weep harder and send him away. I think he wanted to comfort her as much as to be comforted by her."

They kept walking, silently, for a few moments. Claudia was lost in thought, swamped by memories of her parents, by the grief for what was lost and also, it seemed, for the grief of what had never been. For herself, Callie was at a loss. She wanted nothing more than to gather all of those children into her arms and squeeze them and never let go. But confessions like Claudia's didn't happen without reason. There was a warning in them as well, and she needed to know what it was.

"You don't seem the sort to simply bare one's soul. In fact, I don't think if you'd had another choice that you would have told me any of these things. So I must think that there is a reason, Claudia, you're telling me all of this now," Callie observed softly.

"You're quite right. There is a reason. He'll get attached to you, you see? Because you're kind. And so very few people have been kind to William. And I don't want him to be hurt. I know he's a boy and he wants to pretend that he's tough and strong and that nothing bothers him, but I think, in truth, his heart is more fragile than mine or Charlotte's," the girl explained. "And he likes you. He likes you quite a lot."

"I like him quite a lot, too," Callie replied. "I like all of you. And I hope that as the days go along, we will all like each other even more. But I'm not going to run off and leave you the way your last governess did. Nor will I ever tell William that he cannot give me a hug or kiss my cheek. I daresay I will give him hugs and kisses until he becomes utterly sick of them and runs away from me."

"Everyone says they won't leave. But in the end, everyone does," Claudia said.

Callie wanted more than anything to simply hug the child, to take her in her arms and tell her that she knew exactly what that felt like. But that wasn't why Claudia had opened up to her. It wasn't about her. It was about the need she felt to protect her siblings.

Callie sighed. "We'll have to let time tell us how it will all go, won't we?"

"I suppose we will," Claudia agreed.

Changing the subject, Callie gestured toward William who was now climbing the tree he'd apparently conquered during his sword fight. "How long do you suppose it will take for him to expend enough energy to tackle learning his letters?"

Claudia glanced across the distance between them and where her brother played. "A year or so, I would think."

Callie laughed at that. "You read more than a little, don't you?"

Claudia shrugged. "I do. But I hate reading boring school books."

"Then what do you like to read about?"

"Adventure," the little girl answered.

"I think we might be able to squeeze a bit of adventure into our lessons today. You get Charlotte and I will get William and we will head back."

WINN HADN'T GONE to his club, after all. While it had been his destination to start, he'd been waylaid by business. That seemed to always be the way. For weeks, he'd been dodging an acquaintance who wanted to lure him into a risky business venture. Risk wasn't really Winn's cup of tea. Solid, sound, boring investments with smaller but more certain rewards were fine with him. Still, being dragged along with a group of three other fellows to the home of the fourth man being courted for the scheme, he decided anything was better than his own home and the sweet temptation of Miss Calliope St. James' company.

As they reached the elaborate facade of the elegant mansion that belonged to the Gerald Alford, Duke of Averston, Winn couldn't hide his surprise as his brows arched upward in incredulity. "You're courting Averston for this scheme?"

It was a well-known fact that Averston, despite his title and luxurious home, had little ready capital, at least on a personal level. The houses and properties were maintained by the same trust that governed all the wealth left behind by his predecessor. The former Duke of Averston had never married, but had sired a child out of wedlock to whom all of his personal wealth and unentailed properties had been bequeathed. But until that missing heir was found, there was little Averston could do. Indeed, it seemed his only vice was to continually redecorate and "improve" the properties that were in his care. The only other remaining member of the family was the dowager duchess, a woman known by one and all to be a veritable dragon. She had a separate residence but it was widely understood that she kept her grandson on a short leash.

"Well, he's expressed interest and he's in the process of petitioning the House of Lords to declare the previous duke's will void in light of the missing heir's continued missing status. We might get lucky," Charles Burney, the mastermind behind the imports venture, offered with a grin. "Surely no one thinks the child survived at this point!"

Unless Burney had some inside information, Winn was fairly certain the man was set for disappointment. Averston and the dowager duchess had been actively trying to break his late uncle's will since the man's passing. Still, it was a diversion that would keep him from the chaos of his own home, so he gamely followed the group inside.

"His grace awaits you in the library," the butler intoned with all the formality and dignity that a ducal butler should possess.

Winn wondered for a moment if he might steal him away, but then nixed the idea. His young footman would do well enough. His own household was not nearly so high in the instep that he required such a servant, after all. And the young man had been impossibly proud at the prospect of his improved situation. It wouldn't do at all to renege on that offer now.

The library was all the way at the end of a long corridor. Marble floors, art from all over the world and all of it beyond price, along with gilded cornices and elaborate carved moldings combined to create a feeling of opulence and decadence that could only be rivaled by Carlton House itself. It was too much for his taste, too much fuss, too boastful of one's wealth. It made him distinctly uncomfortable. Perhaps because it was such an effrontery when the money being spent so lavishly on such interiors didn't belong to the man who lived amongst them. It seemed to Winn that Averston would rather squander the money than see it go to someone else, even in theory.

"Isn't it a sight?" Burney said, elbowing him in the ribs. "I don't think Golden Ball himself could surpass it!"

"That's hardly an endorsement," Winn said disapprovingly, "Given that Mr. Ball Hughes is now living in France all but penniless after having squandered his very substantial fortune."

That sobered Burney immediately who then straightened and began to speak quietly to his other potential investors. They were halfway down the corridor at that point but Winn simply stopped, struck immediately dumb by the portrait he saw there. The woman in the painting was beautiful—pale, as was the fashion of the day, with powdered hair and elaborately styled hair. But she was also achingly familiar. The bone structure of her heart-shaped face, the fullness of her perfectly bow-shaped pout, and her sparkling eyes all called to mind another woman. It was as if he were being haunted by Calliope St. James, seeing her face everywhere he went.

"Who is this woman in this portrait?" he asked. But no one answered. The men with Burney simply shrugged and the footmen clearly had no idea.

Winn continued to stare at it. There were slight differences in her appearance to Calliope's. The woman in the portrait was older, and there was something more worldly about her, a cunningness in her gaze that his governess lacked. With her hair piled high in the Georgian style and wearing a gown that was daring, to say the least, she was clearly possessed of a less pronounced sense of modesty.

"I see you've discovered the great seductress."

Winn glanced up to see that Averston himself had emerged from his study to greet them or perhaps to send them away. The man was known for somewhat capricious moods. Dressed impeccably, his hair styled artfully and his expression cold and calculating, Winn remembered precisely why he'd never liked the man. "The great seductress?"

"Yes! That is the actress my uncle fell so deeply in love with all those years ago… the one he wished to marry but whom his parents threatened to disown him for even considering," Averston said. He smiled, but the expression never reached his eyes. They remained cold and hard, glittering with resentment. "Her name was Mademoiselle Veronique Delaine. Let us discuss our business first and if you are still curious after, I will tell you the woeful tale of a French harlot and my poor dupe of an uncle. Of course, you cannot let it be known to my grandmother that I uttered her name in this house."

"Thank you," Winn replied. "Let's all get this business sorted out, shall we?" He would certainly find the time to wait for that particular story. He had the distinct impression that he suddenly had a very key piece of the puzzle himself.

"What's this scheme of your, Mr. Burney?" Averston demanded as they all made their way into his study. Like the rest of the house, it was richly appointed and ornate to the point of being obscene. Red velvet on the chairs, thick and heavy brocade on the walls and gold trimming on everything—it looked more like a throne room than a study.

"I've a cousin in Virginia who has recently acquired a tobacco plantation," Burney said.

"How did he acquire this property?" Winn demanded.

Burney shrugged. "I couldn't say."

"Is your cousin Phillip Burney? The one who fled England in disgrace for gambling debts?" Averston asked.

"It is," Burney replied. "But he's doing just smashing in America. Land of opportunity and all that!"

"I'm sure he is. For now, at any rate," Winn said. "Burney, these other gentlemen can do as they wish but I'll not put money on a shipment of tobacco from a farm won on the turn of a card by a man who has never been able to pass up a game of chance in his life. Your cousin is just as likely to lose this plantation tomorrow as he is to see the goods ever set sail for England. Furthermore, I won't do business with anyone who holds slaves, and if he won the plantation, he won them as well. I can't do it."

"I'm in agreement with Montgomery," Averston said. "Your cousin is a bad investment, Burney. I urge you, for the sake of your own fortune, to look elsewhere as a means of making your mark. He'll only see you beggared."

Burney rose, clearly annoyed with the lot of them. "I'll see myself out. Ferris, Sewell?"

The other two gentlemen, toadies of Burney's more so than actual investors, followed him from the Duke of Averston's study as he left in a huff.

"He's a fool," Averston said to Winn.

"Many young men are," Winn agreed.

Averston surveyed him. "But not you. Never you. Though you hardly qualify as young anymore, do you?"

Well, that certainly stung a bit. "I'm not exactly in my dotage," Winn protested.

Averston grinned, but again it wasn't a warm expression. The man didn't seem to do warm, per se. "Not what I meant. You, Montgomery, were born an old man. Always prudent, careful, cautious, you never overspend, over invest, lose at the tables or take extravagant mistresses. In short, you're quite dull."

Winn didn't take offense. Why would he when everything the man said was true? "I never felt the need to do any of those things. Besides, my younger brother had all of that covered for the family. They hardly needed the both of us to do so. Then it would have been redundant. If that makes me dull, so be it," Winn stated. He didn't like Averston but he didn't dislike him either. He found the man cold and they certainly moved in different circles, but there was something about the man he didn't quite trust. Averston struck him as a man with secrets and that always gave him pause.

Averston considered him for a moment, his gaze curious and lingering in a manner that left Winn very uncomfortable. "You wished to know the history of that portrait... of Mademoiselle Veronique Delaine, did you not?"

"I did," Winn agreed.

Averston moved toward the door and back out into the corridor. Winn followed until they were both standing once more before the portrait.

"My uncle, as I'm certain you know, was a confirmed bachelor. Rather like yourself, I think, and myself as well, I suppose. What's your reason for maintaining your bachelor state?"

"I've yet to meet a woman I wish to spend the remainder of my life with," Winn replied. "Though I'm certain I one day shall. Or at the very least, one I don't mind so much."

Averston nodded. "I see. And young Mr. Burney... what do you think his marital prospects are?"

Winn shrugged. It was an odd question, but he answered it regardless. "Burney is little more than a pup yet. I daresay he has plenty of time to sort it out. Why do you ask?"

Averston's mouth turned in a patently false smile. "Just thinking that his poor business acumen may be quite distressing to the future Mrs. Burney. That is all. I wondered if perhaps there was some young miss on the line destined for a disappointment."

Winn frowned. The conversation had taken a turn he was befuddled by. "I couldn't say. I've never discussed the matter with him. Our families are close, but Burney was always more a compatriot of my brother than mine. Though I daresay I shall be in attendance at his sister's debut. It would be a terrible disappointment to her mother if I were to ignore our family's long connection."

"Have you designs on the girl, then? I can't quite see you with a fresh out of the schoolroom miss, Montgomery."

Immediately, the image of Miss St. James appeared in his mind. But not as a prim and proper governess. No, he was imagining her in a gown similar to the one in the portrait, which would bare her shoulders and the creamy swells of her breasts while her brown hair cascaded in rich waves over her back. It was an image that was far too enticing for his own good.

"Well, then," Averston said, "Let us satisfy your curiosity about the portrait. While in Paris, my uncle saw her perform just before the Revolution and was utterly smitten. He begged her to come to England, fearing what might become of her if she remained in France. So she did. And she performed here for many years… but when she became with child, well, he was no longer content simply to have her as his mistress. He wanted her as his wife. Obviously my grandparents refused… my grandmother quite vociferously. As they should have, I suppose."

"Why should they have?" Winn demanded. It was scandalous, certainly, but the previous duke had been a man fully grown.

"Because she was common… an actress, no less, and one with quite a storied and sordid past. Hardly the fitting bride for a duke," Averston said, completely unaware or perhaps uncaring that he sounded like a pompous ass. "Some noblemen might deign to muddy their bloodlines by wedding filth and settling what should be no better than bastards into the House of Lords, but it's a terribly selfish thing, don't you think? Or so, I've always been told."

"No, not really. I think a man ought to marry where, when and how he chooses and I think it ought not matter in the least what anyone else thinks of it," Winn said. *Although, he might not have expressed such an opinion before setting eyes on a pretty governess.*

Averston's eyebrows arched upward and he laughed. "Perhaps you are more like your wild younger brother than I thought! Such radical views to be expressed by a man who has spent the majority of his life making no waves at all. Tell me, Montgomery, will you be searching for a bride in St. Giles? Spitalfields, perhaps? White Chapel? The Devil's Acre? You'll set the *ton* on its collective ear yet!"

"I'm not searching for a bride. I have a nephew who will inherit. I'm content enough with that," Winn insisted. It was what he'd always told himself.

"Ah, but you won't hamstring him as my uncle did me, will you? Saddle him with a title and no funds with which to support it? All of this—all that you see here—it isn't really mine, is it? I just get to borrow it until whatever unworthy bastard he sired is found."

"What became of Mademoiselle Delaine and her child?" Winn asked.

"Lost. I'm afraid my grandmother is quite ruthless," Averston admitted. There was some sympathy in his voice, though it was scant. "Mademoiselle Delaine met a terrible fate at the hands of some brigand... likely hired by dear old granny. Though she'd hardly leave any evidence behind. She's vicious but sly as a fox."

Winn blinked at that. "You think the dowager duchess had your uncle's mistress, the mother of his child, murdered?"

Averston shrugged again. "It wouldn't surprise me. Thank God I wasn't born with some sort of obvious defect... she'd likely have drowned me in the bath."

The day was getting stranger and stranger and all Winn wanted was to be away from Averston and his family dramas which were worthy of any Greek tragedy. But first, he had to know. "And the child? Was she still with child when she was killed?"

Averston laughed. "I should have been so lucky. No. She'd whelped the bastard already and hidden it away. Her dying words to some loud-mouthed vicar were of the child's fate. 'She lives. Find her,' Mademoiselle Delaine reportedly whispered."

Winn looked back at the portrait again, a sick feeling burning in his stomach. It was the weight of dread. Recalling Miss St. James' story to the children about her parentage, or at least what he'd managed to overhear, the similarities were uncanny. "And what did this vicar do?"

"Well, of course, he had to cry hither and yon that her child lived and was safe... hence my current situation. A duke by title, a poor relation to an unknown, bastard heiress by circumstance."

"Your uncle must have been near mad with grief," Winn observed. "To have lost the woman he loved and have no notion of where their child might be."

"Oh, he was. He and my grandfather argued so fiercely that the old man had a heart seizure and passed away right in this very corridor. As for my uncle, all his attempts to locate the child were in vain. He never found it."

"It? You don't even know the sex?" Winn asked, striving for a tone that was only mildly curious and didn't give away his own thoughts on the matter.

"A girl, according to the gossipy vicar, though who knows if it's true or accurate. Useless female... even if she is found, she'll marry and the family's wealth will go elsewhere. I imagine that is my uncle's revenge upon his parents, to beggar the title in their memory," Averston droned, the words muttered low and half to himself. As if realizing what he was doing, he looked up, plastered an urbane and utterly false smile on his face, and said, "At any rate, the child vanished, never to be seen or heard from again. My uncle was distraught and vowed never to marry. And as you know, he did not. So now, I am his heir. But only to the title and one paltry entailed estate. The rest is left to a bastard we cannot find, who has likely died already of the pox or drink in some rookery hovel."

"What if she didn't die? What if she is alive and well and in London?" Winn asked.

Averston's expression was grim and cold. "Then she would do well to stay hidden. I don't mean to let any of this," he swept his arm about to encompass the grandeur that surrounded them, "slip through my grasp, Montgomery, not without one hell of a fight. No matter the cost. And if dear old granny ever finds her, well, suffice to say, she'll regret that the day she was born."

As threats went, it was far from veiled. Winn knew that Averston was ruthless. It appeared it was a family trait. Whatever happened, he'd need to be certain that Calliope St. James never crossed his path or that of the dowager duchess. Otherwise, there would be hell and the devil to pay.

Chapter Five

A T THE END of a long and exhausting day, Callie was actually rather content with her progress. While the children's education was terribly lacking, their intelligence certainly was not. And taking them to the park first, letting them burn off some of their natural exuberance before getting down to their studies, had been an excellent way to begin the day.

Callie had ushered them down the stairs and into the breakfast room where she'd arranged for their dinner to be served. They didn't need the opulence and distance of the formal dining room. Not yet. They needed a place where they could be comfortable and not fearful of breaking things or violating rules they didn't quite understand yet. With a moment to herself, she paused in her task of putting away books and toys and stretched deeply, her back aching from leaning over their smaller desks all day as she corrected penmanship and letters and mathematical sums. She let out a satisfied groan as tense muscles released.

"Has it been that torturous?"

Callie let out a shriek of alarm as she whirled to face the doorway and the man who now occupied it. The Earl of Montgomery stood there, all laconic charm and smug amusement. *And a ridiculous degree of masculine beauty that she could not afford to acknowledge.* "You frightened me half to death."

"You did say I was to have my lessons after the children. I thought we might have them in my study with a light repast. I'm assuming you have not had your supper, Miss St. James."

At the very mention of food, her traitorous stomach growled alarmingly. She blushed furiously. "No, I have not." It was a mistake to share a meal with him, a mistake to create a sense of familiarity between them. And yet, knowing that, she still wanted to be in his presence more than she wished to heed her common sense. If there was proof of just how dangerous he was to her, that was all she required.

"Then come along, Calliope St. James. You may teach me how to be a better human and I will attempt to glean all the information I can about your mysterious past," he said, and stepped clear of the door, holding one arm out in a gesture for her to exit. "The maids can tidy up. It is what I pay them for, after all."

"I hate to make more work for them," she said. It was a pitiful excuse but the only one she could summon.

"I assure you, by keeping those three small ruffians confined to one room in the house for most of the day, you have significantly lightened their workload already," he offered.

"Well in that case," Callie relented. As they walked down the stairs toward his study, she continued, "There are things I must ask you about the children's upbringing thus far… and I am afraid you will not like them."

He sighed heavily. "No doubt they paint a very villainous picture of my brother."

"Not villainous, precisely. But selfish, certainly, and perhaps very immature."

He shrugged then. "An accurate description of him, I think. And one far kinder than he likely deserved."

Callie looked back at him in surprise, stunned by his rueful and regretful tone. It was a mistake, taking her eyes off the stairs. They were unfamiliar to her and she stumbled. She might have fallen had he not reached out to grasp her arm, steadying her. It brought them closer than they previously had been, close enough that when she glanced up at him, she could see the flecks of gold in the depths of his green eyes and the day's growth of whiskers on his face was no longer just an indistinct shadow. She was close enough that she could see the texture of his skin and wonder at what it might feel like against her own.

It was foolish and so very, very dangerous!

A nervous laugh escaped her. "Pardon my clumsiness, my lord. I'm quite all right now."

He cleared his throat and stepped back from her. But he kept his grasp on her elbow as they continued down to the main floor. "We should both be more careful, Miss St. James," he said.

Callie had to wonder if he was talking about more than her near mishap.

As they neared the study, a footman rushed forward to open the door for them and Callie swept inside, Lord Montgomery on her heels. He pushed the door closed, and then apparently thought better of it. He opened it once more, halfway, and left it just so, propped there with a heavy cast iron statue of some sort of poorly rendered terrier.

"That's an odd piece," she commented, gesturing toward the rather homely-looking dog statue.

"We go together," the earl said, as he moved past her toward a small table set before the fire. With a self-deprecating grin, he added, "Odd pieces."

Callie stepped deeper into the room in his wake and took a seat in the chair before his desk that he'd indicated. Two plates heaped with cold meat, cheese and bread had been placed there, along with a bottle of wine and glasses. It was informal, strangely intimate, and might, under different circumstances, have been deemed romantic. Callie was so distracted by that train of thought that it startled her when he pushed the chair in for her. She only just managed to stifle a startled shriek. Even then, he leaned in close enough that she caught the scent of his shaving soap and the hint of something else that was wildly appealing to her. It made her think of the strength and the steadiness of him as he'd caught her on the stairs.

"What is it you wish to know about the children?" he asked, his voice barely more than a whisper. "I'd prefer to speak quietly. The servants know enough about my brother's disgrace."

"What is your brother's disgrace precisely?" she asked.

"All of them. Gambling. Women. Opium. There was not a single vice that he did not indulge to impossible excess," the earl admitted. "Venetia, the children's mother, was young and foolish and allowed him to seduce her. I say allowed because he did not seek her out. She put herself in his very chambers at a house party intending to be seduced by him. She fancied herself in love with him. I believe she had some foolish notion that if she loved him enough, it would save him. Clearly she was mistaken. It was a terrible scandal. They married against my father's wishes but at the pistol-accompanied urging of her own father. Indeed, I daresay if my brother had refused, he'd have been killed outright."

"And afterward? Were they happy together at all?" Callie asked.

He raised his brows in a rather surprised fashion, as if it were something he'd never considered before. "I suppose they were at first. It wasn't long after they married that they announced to the family that she was with child. But by the time Claudia was born, the bloom had certainly worn off the rose. Wills was drinking heavily, gambling incessantly and he'd begun visiting the opium dens. Forgive me, Miss St. James, I should not speak so bluntly of such things."

"I'd prefer you did, my lord," Callie insisted. "For better or for ill, your brother and your sister-in-law spoke very freely of such things in front of the children. I do not have the luxury of being missish about propriety in these very dire circumstances."

He considered it for a moment, clearly weighing the need to be honest with his own sense of propriety. In the end, he continued, "After they married, and while Venetia was in her confinement, there was another scandal. Wills was accused of doing the unthinkable... that he had forced himself upon and compromised an innocent young woman."

Callie let that sink in for a moment. When she did pose the question, her tone was neutral and without condemnation. "Did he? I understand that you may not be able to answer... but do you think he was capable?"

The earl's brows knit together in a thoughtful frown. "I honestly don't know. There are differing accounts of the nature of Wills' relationship with Miss Serena Darlington. Wills always contended that she was a willing participant to seduction and that she was not nearly so chaste as others painted her to be. And Miss Darlington insisted that my brother had forced himself upon her despite the fact that she was in his chambers while clad only in her nightrail. That's only damning because apparently her own guest room was in another wing of the house where they were all gathered for the party. Rather than fight a duel and face terrible social and potential legal consequences for his actions, not to mention the financial consequences if either Mr. Darlington or Miss Darlington's betrothed elected to file suit against him, he took Venetia and Claudia and fled to Spain. From there, I cannot tell you what their life was like." He paused then, his fingers drumming idly on the desk. When he looked at her, there was banked fury in his eyes. His brother might have died, but it was quite obvious that he was still livid with the man. "Though I cannot imagine it was pleasant. Wills was spoiled. He might have been a man grown with a wife and a family, but he was still very much a spoiled boy... all the way to the end."

"I don't wish to say too much," Callie began. She was hesitant, but she couldn't help but think her conversation with Claudia was important in ways she might not understand. "I think much of what Claudia said was uttered in confidence, though that was not stated expressly. Still, I don't wish to betray her trust. But I will say that her parents were not happy together and their unhappiness took a toll on the children. I also think that their father's gaming often left them with very uncertain fortunes and little sense of stability." She stopped speaking when she noted his expression. The fury she'd seen banked in his eyes had suddenly blazed to life.

"I paid for their lodgings," he snapped, the words bitten off sharply. "I paid for their governess. I sent more than adequate funds to see to their comfort."

"Did you pay their landlord directly? Or their grocer?" Callie asked softly.

"Of course not! It would have been impossible to manage such things at a distance! But I was not so foolish as to give the money to my brother, Miss St. James. The money was sent through a third party and was then given to Venetia to see to everyone's needs."

Callie sighed. "She loved him, I think. And she desperately wanted him to love her. So she gave him whatever it was he asked for... that no doubt included the funds you sent to support them all."

⤜⤜⤜✕⤛⤛⤛

WINN ROSE FROM the small table and stalked the length of the room and back. If Wills had been in front of him, he'd have planted his fist right in his brother's face. In retrospect, what Miss St. James proposed made perfect sense. He'd never seen it because he'd never wanted to see it. He'd done the least amount that he had to do and patted himself on the back for it, his duty done and his conscience clear.

"I don't know who I am more angry at... my brother or myself," he said. "I was a fool not to see it."

"I don't think anger in either direction bears considering, my lord.

It's a wasted emotion. Being angry at yourself only creates more misery and unhappiness and your brother, sadly, is not here to face the consequences of his actions. For that matter, neither is your sister-in-law. She is hardly blameless. Any woman who chooses a man over her children, even if it is her husband, cannot be spared censure."

"You have very definite opinions on the matter, Miss St. James," Winn observed, thinking of the woeful tale of Mademoiselle Veronique Delaine. Would she have always put her daughter first? It certainly seemed as if she had in the end, regardless of how it had ended for her. While Calliope St. James' life had been troubled, she had survived to adulthood.

Miss St. James fidgeted with the serviette on her lap. It was clear that she was debating how forthcoming to be with her response. Finally, she said, "I suppose I do. Children are very vulnerable. Smaller, weaker, dependent upon us to care for them and to provide for them, to teach them how to one day provide for themselves. There is nothing so selfish and so worthy of disdain as those who would neglect a child for their own interests."

"I see. And were these ideas formed through your acquaintance with Miss Euphemia Darrow?"

"They were certainly cemented by my acquaintance with her. I have witnessed firsthand what the selfishness of adults does to children. Shuffled from one place to another by those who don't wish to be bothered with you... I understood then that I was being wronged. But I didn't know to what degree until I met Effie. Until she took me into her home and into her heart and offered me a place to belong, to feel safe and sheltered from all the wicked things in this world," Miss St. James said softly. "I owe her my gratitude, and my unwavering loyalty and support."

"You speak of debts, Miss St. James. What of softer feelings? What of the heart?" he asked. It was dangerous territory, to discuss such things with her.

"I love Effie. I could not love her more if we shared a blood kinship. But loyalty and support are a way of showing that affection for her, of demonstrating the depth of my feelings on the matter." Her answer was decisive and firm. She viewed Euphemia Darrow as her family, that much was obvious.

"And what of the woman who birthed you? Do you owe her anything?" Winn challenged. He needed to know what she knew. Did she have any suspicions of her origins that would dispel his own sweeping theories? He fervently hoped so. Heaven knew it would simplify matters greatly.

"I neither know nor care. She is likely long dead and, if so, knowing her fate will not bring her back nor will it engender some feeling in me for a person who is naught but a stranger," Miss St. James said.

"And if she were not dead?"

The pretty governess shrugged, but her hardened expression was in clear opposition to her casual posture. "If she were not dead, then her abandonment of me smacks of the kind of selfishness I have just decried. And I am better for not knowing her."

"You could have other family out there. You could be an heiress," he suggested. "There's been a run of lost heirs turning up these past few years."

Miss St. James laughed at that. "Your imagination runs away with you as much as William's does! An heiress... I was deposited on the doorstep of a workhouse as an infant. Left in a basket in the freezing cold. That is not what becomes of heiresses, my lord."

"Which workhouse?" he asked.

"Does it matter?" she snapped. "Is not one workhouse equally horrific to the next?"

"No, they are not." It was a sad truth and they both knew it.

"Then it is the one whose name I bear. The St. James Workhouse. The very worst of the worst," she said. "It is where I was deposited as an infant, and where I was returned years later, when my foster parents died."

"How long were you there?" he asked.

"I was there for just over three years. I was eight when the vicar took me there and dropped me off. I was nearly twelve when Effie saw me through the slats of the gate and demanded that I be given to her care. I think I weighed less when she took me from that place than when I had gone in," she said flatly. "When you are too small to fight to keep your food, it is quickly taken from you."

Winn said nothing. What could he say to such a thing? The very idea that the beautiful, articulate, and impossibly bright woman before him might have died of starvation in childhood at one of the very institutions that was intended to prevent such a fate was something he dared not contemplate. It was too devastating to consider. But he meant to get to the truth and now he had a place to start.

"Eat your supper, Miss St. James, and I'll have the carriage brought round to see you home."

"I can walk," she protested.

"It would be very unwise. The fog is growing thick out there and it will be dark. Far too dangerous."

"Will you not dine with me?" she asked. "We have much to discuss about the children."

"Tomorrow night, Miss St. James. I find with all these revelations, my time might be better spent sitting in the breakfast room with them while they throw food at one another like wild animals. That is rather the point of your lessons, isn't it? To put me in the position of being a part of their lives rather than a disinterested observer?"

She ducked her head. "You are a good student, my lord."

"Apparently, I have a good teacher," he said. "Enjoy your meal. I shall see you on the morrow."

Chapter Six

"**I** DON'T KNOW why I have to go shopping. I don't like shopping!" William groused as he bounced on the opposite seat of the carriage and kicked his legs.

"Do you like trousers that are too short and coats that are too tight?" Callie asked him pointedly. They'd spent the morning at lessons and the afternoon, by mutual agreement between herself and her employer, was to see the children properly outfitted. It was the beginning of December, after all, and it was already too cold for what the children currently possessed.

"No!"

"William, I do not like shopping either, but there are times in a man's life when he must do things he does not wish to. More often than not, it's shopping," Lord Montgomery said.

Callie gifted him with a baleful stare and he simply turned away to look out the window of the swaying coach. There was little enough room to do anything else. With the earl, Callie, three children and a maid for propriety's sake, they were packed in rather tightly.

"We must shop, William, because you and your sisters are not equipped for an English winter. It also seems that you've all grown quite a bit since you last had new clothes."

"We've never had new clothes," Charlotte said and then immediately went back to playing with the doll her uncle had gifted her.

"You must have!" Callie said.

"No, Claudia is wearing dresses of Mama's that had been cut down and I'm wearing Claudia's old dresses that she can't wear anymore because she's too big!" Charlotte finished proudly.

"Well, you will all have new clothes now," the earl said firmly. "They will be yours and yours alone and they will be made to your measurements as befits proper English gentlemen and ladies."

William looked a little more pleased by that. "Do gentlemen climb trees, Uncle?"

The earl turned to face him, clearly biting back a grin at the boy's concerned question. "When the occasion calls for it."

"What occasions call for it?" William asked.

The earl looked back at Callie and she felt the full weight of his stare. For that split second of time, it was as if there were no one else in the coach with them. He looked at her and she looked at him, and the whole world simply fell away. Oh, that was not good at all. That, she would daresay, was utterly disastrous.

Finally, he spoke and the spell, momentary as it was, had been broken. "What is tomorrow, Miss St. James?"

"Tomorrow will be Wednesday, my lord," she answered, trying to ignore the slight tremor in her voice and the fact that it suddenly felt as if her stays were too tight.

"Wednesdays are such an occasion. I daresay, barring rain and snow, every Wednesday is an occasion to climb trees," he proclaimed.

William let out a whoop of delight. "Can we go back to the park tomorrow so I can climb that big'un, Miss St. James?"

"That big one," she corrected. "And if you're willing to spend at least part of the morning learning the names of the trees you wish to climb, we certainly may."

"All right," he agreed.

The carriage slowed and Lord Montgomery stepped out of it first. He lifted out Charlotte first, then Claudia and William jumped down on his own. He reached back for Callie's hand and helped her down carefully. But he did not linger. As soon as her feet were firmly on the paving stones, he stepped back, putting not an insignificant amount of space between them. The maid followed, assisted by one of the footmen who'd had to cling to the back of the carriage for dear life as they made their way to the shopping district.

"I shall take William with me to the tailor and you may take the girls, along with Maisey, to the dressmaker's, if that plan suits you, Miss St. James," the earl offered.

"It does, my lord. After the dressmaker, we must also go to the milliner and to the cobbler. The girls will both need shoes and, I daresay, William will as well."

"He will not go to a mere cobbler," the earl said, as if offended by the suggestion. "That is all well and good for dancing slippers and women's half boots. No, Miss St. James, he will go to Hoby's and will be fitted for proper boots as any gentleman should."

"Proper boots... to climb trees?" she asked pointedly.

The earl would not be swayed. "I'm certain Hoby has a sensible solution to making boots sturdy enough for the active life of a young boy. If there are any problems, please send for me at once."

"We shouldn't have any problems, my lord," Callie replied. "I have your letter of credit. And I promise, we will not buy out the shops."

"Buy them out if it's needed. Make sure they have everything they require... and that not all of it is terribly functional. They should have a few things just because they are pretty and fun. Don't you think?"

Callie bit back a smile. "I'm glad we're in agreement. I'd planned to do so anyway."

He laughed. "Of course, you did. It dawns on me, Miss St. James, that we've never discussed the specific terms of your salary."

"You'll get a bill, my lord," she said. "Let us hope you are still feeling so generous then. Come along, girls. We have much to do."

Ushering Claudia and Charlotte into one of the more fashionable shops located in the Burlington Arcade, Callie prepared herself for the worst. She fully anticipated that the modiste would be unkind, high in the instep, and very much affronted by having to wait on a mere governess. Luckily, she was pleasantly surprised by the woman who greeted them, a Madame de Beauchamps. The woman looked at Callie with curiosity.

"My dear, you are very familiar to me. Have we met? Perhaps I have dressed you before?" Madame de Beauchamps asked.

"Oh, hardly. I'm a governess to these young ladies... they are wards of their uncle, the Earl of Montgomery. They have only recently arrived in England and, sadly, their Spanish wardrobes are hardly up to snuff for our chilly winters," Callie said with all the friendliness she could muster.

Madame de Beauchamps looked from Claudia to Charlotte. "My goodness! What pretty young girls. It will be like dressing dolls! Come, I have some fabrics. Soft and very warm... if we are lucky enough to see snow this year, you will be able to play in it all day long."

The girls followed Madame de Beauchamps toward a large room filled to overflowing with fabric samples and fashion plates. Several books of fashion plates were placed before them and Callie began looking through them to find sturdy but pretty day dresses for the girls along with a few prettier frocks.

"Can I have a dress for my doll that matches my own?" Charlotte asked.

"Silly," Claudia scolded in a way that sounded very parental, "she makes dresses for ladies and not for dolls!"

"Nonsense," Madame de Beauchamps said. "I have made many dresses for dolls. When I was a little girl, that is how I learned to sew... to make pretty things. I took fabric scraps and made dresses for my own doll, though I do not think she was as pretty as yours."

"She's new. My uncle gave her to me," Charlotte said with a shy smile.

Callie bit back a smile of her own. Of course, he had. He'd seen a little girl without a doll and he'd given her one because that's what kind men did. "Did you get a doll, Claudia?" Callie asked her.

"I did. She's very pretty. I leave her at home though so she doesn't get dirty or get her face all cracked," Claudia said, sparing a warning glance at her younger sister.

"I'm careful," Charlotte insisted, stamping her little foot.

"Girls, Madame de Beauchamps is very busy and she does not need us taking up more of her valuable time by arguing. Now, I've picked out some patterns here that I think you might like. Take a look at them and tell me what you think," Callie said.

Charlotte ran over to her, barreling into Callie's side. She looked at the fashion plates and grinned. "They're pretty!" The word came out "pwetty" as she'd once more tucked her thumb into her mouth. It was utterly charming.

"I like them," Claudia agreed but with much greater reservation. She bit her lip worriedly and added, "Is it too much? We've never had so many dresses! If we get too many, he'll be angry!"

"You've never lived in a house with an earl. I think we might be erring on the side of caution and ordering too little, but you all are growing quickly so it's probably just as well," Callie said as she rose from the settee, selections in hand. She turned to find Madame de Beauchamps staring at her again.

"Forgive me, but I really do feel as if I know you... that I have seen you somewhere before," the modiste insisted.

"I am a governess, Madame de Beauchamps. I could hardly afford to patronize your shop and even if I could, in my line of work, it would be terribly impractical."

"Work..." Madame de Beauchamps murmured. "Yes. It was something to do with work. I think—it's terribly indelicate and I mean no offense at all in asking, but I must ask, Miss, did you have a mother or sister who was in the theater? I worked there for many years as a dresser."

"I have no siblings that I know of, Madame, and my mother is unknown to me, as well," Callie answered. "I am sorry I cannot solve your riddle for you."

Madame de Beauchamps sighed sadly. "Alas, it is my curse that I never forget a face and yet rarely remember a name. Let us choose the fabrics for each of these dresses, no?"

⤜⟫⟫⟫⟪⟪⟪⤛

THEY'D LEFT HOBY'S shop after William had been measured for boots and any other footwear he might need. They were walking back up Piccadilly toward the Arcade where Miss St. James had taken the girls. William walked beside him. He didn't hold on to the boy, but he did keep a close eye on him. Had he never realized how dangerous a London street could be? Horses, carts, costermongers—there were hazards in every direction. Every loud noise had him fighting the urge to snatch the child up lest he dart in front of an oncoming carriage or get trampled under the feet of the crowd.

"Montgomery!"

Winn heard his name and dared take his gaze off William long enough to identify the source. Burney. A curse bubbled inside him, but he wisely held it in check. The last thing he wanted was to get into another argument with Burney about his bloody scheme. He liked the fellow, but investing in Burney's less than upstanding cousin was a surefire way to lose money and sour friendships.

"Hello, Burney," Winn replied.

"Who's this?" Burney asked, gesturing toward William.

"My name is William and I can speak perfectly well," the boy replied.

Winn gave him a warning glower. "Burney, this is my nephew, William. He has only recently arrived from Spain."

"Wills' son? I'll be dam—delighted to make your acquaintance, young man," Burney corrected quickly. "I knew your father quite well. I was at school with him. Will you be off to Eton, then? You're almost of an age!"

"William's education has been somewhat unorthodox, living in Spain as it were," Winn replied. "I've hired an excellent governess for the children and once William is properly prepared, then we will discuss school. For now, I think I'd like to keep the children closer to home until they, and I, feel more settled with our current arrangement."

"Children?" Burney guffawed. "There's more than one? You need to get yourself a wife, Montgomery! Best way to handle children is to let a woman take care of them for you! Children, indeed!"

"You could marry Miss St. James," William offered helpfully.

Winn felt his blood run cold. The last thing he needed was Burney, who was likely still trying to get in the good graces of Averston after that last debacle, to become curious about his governess who—he was almost entirely certain—was the rightful heir to the Averston fortune. If Burney ever saw Miss St. James and put two and two together, it would be disastrous and possibly even deadly for her. It was certainly a long shot in Burney's case, given that he was not the swiftest of fellows. But as the saying went, even a broken clock was right twice a day. "I cannot marry Miss St. James, William. She is your governess."

Burney chortled. "Many a gentleman has made a worse choice than just a governess! At least she's respectable. Of course, most governesses of my acquaintance don't inspire men to make them unrespectable, do they? Plain, if they're lucky, and uglier than a mud fence if they're not!"

William took a step forward. "I don't like you. You laugh very loud and I think you're talking about Miss St. James in a manner that isn't very nice."

Burney blinked at that, then laughed harder. "I say, he's a right knight in shining armor!"

And that was when William kicked him. He drew his foot back, let it fly forward and caught Burney right in the shin. Which wouldn't have been so bad if Burney had been wearing boots. But he wasn't. He was wearing trousers and a pair of leather slippers which meant that kick was felt and heard by everyone around them.

Burney howled in agony, William balled his fists up ready to leap to the defense of his governess and all Winn wanted to do was not have anyone, anywhere wondering about who and what Miss St. James was in order to create such a stir. "Time to go, William. My apologies, Burney," Winn said and then hoisted William under his arm and took off at a brisk pace.

He could hear Burney calling after him, "Blast him!"

"I don't like him," William said. "Put me down."

"I'll put you down if—*if*—you promise not to kick him again," Winn said.

"He deserved to be kicked!"

"Possibly, but you don't need to defend Miss St. James that way. Drawing more attention to his curiosity is not the way to preserve her reputation," Winn admonished as he settled the boy on the ground.

They'd just reached the entrance to the Arcade and had ducked inside when Miss St. James emerged from a shop, the maid behind her carrying several packages, and the footman as well, and one each balanced in Claudia's and Charlotte's hands.

"I'm sorry, Miss St. James. Our outing has been cut short. I've recalled an important business matter I must take care of," Winn said. To the footman, he added, "I'll take those, Maisey, while you go and let the coachman know we need to leave. Immediately."

"Is something wrong, my lord?" Miss St. James asked. It was clear from her rather dubious expression that he was fooling no one.

"Just an urgent matter," he said.

"We met a very bad man, Miss St. James," William offered. "He was very loud and very rude and I kicked him."

Miss St. James' eyes widened with alarm. "Oh, dear. Oh, dear, no. Oh, William, you mustn't simply kick people. Why, it just isn't done!"

"He wasn't nice," William insisted. "You shouldn't have to be nice to not nice people!"

Miss St. James stooped down until she was eye to eye with William. "I know that sometimes it seems like being violent is the only way to make people to listen to you, especially when you're small or young. But not nice people will never learn to be nice if we only ever respond to them in kind. You must be nice so that they can learn by observing you."

William ducked his head. The footman scurried off to retrieve the coachman and carriage and Winn was breathing a sigh of relief. "If there is anything else the children require, we'll have tradesmen come to the house."

Miss St. James smiled. "Did shopping with William prove too much for you, my lord?"

As that excuse was far more palatable than the truth, and far less dangerous, he smiled in agreement. "Certainly. Tell me, Miss St. James, what else will these children require?"

"Claudia needs music lessons. I know the girl who works as a governess next door. I'm certain that their music teacher would take Claudia on, assuming he has availability."

"See that it's done," he said. "And if he doesn't have availability, we will pay him enough that he will be inclined to make room."

Winn was breathing easier, thinking for the moment that they had averted disaster, that they were home free. That perhaps, just perhaps, things would go his way for the moment. Then he heard it. That booming, overly jovial voice that sounded like a death knell.

"There you are! I was wondering where you'd gotten off to so quickly!" Burney all but shouted as he came up behind them.

"Burney," Winn said. "I've got to get the children and their governess home. I'll meet you at the club later."

"I'm afraid I can't get to the club... otherwise engaged! A million things to do before my sister's debut. I say, you are coming to the ball Saturday night, aren't you? Mother will be over the moon to have an earl in attendance!"

Winn grimaced. It was no secret that Burney's mother was hoping for a match between Winn and her young daughter. It was not going to happen. "Yes, yes. I'll be there."

"Children, I have the distinct feeling that your uncle and this man need to have a word in private," Miss St. James said. "We shall walk down to the Arcade entrance and await you there, my lord."

And that was it. That moment, when she spoke in those lovely dulcet tones that were cultured, genteel and yet utterly pragmatic, that was the moment Burney looked at her and recognition flared in his gaze. "I say, you look terribly familiar!"

Miss St. James smiled. "That seems to be the theme of the day. You are the second person to comment on it. Good day to you, sir."

With that, she took the children and strolled toward the end of the row of shops and waited. Burney looked back at Winn. "Where do I know her from?"

"She's a governess, Burney. You can't know her from anywhere."

"But I do. I've seen her somewhere before."

"She just has one of those faces," Winn lied.

Burney guffawed. "There's not more than one face like that in all of England. She's a prime'un!"

Winn bristled. "She's not prime anything. She's the governess to my nieces and nephew and as you stated yourself, respectable. I'll thank you to speak of her as such." Winn walked away from him, shoulders back and head high, furious with Burney, with himself, with Averston.

"Montgomery... it was Averston, wasn't it?"

Winn's blood ran cold. "What about Averston?" he asked.

"It was Averston that made you pull out of the scheme, wasn't it?" Burney demanded.

Relief washed through him. "I was never in the scheme, Burney. I only agreed to hear you out. I wouldn't have bought into it with or without Averston. Good day... and yes, tell your mother, I will arrive on time for the ball Saturday night. I will make an appearance. I will dance with your sister, once and once only, and your mother will leave me firmly off her matchmaking list. Is that understood? I won't drag some schoolroom miss down the aisle!"

Chapter Seven

THEY RETURNED TO the townhouse and the ride was curiously quiet. William was brooding, the earl was lost in thought, Claudia and Charlotte were obviously very sensitive to the mood of their brother and uncle and so said nothing at all save for Charlotte's sweet murmuring as she spoke to her dolly. Finally, Callie'd had enough of it. "Who was that gentleman, Lord Montgomery?"

"His name is Charles Burney. He's an acquaintance, a school friend of the children's father, in fact. Currently, he's trying to get me to invest in some scheme with him that involves his cousin who is a gambler and wastrel. I have declined, but as you see, he is rather insistent," the earl replied.

He was lying. Oh, well, no. He was telling the truth, just not all of it. Of that, Callie was certain. "I see. And is that the man you found to not be nice, William?"

"Yes. He was very rude," the boy said, and proceeded to pick his nose.

"William, that is also rude. Fingers do not belong in noses. If you need a handkerchief, you will find one in your coat pocket," she said.

"How'd it get there?" he asked.

"I put it there this morning," she said. "In fact, I will put one there every day and when you feel the need of it, you have only to look."

"If William doesn't like him, then I don't like him!" Charlotte stated rather emphatically. "He seemed not nice. Too loud. And he showed too many teeth when he smiled… like he was a fake. Papa had friends like him. I didn't like them either. They'd eat all the food in the house and then leave us with nothing!"

Callie realized things were quickly getting out of hand. Speaking more firmly to the children than she had previously, she stated, "It isn't up to you to like him. You don't have to like anyone you don't choose to, but we do have to be polite to him. Don't you agree, my lord?"

"What?" he asked, looking back at her from where he'd been staring out the window. He was quite clearly distracted by something.

"Don't you agree that the children should all be polite to Mr. Burney? He is a family connection, after all."

"Yes," he agreed quickly. "Be polite to him, though I find it unlikely you'll ever have cause to cross paths with him again."

They'd reached the house then. Footmen came out and carried all the packages inside while the earl helped them all down once more, just as he'd done at the beginning of their shopping excursion. Though it was painfully obvious that the mood was entirely different.

"Children, go upstairs to your rooms and wash your hands and faces please. Claudia, will you help Charlotte?"

"Yes, Miss St. James," she said. They all curtsied and bowed and then ran up the stairs like heathens.

The moment they were out of sight, Callie whirled on him. "I don't know what you're playing at. Those children need you and if you think to ignore them in favor of some whey-faced, ne'er-do-well who only means to lead you down the primrose path and divest you of your fortune, I will not have it. That man is clearly not trustworthy!"

"Charles Burney is a family friend, Miss St. James. That is all. Furthermore, I think you may be laboring under some confusion about exactly who is in charge here. I'm not to be ordered about by you or anyone else," Winn snapped.

Callie wasn't about to be bowed by his temper. He could get as angry as he liked, but she wasn't going to back down. The children needed someone to stand up for them, and good or ill, that would always be her. "Very well, my lord. You are certainly in charge. But I am still entitled to my opinions, especially when they concern the children and their welfare. You heard Charlotte. He reminds them of their father and his feckless friends and associates. The last thing they need is to feel that you are as unreliable as their father was."

If he was taken aback by her rather inappropriate and highly ill-advised taking him to task, his expression, save for a minor arching of his eyebrows, did not reveal it. "I do not trust Burney. And I've no intention of investing with him. I will go to the ball this weekend because his sister, Amelia, is a sweet and very shy girl and her mother will thrust her at every single, titled gentleman who darkens their door, be he eighteen or eighty. The presence of loftier titles assures her success as a debutante and for that reason alone, I am going. Trust me when I tell you, Miss St. James, I'd rather do anything else. In fact, I'm thinking we should leave London. I'll take the children to my estate in the country. You should invite Miss Darrow to come along and the both of you can reside with us there. Two governesses are surely better than one with that lot."

"Effie cannot possibly leave her school."

"Then I will arrange for a chaperone so that you may join us," he insisted.

Callie realized then that he wanted them out of town for a very specific reason. "Is he blackmailing you?"

The earl's eyebrows more than arched. They rose nearly to his hairline in shock. "I've done nothing to be blackmailed with, Miss St. James!"

"Then tell me what this is about! And please do not give me some flimsy story about investments and debutantes. I want the truth from you, my lord. However ugly it may be! Are you sending them away?"

"Sending who away?" he asked, clearly perplexed.

"The children, of course. I understand that, as a bachelor, it cannot be easy to suddenly have the care of three young people thrust upon you, but I cannot tell you how damaging it would be to these children. Given the strained relationships they had with their parents prior to their illnesses and tragic deaths, I can only say that experiencing such a rejection from you, now their nearest living relative... I fear it would be catastrophic to them. Especially poor William. He looks up to you so!" Callie cried. She was terrified to think what it might do to them. In only a matter of days, she'd grown terribly attached to the children. Perhaps because she saw so much of her own childhood pain reflected in each one of them. And the disappointment she felt at the thought of him doing something so lacking in compassion also weighed heavily on her.

"I'm not sending them away," he said. Then the accusation seemed to sink in a bit deeper, deep enough to raise his ire. "I would never send them away! They are my family and I will not shuffle them off to others. I meet my responsibilities, Miss St. James!"

Responsibilities. Callie wanted to shake the man. Winn Hamilton, Earl of Montgomery, was utterly infuriating. And he was also hiding something from her. Of that, she was certain. "They are more than responsibilities. They do not need to be simply added to your list of daily tasks! They are children, my lord, and what they require from you is your love. Your guidance. The sense of safety and security that can only be achieved through having an adult figure in a young person's life who cares for them and protects them... even if it is from themselves! They need to know they are wanted!"

His eyes narrowed and he stepped closer, not menacing exactly, but clearly furious with her. "Do you presume, Miss St. James, to proclaim that you are in possession of the ability to know precisely what I feel for another person? If so, I should imagine that you would realize by now just how deeply you have insulted me—beyond measure, in fact. Were you a man, I would call you out for it!"

"Were I a man, I would never presume to know how anyone feels!" she snapped. "As we all know, men rarely deign to acknowledge such a trifling thing as another person's emotions, especially if that other person is either a female or a child!"

WINN HAD NEVER been so angry in his life. In fact, he'd never known another person who had the ability to make him as angry as Miss St. James, *his* employee, just had. Where in the devil had that come from? He was torn between wanting to throttle her and wanting to—he stopped the thought. He knew precisely what it was he wished to do with Miss St. James and he also knew that even considering it was nothing more than the path to ruination. Kissing Calliope St. James would surely bring about nothing less than his doom. Yet he could think of nothing else.

Perhaps it was the fact that through the course of their angry and heated exchange they had somehow closed the distance that separated them until they were facing off toe to toe. He wanted to step back. There was no question that he should step back. But he didn't. Instead, he inched forward until he could see her pupils dilate, until he could hear the soft hitch in her breathing and feel the rush of it as she finally exhaled. But she didn't back away either. And as her head tipped back, her face lifting toward his, her lashes drifted lower. He was lost. Even knowing it was a mistake, he was unable to resist.

He leaned in and touched his lips to hers. It was only a whisper of a kiss, but it felled him as surely as a volley from a cannon. Against every urge that gripped him, he didn't take her into his arms. He didn't deepen the kiss. Instead, he simply settled his lips more firmly upon hers and committed the texture of them, the taste of them and the lightning bolt sensations they stirred in him, to memory. Because even as he kissed her, he knew it was an error that could never be repeated but would often be remembered.

It lasted only seconds, although it altered him forever. Some things, once done, could never be undone. And having tasted her lips once, it would now haunt him for all his days. He acknowledged that, acknowledged that he'd made a terrible error in judgment, and that he regretted it not in the least. Then he simply drew back from her and stared down into her upturned face and confused gaze.

She stared up at him for a moment, one hand drawn up to her plump, rosy lips. "Why did you do that?"

Winn shrugged. "I cannot say."

"You don't know why you kissed me?" she demanded, as if that were somehow more offensive than the liberties he had just taken.

A heavy sigh escaped him and he looked away from her for just a moment, long enough to get his bearings. Then he answered, "I know why I kissed you, Miss St. James. And I know why I would very much like to kiss you again. But those explanations are even more inappropriate than my behavior has been. So, no, Miss St. James, I *cannot* say."

"Oh," she said, apparently mollified by that. But there was also a spark of curiosity in her gaze. "Well, you can't do it again. Not ever. I don't want to leave the children, but I can't—I just can't. It would mark me the worst sort of fool."

"And what would it mark me, Miss St. James?" he asked.

"You said it yourself, my lord... I am incapable of reading your thoughts. What it makes of you is determined by your intentions. And while it may have been unwise, I do not think it was intended. Simply an impulse."

"That it was," he agreed.

"And it was one we simply must never repeat," she stated firmly.

"I know," he agreed. And it gutted him. "You should go upstairs and see to them."

She started to walk away, but then turned back to him. "I was very harsh with you, judging you unfairly before because I was afraid for the children. But my concern isn't only for them. They could be very good for you if you let them."

Winn felt a smile tugging at his lips in spite of everything that had occurred that afternoon. "They already have been, Miss St. James. I'm aware of that."

"Then tell me the truth, so that I may know if they require protection from it. What are you hiding, my lord?"

"Call me Winn," he said. "At least when we are alone."

"It would be a mistake," she said, the declination quick to her lips.

"I know that, too. But I want you to do so anyway. I cannot tell you. I can promise you, Miss St. James, that everything I am doing is for the best interests of every person in this household and, right now, that includes you. Please do not ask me. I've no wish to lie to you but the truth is more dangerous than you know," he said.

"And was that kiss in my best interests?" she asked.

"No... but it was in mine," Winn admitted. There was a sense of inevitability for him, in kissing her, as if it were simply meant to be. It was both terrifying and exhilarating. As a man who was used to being in control of everything about himself, including his passions, being swept away by impulse was a novel experience. "Please, go to the children. They'll be climbing the walls by now... and we've tempted fate and ourselves enough already."

She turned away and moved toward the door, her steps slow and uncertain. When she reached it, she turned back to him, glancing at him over her shoulder, her face a study in confusion. "I've never been kissed before."

He smiled, a gentle curving of his lips. "I know that, as well, Miss St. James."

"I can't say for certain, as I've no basis for comparison, but I thought it was a very nice kiss... Winn."

With that, she fled, the door closing soundly behind her. Crossing the expanse of the Persian carpet, Winn sank into the chair behind his desk and put his head in his hands. He'd had a simple life once. Clubs, investments, the occasional ball, riding and shooting when he felt like it. Now, he was overrun with wild children who acted like animals half the time and he was bedeviled by a governess who'd tied him in knots in a matter of days. And if she was who he truly believed her to be, her very existence put her in the sights of the most ruthless family in London, a family who would not hesitate to see her killed rather than face the scandal of her ignoble birth. Not to mention, they'd have to give up a sizable inheritance that was never meant to be theirs anyway.

"Bloody, everlasting hell," he muttered.

And then Winn did something he rarely ever did. He reached for a decanter of brandy and took a deep drink of it, straight from the crystal vessel. It might only be the middle of the afternoon, but a day had never called for spirits more. He meant to drink every last drop of it and banish her from his mind, at least until the morrow.

BURNEY WAITED IN the elaborate foyer of the Duke of Averston's Mayfair mansion. It could not be called a townhome as it was at least triple the size of most. Not to mention that the elaborate decor made him feel more as if he were being presented at court rather than courting an investor. Shifting from one foot to the other as he waited, Burney considered his options. They were slim, to be sure. If he didn't get the money to invest in his cousin's scheme then his cousin would disclose the terrible truth about Burney's bachelorhood—that he preferred lovers of a more masculine persuasion.

If the truth came out, Burney would be ruined. His whole family would be ruined. Poverty would be the least of his concerns. Fleeing to France would be his only course of action and that would take him away from everything and everyone he held dear.

The butler appeared at the end of the hall and walked toward him with slow, measured steps. The man certainly was in no hurry. By the time he'd traversed the length of the corridor, Burney was on pins and needles. Would Averston even see him or would he be sent away… again?

"His grace will see you in his study, Mr. Burney," the butler said in a slightly disapproving tone. "This way, sir."

Burney followed the man down the corridor, measuring his steps and his pace to the servant's. It was torture. They were no more than halfway down the corridor, when out of boredom, Burney's eyes began to wander. The portrait jumped out at him. And recognition was instantaneous. The woman in the portrait looked almost identical to Montgomery's new governess. The likeness was uncanny. His gaze remained on that telling piece of art, even as they walked on.

Finally, they reached the study and Burney was ushered once more into the dark, richly appointed room. It was a masculine sanctuary, full of dark wood, lush velvet and rich leather. It smelled of old books, tobacco and the burning wood in the hearth. No coal fires for a duke, it would seem.

"The Right Honorable Mr. Charles Burney, Esquire to see you, your grace," the butler intoned with grandiosity before backing through the door and closing it firmly after him.

It was silent for a moment after the servant left. Then slowly, Averston took the cheroot from his lips and settled it in a crystal dish on the top of his desk. "What are you doing here, Burney? I told you that I won't invest in your scheme."

"I'm not here for that," Burney said. "I'm here for other reasons."

Averston's eyes narrowed. "And what reasons are those?"

Doubt hit him then. Yes, he'd caught a look, he'd seen Averston studying him in a way that was usually reserved for only those one was attracted to. But that didn't mean Averston would be pleased to have it pointed out. "I thought we might further our friendship, your grace."

Averston smiled, coldly and with a hint of cruelty. "I've friends enough, Mr. Burney. I have no need of more."

"Then I should go," Burney said and turned away to do just that.

"I said that I have no need of friends, Mr. Burney. I did not say that I have no need of you," Averston said.

Excited but still hesitant, Burney hedged, "I'm not sure I understand your meaning, your grace."

Averston rose and walked around his massive desk to perch on the corner of it. "I asked about you. Discreetly, of course. I made inquiries so that I might know whether or not we were... like-minded, shall we say?"

Burney's heart began to pound. "And are we... like-minded, your grace?"

"As you frequent a certain establishment near Lincoln's Inn, and yet another near the Arcades of Covent Garden, I think it safe to assume that we are," Averston replied. "The question is whether or not our personal preferences are as compatible as our broader persuasion. Tell me, Charles Burney, do you possess the ability to be discreet?"

Burney swallowed convulsively. "I do, your grace. Living as we are in this city full of gossips and hypocrites, I could hardly be less."

Averston's lips pursed in the faintest imitation of a smile. "Quite true, of course. There's a coffee house on Grate Street near Lincoln's Inn Field. It is called Dasher's. Do you know it?"

"I know of it, but I have never been," Burney admitted.

"There is a door off the main room that leads upstairs. I keep a set of rooms there for when I need to be more discreet in my pleasures. Be there tonight at eight o'clock sharp. When you arrive, greet the woman at the counter and tell her you are a friend of Patroclus," he instructed. "She will give you a key. I will join you there at nine."

"And what should I do with the hour between?"

Averston smiled. "You will wait for me… and I will join you at my leisure. That is all."

"Until tonight, your grace," Burney said, trying to keep the anticipation from his voice. There was something about Averston that fascinated him as much as it frightened him. Cold, calculating,—yet impossibly handsome and clearly interested, how could Burney be anything less than flattered.

"Indeed, Mr. Burney. Until tonight," the duke agreed with a slight quirking of his lips.

Burney nodded and turned to leave, recalling as he did so that he had questions about the portrait. "The woman in the portrait in hall… the one Montgomery was so interested in the other day, who is she?"

"My late uncle's whore," Averston replied. "And mother to the bastard whelp who could claim all of this if they ever dare to step forward."

"What would you do if someone did step forward?" Burney asked.

Averston's eyes flashed with anger. "It will never happen. Even if they tried, they'd no doubt meet some unfortunate *accident* courtesy of my ruthless grandmother before the claim could even be investigated."

Burney felt a shiver of fear, but also a shiver of excitement. He knew how to get the money for his wretched cousin, after all. And he understood now why Montgomery had been so desperate to get his pretty governess out of sight. "Until tonight, your grace."

As Burney fled the home, he glanced once more at the portrait. He was so intent upon it that he didn't see the small, steely-eyed woman walking along the corridor until he'd very nearly run her down.

"A thousand pardons, your grace," he mumbled, helping to right her.

"Do not touch me, you impudent whelp," the dowager duchess snapped. Her gaze flew past him to the portrait that had fascinated him so. Continuing in a tone that was laden with her obvious disdain, she added, "Dead twenty years and still she has the power to render men stupid!"

"I was only thinking she looked familiar, you grace," Burney stated. "Again, my apologies for being so clumsy."

"Familiar? You have seen someone who looks like her?" the dowager duchess demanded, her eyes flashing as she reached out and gripped his arm with rather surprising strength. Her nails, thick with age, dug into his flesh like the talons of a hawk.

"I don't think so, your grace. Perhaps I saw her as a child. She was an actress, was she not?" Burney said.

The dowager duchess released him abruptly. "Indeed. It's a filthy trade plied by filthy women. My son was a fool. That portrait remains here, in a place of honor, because he put it in his will that if we ever removed it, all his wealth should be given to charities. Can you believe the nerve?"

"No, your grace, I certainly cannot," Burney replied. He wanted nothing more than to be away from her. He'd heard tales of haunted places in his life, where the presence of a ghost would render the room the ice cold. It appeared there were certain living people who possessed that ability, as well.

Her eyes narrowed and she looked at him as if he were something unpleasant she might have stepped in on the street. "What is your business here, young man?"

"I was speaking to his grace about a potential investment," Burney lied.

She laughed bitterly. "Well, he has no money to invest unless I convince the trustees of the estate to release funds to him. You'd best talk to me about the investment." There was a triumphant note in her voice, as if she enjoyed the power she held over her grandson.

"I would, your grace, but the duke has already declined," Burney replied evenly. The woman made him terribly uncomfortable. She was, despite her diminutive stature, the most formidable woman he'd ever met. Her dress was somewhat old fashioned and she still wore her hair piled up in the intricate fashions popularized decades earlier. On some women, it might have looked ridiculous. On her, it simply made her more terrifying, as if time itself could hold no dominion over her. Certainly society could not. Such would never be permitted.

She harrumphed loudly before sailing past him. Over her shoulder, she tossed one parting insult. "Then you may go, sir... and please do not darken our door again. We've little patience for beggars here."

Dismissed and chastened, Burney made his escape.

In his study, Averston let out a groan. He'd heard her before he saw her. His grandmother. The dragon. He pinched the bridge of his nose to stave off the headache that her presence always created. Retreating to his desk, he poured some of the brandy stashed there into a glass and quickly tossed it back. There was no time to savor the burn of the fiery liquid. He wasn't drinking for the pleasure of it but as an anesthetic, after all.

He'd just managed to stash the glass and the brandy away when she entered, sailing toward him with a look of disapproval on her face.

"Who was that man who was just here?" she demanded.

"He had an investment proposition... I declined," Averston stated. It wasn't untrue, after all, just less than completely forthcoming.

She strode forward and seated herself before his desk. "I see. And is business the only proposition he had for you?"

He had no intention of discussing his sex life or his potential part-ners with her. "What are you doing here? I was under the impression we'd agreed to avoid one another as much as possible."

"So we had... and in the interim you were supposed to seek a wife and start living a less... debauched life. Certainly a more natural one!" The last was uttered with a snap to her voice, her disapproval of him quite obvious.

"I will marry when I am ready and not before," he retorted. "State your business and leave. We keep separate households for a reason. Namely that we cannot abide one another."

"I'm no longer content to let you marry when you are ready to do so. Given your proclivities, it doesn't suit me to allow you to continue living as an abomination... I also won't allow the risk of scandal which you court as recklessly as you do your young men." She hissed the last part of it with a malice that few saw in her save for those closest.

"And what will you do if I refuse?"

She smiled coldly. "My dear boy, it is not in your power to do so. I have the ear of the trustees. At the merest snap of my fingers, I could see your lifestyle curtailed to the point of penury. If you wish to continue receiving the generous annuity that has been provided for you, you will do as you are bid. Find a woman, get yourself married and stop courting scandal by indulging your... unnatural urges."

Averston said nothing. He simply stared at the woman before him with disgust. "You know nothing of what you speak."

"I know that if word gets out about your proclivities, we will be ruined!"

"Hardly that," he said. "I certainly wouldn't be the first gentleman in society whose romantic interests raised eyebrows!"

"You think I care about raised eyebrows?" Her voice was a low hiss, a sure sign of just how furious she was. "I have devoted my life to the cultivation of a kind of power few will ever have. I am not fearful of society because *I am* society! I determine who gets the cut. I determine who has success. Who is deemed eligible or ineligible! But that power is predicated on the fact that, save for your late uncle, we are above reproach! I will not see it jeopardized so you can cavort with some pretty young man!"

He rose to his feet, pacing with anger. "And if it was more than that? If it was more than simply cavorting? What if I loved him?"

She laughed. "Do you?"

He didn't answer. He didn't have to. They both knew the truth.

A cool smile curved her lips, brimming with triumph. "Of course not. Whatever flaws and perversions you may possess, you are still very much an Alford, Gerald. Your uncle was the outlier. He truly did love that worthless trollop. But you… you're like the rest of us. Such a tender emotion will never take root in your dark heart."

"I hate you," he said.

"I know you do," she replied evenly. "But you do respect me and you do fear me. That is preferable to being loved. Now, mark me, Gerald, I have not done all that I have and courted a seat at the devil's right hand in order that you might throw it all away! Do your duty and find solace in it," she said in parting and sailed from the room once more.

How he despised her, he thought. What rankled more was that, in this instance, she was right. People were beginning to talk. Whispers had begun regarding his bachelor status. He thought of Charles Burney. Handsome, eager in the way only the young and not yet jaded can be, he'd been drawn to the man instantly. It wasn't just that he was handsome and affable. Burney appeared to be a man who was quite capable of love, of a depth of feeling that he himself lacked. From the moment they'd first been introduced in his club the week before, he'd wanted to know him better. But as with everyone else in his life, he tempered any outward display of emotion or even excitement. To let anyone know that he had feelings for a person or a thing was to give his grandmother a weapon. She had enough of those, already.

He should write to the young man and cancel their assignation. He knew that he should. Yet, even as he reached for the quill on his desk, he hesitated. What could it hurt, he reasoned, to indulge their mutual attraction just the once?

Chapter Eight

"**I** DIDN'T LIKE that man the day before yesterday," William said.

"I didn't like him either," Charlotte seconded, crossing her little arms over her chest in a fair approximation of her brother's rebellious stance.

Callie sighed. "It isn't nice to say such things. We do not know anything about Mr. Burney and he may be a perfectly fine gentleman. We should not rush to judgment." She hadn't disliked him. But she didn't trust him. It wasn't that he'd done anything wrong, exactly. It was more that he'd seemed to be false. He laughed too loud and tried too hard and in general. It was uncomfortable to be in the presence of a person who was so obviously not comfortable with themselves.

"I don't care if it's nice. He's not a gentleman! He said—" William stopped abruptly, obviously not willing to repeat what had been said.

Callie would have pressed him but decided for the sake of Charlotte's innocent ears, which in truth probably were not so innocent, it would be best not to encourage him. "It doesn't matter. He's an adult and, as your elder, he deserves a certain amount of respect. You don't have to like him, but that doesn't mean it's all right to talk about him. Are we in agreement?"

William shuffled his feet on the rug for a moment. "Fine."

"Thank you. Your willingness to overlook your dislike of him indicates a remarkably generous nature and a good character,

William," Callie said with a smile. "And as for you, Miss Charlotte, the same goes! No saying mean things about adults!"

"What if adults do mean things to us?" she asked.

Callie's heart clenched at the thought of it. She fervently hoped none ever would. "Then you must immediately tell me or your uncle... no matter what. All right?"

Charlotte nodded solemnly and immediately popped her thumb into her mouth. Callie gave her a warning look and she removed it. "I know, I know," the little girl said, perfectly capturing Callie's own tone and inflection as she repeated the words that had been uttered to her so frequently. "It's a terrible habit and I'm too big for it."

Callie smiled. "It is and you are. Furthermore, you are a strong and capable young girl. You do not need to suck your thumb in order to feel safe and secure. You have everything and everyone you need. Don't you?"

"I miss Mama," Charlotte said.

Callie's felt that terrible hollow feeling inside her as she looked at the sad, sweet face. "I know you do. Come here and sit with me for a moment."

Taking a seat at the small table she used, she pulled Charlotte on her lap and looked to William. "Today, we're going to work on letters."

"Why doesn't Claudia have to?" he demanded.

"Because she knows her letters," Callie replied. "Also, she is preparing to meet her music instructor. Your uncle hired him just this morning and she will have her first lesson in only a few short moments. All young ladies should know how to play the pianoforte and she is getting a very late start."

"Where's he coming from?" William asked.

"When was he hired?" Charlotte demanded.

"Why don't we get music lessons?"

"Is he nice?"

Callie held up her hand lest the barrage of questions continue. "He teaches the children next door," Callie replied to William. "He comes very highly recommended. Your uncle hired him just this morning and you won't be getting lessons unless you want to have them because boys generally are not required to learn an instrument. Charlotte will have lessons beginning in the next year or so. And before you can protest further or suggest that the man is a murderer or thief, I will check in on them later. But only after I get you and Charlotte settled in doing your letters."

William grumbled more, but didn't protest overmuch. Charlotte, so long as she was being cuddled, was perfectly content to practice anything. Preparing the sheafs of paper for them to practice their letters, Callie painstakingly lined the paper with the compass and ruler and then wrote one row of letters across the top for them to repeat beneath. When the task was done, she rose and placed Charlotte in her chair.

Once the children were settled in, attempting to recreate the strokes of the letters, Callie's mind drifted. It had drifted often over the last twenty-four hours, so much so that she'd been robbed of any chance at actual sleep. The memory of that brief—too brief—and painfully gentle kiss, administered even in the midst of a heated argument, left her reeling. She still didn't know why he had kissed her, but perhaps her greatest shame lay in that she desperately wanted him to do so again.

It had been a tease, that delicate kiss. So light, so tender that it seemed almost as if she had imagined it. Yet, she knew she had not. And she also knew that kissing was so much more than that single feathery brush of his lips over hers. The man, blast him, had given her just enough to stir her curiosity.

"I can't do this one," Charlotte whined. "I can't make it look right!"

Callie rose and moved over to where the little girl sat. "Start from the bottom," she instructed patiently and guided the child's hand through the motions of the letter once, then again, and a third time. "Now you try."

Charlotte looked up at her nonplussed. "It won't look as good."

"It doesn't have to. You're practicing, Charlotte. And every time you practice something, you get better at," Callie said. Immediately, her traitorous mind thought of kissing again. Would that get better with practice, also? Drat him!

A movement at the door drew her eyes and Callie glanced over to see one of the maids frantically trying to get her attention. "Wait here, children. Keep working on your letters and I'll return shortly."

Stepping into the corridor, she closed the door firmly behind her and met the maid's worried gaze. "What is the matter?"

"Oh, Miss St. James, I know it's not my place and I know I'm not supposed to say anything, but it's just awful!"

"What is your name?"

"Bea, Miss. Beatrice, but everyone calls me Bea," the girl said. She was still breathless and clearly distraught.

"What has happened, Bea?"

"It's the little girl, Miss. Miss Claudia. That fellow belowstairs, giving her lessons... I've never heard or seen such in my life. He's a monster, Miss. A monster!"

Callie's stomach dropped. "Wait here. Do not let the other children come below. No matter what. All right?"

"Yes, Miss!"

Callie didn't waste another second. She raced down the stairs as quickly as she could, her feet flying over the polished wood until she reached the marble floors of the foyer. From there, she headed directly for the small music room. At the door, she paused to catch her breath and also to listen. She heard a few halting notes and then one discordant one. It was immediately followed by a sharp crack. It was a sound she knew well and one she'd felt the sting of far too frequently during her younger days. He was striking her with a cane.

A dozen conflicting emotions swamped her. Fear. Anger. But it was guilt that made her stomach turn and her knees go weak. She had insisted that Claudia have music lessons, after all, that there was no time to waste. Now Claudia was being tormented by him and it was entirely her fault.

Callie placed a shaking hand on the door knob, turned it and found it locked. Fury swept through her, burning so hotly that even the guilt faded beneath it.

"Monsieur Dumont, you will open this door immediately," she called out.

When there was no reply, she turned to the butler. He was not the stuffy gentleman who'd first greeted her but the younger man who'd shadowed him. Foster. "Do you have a key to this room?"

"My aunt, the new housekeeper does, Miss St. James," he said and waved to one of the footmen to fetch her. He didn't have to go far. The newly hired housekeeper had apparently been listening at the door along with a bevy of kitchen girls and parlor maids. She came bustling in, key at the ready.

"Here you are, Miss," she said and bobbed a curtsy.

Callie didn't bother correcting her that she did not need to curtsy to another servant. There were more important matters to deal with. Fitting the key into the lock, she turned it and pushed the door open. Claudia was seated at the pianoforte, her face red and wet with tears. Her hands were placed on the keys and a heavy board was strapped across them, holding them in position there so that she wouldn't be able to withdraw them even if she wanted to.

"You will get your things and leave this house immediately," Callie said.

"By whose authority?" the man sneered. "That of a mere governess? I should think not!"

Callie drew in a deep, fortifying breath and then, with all the haughty dignity she could muster, she said, "I am not merely *a* governess, Monsieur Dumont. I am *the* governess. I am a graduate of the Darrow School... one of the most highly sought after governesses in all of England. It will take but a whispered word into the ear of my mentor, Miss Euphemia Darrow, and you will find yourself without any employment whatsoever. Is that really what you wish to do?"

"You wouldn't dare," he said, stepping forward until he loomed over her.

Callie squared her shoulders and met his gaze steadily. "I would. I most certainly would! Now, remove whatever barbaric contraption that is from this child and remove yourself from this house immediately. I will not tolerate bullies and abusers!"

He raised the cane high. Callie braced herself for the blow. It wouldn't be the first time she'd been struck with one. But the blow never fell. Instead, Monsieur Dumont tumbled backward, propelled by the violent blow struck by Lord Montgomery.

"Get out," the earl growled. "And if you ever darken my door again, so help me, you will not live to regret it."

"My lord," the man began, all but groveling, "This is the only way a child can learn. They must fear consequences for misbehavior!"

"Misbehavior? This child has never played an instrument before in her life!" Callie shouted. "And you feel that warrants you striking her every time she plays a wrong chord? You are worse than despicable! I do not possess the vocabulary to adequately describe you!"

"Get out," the earl repeated. "If I look at you for a moment longer, I will not wait until you darken my door again."

Monsieur Dumont scrambled to his feet. He didn't bother to gather his items, but left them as he scurried from the house.

Callie immediately went to the pianoforte and began unbuckling the heavy straps that held the board to Claudia's arms. Once she'd managed to free the restraints from the terrible device, Callie tossed it aside and hugged the little girl to her. "I would never have let him hurt you if I'd known!"

"It's my fault."

Callie looked back to see the earl standing there, his face dark with guilt and anger, much of it self-directed. "It is not your fault. It is mine."

He shook his head. "The children are my responsibility, Miss St. James. Anything that befalls them is my responsibility, as well."

Rubbing her hand soothingly over Claudia's back while the child leaned against her, Callie stated as reasonably as possible, "I daresay when he was interviewed that Monsieur Dumont never stated that beating children was part of his teaching methods." The words weren't just absolution for him but for herself, as well. No one knew better than she did the kind of wickedness men such as Dumont, men with power and no conscience, could indulge in.

"Of course, he didn't... but I didn't like him from the start and I should have trusted my judgment."

"Not liking someone is hardly grounds for thinking they are the devil incarnate," she said. "He is a monster and monsters always hide their faces until they have an opportunity to inflict pain on someone weaker and less powerful than they are."

Something in her tone must have given away that she was speaking from experience. His eyes narrowed as he looked at her. Their gazes locked. She could see the questions in his expression, but she had no intention of answering them. Not today and likely not ever. There were parts of her story, of all the things she'd endured before Effie had taken her in, that she would not share with anyone.

"Where did he strike you?" Callie asked, turning her attention back to Claudia. The earl needed comfort, of course, but he was not alone in that. It was clear that the earl needed reassurance, as well. But for the moment, she had to focus on the child.

Claudia held up her hands. Her palms were blood red and there were other welts across the backs of her hands and her knuckles.

"You're to go to the kitchen and let the cook put something on them for you. She'll have a salve that will make them feel better and while you're there, perhaps she can give you a cup of hot chocolate? Would you like that?" Callie asked.

Claudia nodded but still wasn't talking. It was obvious that the little girl was struggling not to cry, not to show how much pain she was in and how frightened she must have been. Claudia hadn't even made it to the door when the new housekeeper, Mrs. Marler, rushed forward, wrapped her arm around the little girl's shoulders and whisked her toward the kitchen.

When the servants had gone, amid lots of whispers and head shaking, Callie looked back at the earl. He had crossed the room and was standing at the window, staring out at the street beyond. His hands were on his hips and he'd ducked his head. But it wasn't defeat. She knew that. It was temper. He was furious with Monsieur Dumont, with himself, and quite possibly with her. She had insisted, after all, that Claudia needed music lessons.

"It wasn't your fault," she said softly.

"Wasn't it? I took an instant dislike to the man, but I hired him anyway... because it was expedient. Because I wouldn't have to spend any further time looking for a music teacher for her. I put her in jeopardy, Miss St. James. I placed that child directly in the path of a man who clearly glories in inflicting pain and torment upon others... all because I couldn't be bothered," he stated.

"Then it's my fault, as well. Because I insisted that she had to have lessons and that they needed to begin as soon as possible," Callie stated.

"These children are your charges but, ultimately, they are my responsibility," he stated. "I shoulder the blame alone."

"And what of Monsieur Dumont? Does he not shoulder any of this blame? What of your neighbor who wrote him such a glowing letter of recommendation, or the other letters of recommendation that he had?

Do they not shoulder the blame as well?"

He looked back at her then, his eyes still glittering with fury. "You will not let this be, will you?"

"No. I will not. You cannot take it all upon yourself, my lord."

"Why not?"

Callie smiled sadly. "Because you cannot control everything... no matter how much you like to believe that you can. He was a highly respected, highly recommended music instructor and we had no reason to suppose that he was cruel and wicked enough to willfully abuse a child in her own home. It is an unfortunate way to learn a lesson, but it is a lesson learned nonetheless. We will both be more careful going forward."

"There is no going forward. I will never entrust these children to anyone in such a manner again."

"Claudia must learn an instrument, my lord. I know it seems silly to you, but she will be in society in a very short number of years. To not have such an accomplishment would place her at a disadvantage. And I cannot teach the other children and her what they require academically and teach music, as well."

"Then I will teach her," he said.

"You play?"

"Yes... and rather well," he said, crossing the room to the piano-forte.

Callie was rather surprised when he walked toward her and seated himself on the bench next to her. He was close enough that she could feel the heat of him. When he placed his hands on the keys, she could see blood on his knuckles where he'd struck the worthless Monsieur Dumont. Then his fingers began to fly over the keys, playing a tune she'd never heard before. And she was simply spellbound by it. The notes surrounded her, transported her, and the very complicated man who played them... well, he held her spellbound as much as the music did. He filled her senses and left her reeling. She was treading in very deep waters that she had no notion of how to navigate.

"I need to go," Callie finally managed.

His hands stilled on the keys and then he turned to her. It wasn't regret that she saw in his expression. In fact, it was so guarded that it was entirely unreadable.

"You don't have to fear me," he said. "I know my behavior yesterday was inappropriate, Miss St. James. I cannot and will not deny that I find you very appealing... more so than any woman I have encountered in years."

Callie's heart thundered in her chest. Those words pierced her deep and made her long for things she had never thought she wanted. "You should not say such things to me, my lord."

"No. I shouldn't. But I—it doesn't matter. Go back to William and Charlotte. I'll take Claudia to Gunter's for an ice. She certainly deserves it after the experience of this morning and I have amends to make."

"It was a mistake, my lord... nothing more than that. Luckily, we were here to intervene and halt his abuse of her. She will recover."

"Will she?" he asked. "Did you?"

Callie looked away. "It was very different for me, my lord. When I was a child, there was no one to intervene. Not until Effie discovered me. But we all survive terrible things, do we not? Claudia will be fine once she feels secure again."

She rose and turned to walk away, but his hand closed over her wrist and held her there for a moment. "Thank you," he murmured softly.

"For what?"

"For being willing to risk everything for a child that you barely know. For being you, Miss St. James. Thank you simply for being you."

Chapter Nine

A VERSTON PAUSED OUTSIDE the door to the set of rooms he kept above the coffee house. Glancing to the right and then the left, certain he wasn't being observed, he fitted the key into the lock and then entered. Lamps had already been lit and coals glowed warmly in the grate. Burney was there already, seated at the small table before the fire enjoying a glass of brandy.

"I'd rather thought you might not show," Burney said, his expression clearly displaying his surprise.

"It's not outside the realm of possibility. I had second thoughts, obviously. There are always second thoughts about these sorts of things. Don't you find that to be the case?"

Burney shrugged, obviously attempting to appear casual. "I wouldn't really know. I haven't indulged in these sorts of assignations before."

Averston was somewhat surprised by that. Stepping deeper into the room, he shrugged out of his heavy redingote and settled himself on the chair opposite Burney. "How did you know?"

There was no real question of what they were talking about it. The unspoken thing hovered in the air between them. The tension was palpable and yet strangely comfortable.

"How did I know that I was different?" Burney asked.

Averston wasn't about to let him get away with being so vague. It needed to be spoken and plainly. "How did you know that you preferred men to women? Was it just something that you were always aware of or was there some great epiphany for you?"

Burney settled back, suddenly at ease now that things were so very much out in the open. "A bit of both, I suspect. I always felt different, I suppose. When I was growing up in the countryside, all the boys were taking bets on who could kiss a girl first. I won the bet, but I hated all of it. She was a lovely girl... baker's daughter." The last was offered with a self-deprecating laugh. "But it didn't feel right to me. Then I was sent away to school. And if there is one thing that you can count on occurring at a boy's boarding school, it's a certain degree of... let's call it experimentation, shall we?"

"And that did feel natural to you?" Averston questioned.

"Yes," Burney replied. "And you... how did you know?"

"I've always known," Averston said. "From the moment I understood that one day I would be expected to marry a woman and produce an heir, I've known."

Burney placed his glass on the table. "Do you ever think a time will come when we're not persecuted for not loving at the direction of others?"

"Is that what this is? Love?" Averston asked, his lips quirking in a sardonic half-smile. His grandmother's words returned to him, taunting him from the darkest and deepest shadows of his mind.

"Lust, then. But surely two men can love one another, or two women, just as easily as a man and woman can love one another. Can't they?"

Averston shrugged. "Love is hardly something I'd hazard to have an opinion on as it is not something I have ever experienced."

"Never?" Burney asked. "You've really never fancied yourself in love with anyone... man or woman?"

"No," Averston said. "I don't think love exists. I think it's a pretty word people wrap around the dirty things they want to do in private so they don't have to feel guilt or shame."

Burney shook his head. "That's a very sad way of looking at things."

"Perhaps. But it is a realistic one... don't fancy us in love, Mr. Burney. I'm not even certain I like you yet," Averston stated. "But you are remarkably handsome and you remind me what it felt like to be a younger man, not quite so burdened with bitterness."

"Then how do I make you like me? For that's a start, isn't it?"

Averston smiled. "So it is." But he said nothing further, he simply rose to his feet and grasped the other man's hand, pulling him to standing as well. They were of similar height, so much so that they were nose to nose and only the space of a breath separated their lips. "I find that a kiss is usually a good way to start."

"Come to my sister's debut tomorrow night," Burney said. From the widening of his eyes, it was quite apparent that it had been an impulsive invitation.

Averston cocked one eyebrow. "Why would I do that?"

"Because we are friends," Burney said. "Because we might be able to slip away for a moment alone together."

"And because having a duke in attendance, even one on a tight string such as I am, would cement your sister's success?" Averston suggested.

"I won't deny that it would help Amelia... but that isn't why I asked," Burney said. "It is possible that I like you just for you."

Averston's smile had chilled. "We shall see about that, Charles Burney. We shall see. Tell me, how are you managing this great expense when we both know you've pockets to let?"

"How else? Credit, of course," Burney admitted.

Averston clucked his tongue. "You've overextended yourself."

"My father did. I inherited more debt than funds," Burney admitted. "But that isn't Amelia's fault. If I can keep up appearances just long enough for her to find a husband—I just need a little time."

"And the ability to claim a friendly connection to a powerful duke would only aid her chances. Wouldn't it?" Averston demanded.

"It would," Burney said. "What do you want from me? Do you want me to beg?"

Averston pulled him closer. "No. You've pleaded your case well enough. I'll consider it. But I'm done talking about your sister, Charles Burney. I've other plans for you."

⇛⟩⟨⇚

IT WAS LATE. The wee hours of the morning, in fact. Burney rolled over in the bed and found it not only empty but cold. Averston was long gone and had been for hours. He tried not to be disappointed, not to feel used by the other man. But he did regardless. And the truth was that he had been used. Averston wasn't the sort for sentimental attachments. They could share pleasure, had shared it and likely would again, but it would never be more than that. It was impossible anyway. He'd stated it very clearly. The man would have to find a wife and produce an heir. Burney was in much the same boat, assuming there was anything left in the family coffers for any would-be children to inherit.

Getting up from the bed, Burney began to gather his clothes, dressing quickly and quietly in the dim light that filtered in through the colored glass panes of the window. It was as discreet a location for a molly-house as one could ever hope for. Well protected, invisible to the outside world, the rooms all sealed behind locked doors. For men of their persuasion, that kind of security was hard to come by. He wondered if perhaps he'd ever be in that room again, or if having had his fill, the Duke of Averston was now done with him.

He sincerely hoped not. Cold, yes. Enigmatic, of a certain. But there was something compelling about the duke, something he couldn't quite resist. Wanting a memento, something to remind him of the man and the hours they'd spent together, Burney moved toward the small desk that occupied one corner of the room. It contained a small writing box. Lifting the lid, he saw that the paper was of fine quality but lacked any distinguishing marks. Disappointment filled him. It was not Averston's personal stationery but something discreet, intended for arranging assignations and communicating with lovers without risk of discovery.

Muttering a soft curse, Burney settled back in the chair once more. His eyes drifted to that discreet stationery as he wondered how many men Averston had entertained in that room. More than he wanted to consider, certainly. And when he was rotting in debtor's prison, someone else would most assuredly be enjoying his attentions there in that lovely bower. He had to find a way to pay off the debts quickly and getting people to invest in his cousin's scheme was clearly not going to do the trick.

But there was always another option. The portrait in the corridor of the duke's residence came to mind, as did Montgomery's lovely governess. The stationery, Burney thought, glancing back at it again, was also perfect for blackmail.

Broke, with no hope of raising the funds needed on his own merit, desperation had Burney reaching for one piece of the heavy paper and the quill and ink in their elaborate stand. He wrote carefully, camouflaging his own hand as much as possible. When it was done, he scattered fine sand over the surface to prevent the ink from smudging. With it completed, he slipped it into the pocket of his coat after donning it and quickly exited the secreted apartment via the same door he'd entered through hours earlier. On the street, it was still dark but dawn approached. The lamplighters were on the tail end of their nightly tasks and were now dousing the gas lamps and rapping on windows to wake those who paid for the service.

A small boy was assisting another boy, older and harder in appearance, a boy who had clearly seen far too much during his tenure on the streets. Taking a precious coin and the letter from his pocket, Burney approached the pair. "I have a job for you."

"We know what that coffee house really is," the older boy said. "We'll not be doing any work for you in there."

"I only need a note delivered," Burney said casually. "And I've coin to pay you for it."

"That's it?" the younger of the two said. "Just knock on the door and hand 'em the note?"

"Not at all. I want you to wrap this note about a rock and toss it through a window. You can throw well enough to do that, can't you?"

"We'll go to the gaol if we're caught!" the older boy protested.

Burney smiled. "Then do not get caught. At this hour, if you hurry, you'll be able to get away before the house stirs enough to even discover what actually happened. Toss it and run... and get a guinea for you troubles."

"A guinea? I don't believe it!" the older boy snapped.

Burney held up the coin. "And do you believe it now?"

"You pay us up front," the older boy said.

"You do as you've been asked and I'll be waiting at Piccadilly Circus to pay you," he said. Handing the note to the smaller boy, he added, "And if you don't do it, I will find out."

"We ain't crooks," the younger one replied and took the note.

"Do not open that," Burney warned.

"Can't read no way," the boy answered flippantly.

"House number 114 on Piccadilly. Do you understand?"

"Aye, sir. We understand," the older boy answered. "And we'll get it done."

With that taken care of, Burney wandered aimlessly toward Piccadilly Circus, prepared to wait for his reluctant accomplices. It was a dangerous thing to make an enemy of Montgomery. And the truth was, he liked Montgomery. But friends were a luxury he couldn't afford at the moment. If he didn't get the money to his cousin, he'd be ruined. Then the credit they were living on would be revoked. He'd wind up in debtor's prison. He didn't have the protection of a title to keep him from it.

>>>><<<<

THE SOUND OF breaking glass awakened the servants. They, in turn, awakened the remainder of the house. Clad only in a banyan, which he'd only taken to wearing now that there were children roaming the halls at all hours of the day and night, Winn left his chamber and headed toward the morning room that faced the street. Broken glass littered the floor and a rock lay on the carpet, bound with twine and wrapped in a note.

"I thought it best to let you examine the item, my lord," the new butler, Foster he recalled, said. "I thought perhaps it might be personal in nature."

"It's a rock through my bloody window. I'd say it's definitely personal," Winn groused as he strode toward it. Glass crunched beneath his leather-soled slippers as he stooped to retrieve it. He didn't open the note in front of anyone. Instead, he took it and retreated to his study with it. Was this some retaliation from Monsieur Dumont? It seemed unlikely. The man was a coward, after all, and a bully. Had it been only the rock, minus any form of communication, he might have leaned more heavily in that direction.

Taking a seat at his desk, he carefully untangled the twine, noting that it had been tied rather clumsily. Almost childishly. Should he check to see that William was still abed? But then he unpeeled the slightly damp paper from the stone and unfolded it carefully.

It wasn't William's doing. In fact, despite the rather elaborate efforts taken to disguise the penmanship, it was obvious to him immediately that it was Burney. Not because he recognized the hand, but because Burney was the only other person who had been in

Averston's home to see the portrait of Mademoiselle Delaine and who had also seen Calliope St. James' face. Recalling Burney's desperation to seal the deal for his cousin's tobacco shipments, it was obvious that he was in need of funds. And now it was equally obvious that he would not hesitate to procure them through unscrupulous means.

Crumpling the note, Winn considered his options. The first thing he'd have to do is be completely honest with Miss St. James. He'd hoped to shield her from the truth and, in doing so, shield her from Averston. But if Burney exposed her, Averston would not stop until the girl was dead. He knew that. She posed too great a threat to all that the duke held dear.

Cursing, he rose and left the study. Climbing the stairs to his chamber, he began dressing. It wasn't quite dawn yet, but he had no intention of waiting. He meant to beard the lion in his den, so to speak. His valet entered, sleepy-eyed and clearly concerned by all the commotion of the early morning vandalism.

"May I be of assistance, my lord?"

Winn shook his head as he hastily tied his cravat. "I'm not concerned about whether or not I'm fashionable at the moment. It's hardly a requirement for beating another so-called gentleman to a pulp."

The valet inhaled sharply, clearly appalled by such ungentlemanly violence. "Surely a duel would be more the thing, my lord."

Winn rolled his eyes. "I don't want to kill him… nor do I have any great desire to be shot myself. No. A sound thrashing ought to take care of it. But thank you for the advice, Smithton. It's greatly appreciated. Should I ever need clarification on whether blackening someone's eyes or sending them to meet their maker is the most gentlemanly course of action, I'll be certain to seek out your wise counsel."

The valet, giving every appearance of being chastened when nothing could be further from the truth, ducked his head. "Very well, my lord. And should this gentleman manage to thrash you instead, I will have poultices at the ready to treat your wounds."

"Your faith in me is astonishing, Smithton, and I thank you for it," Winn said as he headed out the door. Down the stairs and into the darkened streets beyond, he made straight for the set of rooms that Burney kept on Church Street. With his brisk pace, fueled by anger, he actually reached those rooms in time to see Burney disappearing through the front door. If there had been any doubt at all that the man was responsible, seeing him out and about at such an ungodly hour was all the proof Winn required.

Quickening his pace, he crossed the street, all but abandoned at such an hour, and entered the building just behind Burney who was already at the top of the stairs. The other man looked back at him and Winn saw the guilt in his expression. "I'd like a word with you, Burney."

"Now isn't a good time, Montgomery. Heavens, I'm only just getting to bed."

"I wasn't aware blackmail required such late hours," Winn snapped. "And it wasn't a request, Burney. We will have those words and we will have them now... here in the corridor or in the privacy of your rooms. I'll let you decide."

Burney hesitated, but only for a moment. He opened the door, stepped aside and waved for Winn to precede him into his small apartment. Once inside, Burney closed the door, and Winn whirled on him immediately. The punch landed squarely, sending Burney stumbling backwards and clutching his nose.

"Were it not for decades of friendship between our families, I would call you out on the spot!" Winn snapped. "You dare to blackmail me? To extort funds from me? Not to mention that you are very likely risking the life of an innocent woman in the process!"

Burney shook his head, still clutching his nose. "I've no notion what you're talking about. But clearly you are upset about something you think I've done." There was panic rising in his voice.

"I think you or some miscreant you hired threw a rock through my window with a note wrapped about it attempting the most ridiculous extortion imaginable... demanding a sum of four thousand pounds or the Duke of Averston will be told that the missing heir to the Averston fortune is acting as governess to my nieces and nephew. Did you really think I wouldn't piece together that it was you, Burney?"

"You can't prove it," Burney denied.

"I don't have to prove it... and I certainly don't have to pay you. You'll not see a pence from this, Burney. I'll tell Miss St. James myself about her parentage and I'll see to it that Averston will never get near enough to her to do her harm." Winn was too disgusted with the man to even want to hit him again. He just wanted to be away from the man. "If you approach me in society, it will go badly for you. Do not think to trade on our friendship or my long-held respect for the remainder of your family. In short, Burney, do not make me embarrass them that way... and stay the hell away from mine. Is that understood?"

"You have it all wrong, Montgomery," Burney implored. "I'm not the villain here."

"No. You're not a villain. You lack the courage to be a villain, Burney. What you are is a coward and that is even worse. If you ever think to threaten me or mine, and that includes those in my employ, I will make you regret it."

"Please!" Burney cried out.

Winn turned back to him. "What?"

"Amelia's debut is tomorrow... please don't disappoint her or mother by not coming. I know what I did was wrong, but I'm desperate, dammit! You've no idea the dire straits we're in!"

"I know that hosting an elaborate ball is hardly the way to get yourself out of them! Think man! You've spent a bloody fortune on this ball and I know Amelia would have understood if you'd needed to postpone her coming out."

"It is all worth it if Amelia can marry well! I need to see her settled so that she is safe from scandal!" Burney snapped.

"What scandal, Burney? Dammit, I've been a friend to you all your life! I would help you if you only told me what you needed," Winn replied.

Burney laughed bitterly. "There are some things that cannot be helped. Promise me you will come to the ball. If I had to explain to Mother why you weren't there—please... having you there would help to cement her status as an incomparable."

Amelia Burney would never be an incomparable. She was a pretty enough girl, but painfully shy and far too sweet for her own good. Society would eat her alive and Burney was too damned foolish to see it. "I'll be there. I'll dance with her one time and one time only, as agreed. And then we are done... and you will leave Miss St. James be. I can help you, Burney, but if you cause that girl harm—"

"They wouldn't really hurt her!"

Winn shook his head. "My God, but you are stupid. Yes, Burney, they would hurt her. They would hurt anyone who opposed them... or at the very least the dowager duchess would. What Averston is capable of, I've no notion. But I wouldn't trust him any further than I could throw him."

"You're wrong about him."

"Perhaps. I was certainly wrong about you. We might not have been close but, at one time, I would have counted you as a friend." Winn turned on his heel and left, the younger man sputtering behind him. As he left, he did not return to his house on Piccadilly but instead made his way toward Jermyn Street and the Darrow School for Girls. He needed to speak to Calliope St. James about her parentage and the potential threat she now faced because of it. It was definitely a conversation that needed to take place somewhere that his nieces and nephew were not.

Chapter Ten

C ALLIE WAS DONNING her pelisse with the assistance of one of the maids when a knock sounded at the door. The housekeeper, Mrs. Wheaton, who in their unusual house also fulfilled the role of butler, appeared scandalized that anyone would dare knock upon their door so early. It was unusual to Callie's mind, but far from unheard of. Mrs. Wheaton opened the door and a familiar voice greeted Callie's ears.

"I'm sorry to have called so early but it is imperative that I speak with Miss St. James immediately." From his tone, he was clearly unhappy about something.

"Then I suggest you make an appointment to meet with her during the hours when it is acceptable to pay calls," the housekeeper replied sternly.

"It is urgent, Madam, or I would never dare to presume… please. I daresay it could be a matter of life and death," he insisted.

Worried, Callie stepped forward. "It's fine, Mrs. Wheaton. Send one of the maids to fetch Effie and I'll see his lordship in her study."

"It's very irregular, Miss," the housekeeper warned.

"I understand that, Mrs. Wheaton, but I daresay the Earl of Montgomery would not be here if he did not consider the situation to be of a most urgent nature," Callie replied.

The housekeeper walked away, grumbling under her breath about lords and their urgencies. It was followed closely by something that sounded rather like "my eye".

"Not a trusting sort, is she?" he asked.

Callie smiled but it was a cool expression and, with it, she conveyed a warning. "We are standing in the entryway of a home that functions primarily as a school for the illegitimate offspring of gentleman of your standing, my lord. I'd say she's entitled to her skepticism."

"Touché, Miss St. James," he conceded as he stepped fully into the entryway.

Turning on her heel, Callie led the way down the corridor to the small study that Effie had converted into an office of sorts for herself. "The children are well?" she asked as the door closed behind them. She was giving voice to the fear that had been plaguing her since she'd first recognized his voice. What other reason would he have to come there, after all?

"They are quite well, though I daresay they are already tearing my house apart without you there to guide them… but this is a matter of some urgency, Miss St. James," he said, his tone grave. He moved away from her, crossing the expanse of carpet to stare out the window into the back garden. When he looked back at her, his expression was one of grim resolve. "The threat is not to the children in this instance, but to you."

If he'd said the grass was blue and the sky green, she wouldn't have been more surprised. "To me? You can't be serious!" she protested.

"What do you really know of your parentage, Miss St. James?"

Callie shook her head. "Nothing. I have no notion of who my mother or father are… or were. I was left at the gate of the St. James Workhouse. Someone rang the bell and departed before the attendant even discovered me."

"Was there any identifying information with you? Anything significant about the basket or the clothing that you were dressed in?"

Callie shook her head. She didn't know honestly and there was likely no way to obtain any such information now. "There's nothing... not so far as I am aware, at any rate. Before I answer any more of your questions, I think it's time you answered mine! What is this about, my lord?"

He was silent for a moment, staring at her in a considering way, thoughtful and focused. After that long silence stretched to the point of discomfort, he began speaking abruptly, "I may know who your mother was... and your father. It was strange coincidence that shortly after you came into my employ, I was attending a meeting with several gentleman at the home of the Duke of Averston. Do you know him?"

Callie blinked. Then she blinked again and again, as if doing so would force the words he'd uttered to penetrate the fog that had claimed her mind. With no clarity forthcoming, she managed to utter, "No. Why on earth would I be acquainted with a duke? But do go on."

He cleared his throat and began to pace as he talked. "Burney, Mr. Charles Burney, whom we happened to run into while shopping the other day was the gentleman responsible for putting together a prospective business deal that he hoped I, and the Duke of Averston, would be willing to invest in. While there—at the duke's residence— to discuss the matter, I saw a portrait of a woman and the resemblance between you is so marked that it cannot be mere happenstance. There must be some familial link... because it is undeniable."

"And who is this woman?" Callie asked.

His expression shifted once more, to one that was tinged with compassion. "Who was this woman... I'm afraid she is long dead, Miss St. James. And I fear her death was not one of natural causes. Her name was Mademoiselle Veronique Delaine. She was a French actress and a very successful one. She was also the mistress of the former Duke of Averston... your father."

Callie stared at him for a moment as if he'd gone utterly mad. Then she began to laugh. "If I were the daughter of a duke and his mistress, why would I have been left at a workhouse, my lord? Surely they would have made other arrangements even if, due to societal and family pressure, they could not raise me themselves!"

"The former duke made it clear that he planned to marry her, Mademoiselle Delaine... but his mother, *your grandmother*, had other ideas. Your mother left you on the steps of the workhouse, I'm assuming, because she was literally running for her life and... yours. The dowager duchess is a formidable woman, Miss St. James, and I have no difficulty at all believing that she is capable of everything that Averston admitted to me, albeit in a vague fashion. She killed or had your mother killed and would likely have done the same to you had your mother not placed you on the steps of the St. James Workhouse and left you to whatever mercy might be had within those walls."

"Why would he tell you such things?" Callie demanded. She couldn't fathom what he was saying. The words all made sense, she understood them, but the meaning behind them and what they signified about her own life was not something that she could grasp in that moment. "Who admits such monstrous things to someone that, by your account, would only qualify as an acquaintance? You must have misunderstood."

"The current Duke of Averston is in an untenable situation... he inherited the title, but the wealth is not his. It's in trust, for the missing illegitimate daughter of his uncle. A woman, he as much as admitted to me, that he would see dead in the same manner his grandmother had done for her mother. He has no reason to fear consequences. Why would he? Wealth or no, he's powerful and all but untouchable by the courts," the earl continued. "And at the Arcade, when Burney commented on how familiar you were to him, he did so because he had seen the portrait as well."

Something about the statement bothered her, creating a sense of déjà vu almost, as if she'd heard that sentiment expressed before. "You really believe this?"

"I do," he said. "And what's more, Burney believes it. He had some miscreant throw a rock through the window this morning with a blackmail demand tied about it. Burney is desperate but not especially clever. He's threatened to expose your identity to the Duke of Averston if I don't pay him."

Callie couldn't quite comprehend all that was coming at her. "Why on earth would he think that you would ever do such a ridiculous thing for someone who is only a governess?"

BECAUSE SHE WAS so much more than just a governess, and Burney, blockhead that he was, had at least managed to glean that correctly. Still, he couldn't afford for her to be. He certainly had not planned that she would be. But from the moment he'd first laid his eyes upon her, he'd been drawn to her. Watching her with the children, literally the only family he had left, had made him realize just what was missing from his existence as a confirmed bachelor. And now, facing the possibility that she might be in danger, he knew that he would do whatever was necessary to ensure her safety.

How was he to keep her safe from harm? While others might assume he was being overprotective or jumping at shadows, he had seen the truth of it in Averston's cold gaze. The man was capable of a ruthlessness most would not imagine. And given the incentive of the fortune he currently had access to, even in a limited capacity, he would not easily give that up.

But how could he protect her? He couldn't even keep her under his own roof, for heaven's sake.

You could marry Miss St. James. William's suggestion, made from innocence and ignorance, immediately came to mind. It was not out of the question. He had no need to marry for wealth nor did he particularly care for the notion of marrying for prestige. The simple truth was, he'd never considered marriage at all. He'd been utterly content with his bachelor status. But there were many things about his life in that current moment that had changed inexorably. Why should his marital status not be amongst them?

Still, no offer was forthcoming. In part because they barely knew one another and that was a very permanent arrangement to enter into for the sake of what could prove to be temporary danger. Also, he wasn't entirely certain of what her answer would be. And if Burney did as advised and kept his rather large mouth shut, there would be no need to go to such extremes. And if, in time, he did decide to pursue Miss St. James as something other than simply the children's governess, they would both know he did so for the right reasons—that he wanted her solely for her own sake and not for any claim she might have to a fortune that rivaled the Crown's.

"William might have said, in front of Charles Burney, that I should marry you," Winn admitted.

Miss St. James laughed at that after the shock of it settled. "Why on earth would the boy have said such a ridiculous thing?"

"Because William doesn't understand the idea of 'just' a governess," Winn replied, trying not to let her disparaging tone sting overly much. "Nor should he. I should hope that he will continue, in this life, to judge people more by their actions and character than any title that might be attached to them. He thinks you're pretty and he thinks you're nice... and he is correct on both counts. To his mind, and indeed to the mind of most men, that would make you an exceptional choice as a bride."

"But not for you," she surmised.

"I did not say that. I've never considered myself the marrying sort. I knew Wills had provided the requisite heir and expected that more children, still, would be forthcoming from my brother's union. I was free to live in my bachelor state as long as I desired." And until three miscreant children and one utterly enticing governess had turned his world upside down, he'd thought that would be forever.

"I see. So you don't object to marrying me, you just object to marriage in general," she summed up.

Winn had the distinct impression that she was somehow insulted. "Let us just say, Miss St. James, that were I to ever enter into the state of holy matrimony, I should hope that I had thought out my actions well, chosen my bride carefully, and that I should be lucky enough for her to possess even a portion of your beauty, intelligence and kindness. Where is Miss Darrow?"

"I'm here, Lord Montgomery," Euphemia Darrow said as she opened the door to the office and stepped inside. "Whatever could have been so urgent this morning?"

"Good morning, Effie," Callie said. "His lordship seems to have potentially identified, albeit inadvertently, who my parents were. And now he thinks I may be in danger because of it."

Effie's face paled. "What? In danger? In danger from who? That is a great deal to impart without actually telling me anything at all, Calliope!"

"I believe that Miss St. James is the daughter of the former Duke of Averston and his late mistress. According to Averston, his very own grandmother had his uncle's mistress murdered to prevent the former duke form marrying her and bringing scandal down upon the family... the child she bore him, a daughter, has been missing since," Winn answered.

Effie nodded. "I'm going to require more details than that."

Winn shook his head. Of course, she would. Women, all of them, were maddening. "Averston is the coldest of fish and the dowager duchess... well, she is as ruthless as they come. Because of Veronique Delaine's occupation, she was deemed unworthy of the former duke's affections. The intent, based upon what Averston relayed to me, was to eliminate her and the child. Mademoiselle Delaine perished in a terrible accident, but the child was unaccounted for. And all these years on, this child, a daughter, has been rumored to have survived... and I believe, with all my heart, that Calliope St. James is the lost heir to the former Duke of Averston."

"What has led you to this belief? There must be something!"

"Another gentleman and I who were both in attendance at the current duke's residence saw the portrait of Mademoiselle Delaine. Shortly, thereafter, Miss St. James, the children and I bumped into this gentleman, Charles Burney, while shopping. He has since noted the remarkable resemblance between Miss St. James and the woman whom I now believe was her mother."

Both Callie and Effie Darrow blinked at him in surprise at that very succinct retelling of the events.

"Mademoiselle Veronique Delaine?" Effie asked, shaking her head as if to clear it of cobwebs. "I saw her once when I was very, very young. In a play on Drury Lane. But we were, of course, seated so far away that I could not even begin to describe her face other than to say that I had the impression she was rather beautiful."

"And if the portrait is an accurate representation of how she appeared in life, then I daresay your impression was quite correct," Winn said.

"Drury Lane," Callie said, her voice distant and seeming lost in thought. "I recall now that the dressmaker I took Claudia and Charlotte to, Madame de Beauchamps—she asked me if anyone in my family had ever worked in the theater because she said I looked terribly familiar to her. She mentioned Drury Lane."

"Then we should go to see Madame de Beauchamps," Winn stated.

"No," Effie said. "You should take Callie to your home. She should instruct the children as planned and, above all, stay indoors with them the entire time. No trips to the park. Not today. Not any day until this is sorted out. I will go see Madame de Beauchamps myself."

"But what will you say to her?" Callie asked. "I don't think you should involve yourself if there is danger, Effie!"

"Yes, Miss Darrow," Winn interjected. "While I certainly have no say in allowing you to do anything, I must protest. Miss St. James is correct and you could be putting yourself in danger."

"My lord, how could I do anything else? While I understand most people view the Darrow School as just that... a school, it is, in fact, so much more. The girls who come here are like my own children. They are my family and I would never dream of not doing all that was in my power to protect them," Effie replied. "I assure you, my lord, that I will have all the assistance I require to see to my own safety. You, however, are charged with Miss St. James' safety, and I hope you realize just how much she means... to all of us."

"I do, Miss Darrow," Winn answered. "If you are ready, Miss St. James, I will hire a hack to transport us to the house. The less we are both walking about the streets of London right now, the better."

Chapter Eleven

THE INTERIOR OF the hired hack was quiet, neither of them speaking. The silence between them was neither comfortable nor awkward. It was present and noted, significant, but also necessary. Winn understood that. There was a great deal for Miss St. James to consider, a great deal to take in, and as for himself, he had his own plotting and planning to do.

Finally, when they had almost reached the house, she asked, "Do you really believe that I am in danger?"

"I think the possibility exists and it would be imprudent not to treat that possibility with all the respect and caution it deserves," he answered honestly.

"Then perhaps I shouldn't continue working for you, my lord. I don't want to place the children in harm's way," she said.

"I don't want them in harm's way, Miss St. James, but I'm not willing to let you be either. Sometimes, danger must be eliminated rather than simply avoided," Winn insisted. "And I daresay if you were to attempt to leave them, you'd face greater danger from the three of those imps than anything Averston might devise."

The comment coaxed a soft smile from her. That gentle curving of her lips called to mind their all too brief kiss. It had been a mistake. He knew that. It was a lapse in judgment and a lapse in propriety from him that was out of character. But he didn't regret it. He couldn't. Not when all he wanted, more than anything else, was to repeat it. Of course, it wouldn't be a simple brushing of his lips against hers if the opportunity presented itself once more. If he kissed her again, he meant to kiss her in a manner that neither of them would ever forget.

"We shouldn't mention any of this to the children," Callie insisted. "I won't have them worry... and I certainly won't have William doing something reckless because he thinks it's his duty to protect me."

"And he most assuredly would," Winn agreed. "We will say nothing to them. As for reasons for you not taking them to the park, blame it on a megrim or some other simple malady. Or lay the blame at my door. Heaven knows they've all certainly done something that warrants a restriction of some sort."

"Absolutely not! I won't have them thinking they are being punished without just cause."

"Whatever it takes to keep them safe," he said. "And you."

She eyed him curiously, her gaze direct and unwavering. "Why does it matter so much to you?"

"Because it does," Winn stated. "Because you work for me and that places you under my protection. Because the children care for you and need you. Because... because I very much want to kiss you again, Calliope St. James, and I plan on ensuring that there is ample opportunity for me to do so." It wasn't something he should say, nor was it something he should feel. But it was there nonetheless and he didn't mean to hide it from himself or from her.

Her lips formed a soft "O". "My lord... that is, I hardly think this is an appropriate topic of conversation. And it's hardly an altruistic motive!"

"I'm not an altruistic man, Miss St. James," he admitted. "I'm not a bounder or a rogue by any means, but I'm not a saint either. And I think, if you're perfectly honest with yourself and with me, you want the same."

"That hardly signifies."

Winn leaned forward and captured her hand in his. He made no other move, simply held her delicate hand in his for a moment, feeling the slightness of it, the impression of fragility that could only be misleading. "It does signify. Tell me the truth."

"I shouldn't."

He needed to know. As much as he needed his next breath, he needed to know that she felt at least some stirring of attraction for him. "Do it anyway."

"I liked it when you kissed me," she admitted, almost defiantly. "And while the thought of repeating it does appeal to me, it is unwise and we should not even be discussing it much less contemplating it."

Satisfied with that, Winn relented. "Fair enough, Miss St. James... for now. I'll take my victory, no matter how small it is."

Callie rolled her eyes. "We are not at war, my lord."

"Aren't we? I certainly feel as if I am under siege. I think of you constantly," he admitted.

For the longest moment, she simply blinked at him, apparently stunned by his admission. When she'd managed to regain her composure, she pointed out, "You've known me for less than a week."

He felt the tug of a grin at his lips, though it was certainly a rueful one. "To borrow your own phrasing, Miss St. James, that hardly signifies. Whether I've known you for ten minutes or ten days or ten years... I daresay you are the type of woman a man never forgets. You invade us... our thoughts, our dreams, until we're nothing but hollowed out wrecks of our former selves."

She stammered for a moment, attempting to formulate a reply. But wide-eyed, she eventually gave up and simply stared at him. He'd caught her off guard that morning, in more ways than one. Finally, she managed to say, "That's hardly a flattering assessment."

"Isn't it? I had thought myself immune to such things... that no woman could ever get under my skin in quite that way. And yet here we are. In short, Miss St. James, you've turned me into a jabbering, calf-eyed fool like some fresh out of the schoolroom lad who doesn't know his head from his—well, regardless. You have a singular kind of power, Calliope St. James. I urge you to wield it wisely."

"I don't feel powerful," she admitted. "I feel confused and frightened and out of my depth at every turn. But the one thing I am certain of is that the kiss we shared, as such things go, was fairly benign."

Winn shook his head. "I wouldn't say it was benign. It was relatively chaste in the overall scheme of things, but no less potent for it."

She nodded. "I suppose that's an accurate assessment. You said you wanted to kiss me again... why haven't you? There has certainly been opportunity to do so."

"I suppose I'm waiting for you to decide that you'd like to be kissed."

"Oh. Would it be only a kiss?"

"If that is what you desire," Winn replied.

"Then perhaps you should kiss me now. It might be that the first one was an aberration of sorts," she suggested.

He didn't laugh. In fact, he half-hoped she was right. Yet, he knew that if he kissed her again, it would only solidify one truth for him. Calliope St. James had the power to tie him in knots.

Winn pulled her across the small distance separating their seats until she was pressed against his chest. His arms closed around her and she leaned into him, her lashes fluttering as she closed her eyes. Unable to resist a moment longer, he claimed her lips. Despite his desire to take, to plunder, he kept his touch gentle—coaxing and seductive rather than forceful. When her lips parted under the gentle pressure of his, he teased them with his tongue, nipping at the plump curve of her lower lip. But there was nothing that prepared him for when she returned his kiss, when she mimicked those same strategies.

But there was no time to ponder it further. The hack was slowing to a stop. They had arrived.

Easing back from her, Winn straightened her hair, tucking one wayward strand behind her ear. "Not an aberration then."

"So it would seem," she said, looking somewhat poleaxed by the whole experience. "I always thought kissing was something done as a sign of affection... as a sweet gesture."

"It can be. But it can also be so much more," he answered, taking note of her slightly panicked expression. Taking pity on her, he said, "Come on, then. No more kissing or talk of kissing, not today at any rate. We should get inside and see what catastrophe awaits us."

Winn stepped down from the carriage and reached back to assist her. Holding her gloved hand in his, even for that brief moment, brought home to him just how true his earlier statement had been. Somehow, she had invaded every aspect of his being. No part of him remained unaffected by her—heart, mind, body and soul.

⟫⟫⟪⟪

EFFIE WAITED PATIENTLY in the small coffee house near the Royal Arcade. She knew the moment he walked in. So perfectly attuned to him was she, she could feel his presence. As he approached, she took a deep and steadying breath. When he rounded the table and took a seat at the one adjacent to hers, she knew he did so for her benefit. He was mindful of her reputation at all times.

"You summoned," Highcliff said, his voice deep and rumbling.

"I asked you to join me," Effie pointed out. "That's hardly the same thing."

"I have no choice but to heed the call, Miss Darrow. I'd say it is exactly the same," he replied. "To what do I owe the honor? If you're expecting an apology for what transpired at our last meeting, I won't offer it. I'd just as soon cut out my own tongue."

Recalling just how skillfully he'd kissed her with the appendage offered up as sacrifice, Effie thought that would be a terrible waste. But she wouldn't encourage him by saying so. Instead, Effie cast a quelling glance in his direction. "Despite your supreme arrogance and conceit, my invitation has nothing to do with the new complexities of our very old acquaintance. It's about Calliope and the Earl of Montgomery."

"For what it's worth," Highcliff replied, "He's perfectly acceptable. I couldn't find a shred of dirt about him. His business dealings are above board. He doesn't wager heavily, nor drink heavily. He doesn't frequent bawdy houses and hasn't maintained a regular mistress for years. The man is practically a monk by society's standards. If there's anything about him untoward, he's managed to be the soul of discretion... and I always find the dirt, Effie, no matter how well hidden it is."

"This is more about Calliope than about him, I suppose... the earl has inadvertently discovered her parentage and it could very well put her in danger."

"Well, all he has to do is keep it a secret," Highcliff sneered. "Problem solved."

"Unfortunately, that cat is out of the proverbial bag thanks to a gentleman of the earl's acquaintance by the name of Charles Burney."

He muttered something under his breath.

"What was that?" she asked.

"Not fit for your ears," he answered. "Burney is trouble... trouble of the worst sort."

"What sort is that?"

"The desperate sort. To say his pockets are to let is an overstatement. They're no longer even his pockets," Highcliff replied. "Desperate men are dangerous men."

It was something she knew well. The past few months, it seemed one or another of her girls was always in some sort of jeopardy. "Then you should accompany me on my next errand, Lord Highcliff."

"What sort of errand?"

"We're going to speak with Madame de Beauchamps. It seems she may have known Calliope's mother long ago."

Effie dropped a few coins on the table and rose. Walking out of the coffee house, she waited until he exited a few moments after her. When she was certain he was following, she made her way along the Arcade to the entrance to Madame de Beauchamps' shop. As she opened the door and stepped inside, a bell tinkled above the door. The woman in question came out to greet her.

"Miss Darrow! How good it is to see you! It has been some time. Are you in need of a new gown?" the shopkeeper and most fashionable modiste in London asked with a beaming smile.

"No, Madame, not today," Effie said. The bell tinkled again, signifying that Highcliff had entered. "But is there a place where you and I—and my friend—might speak privately?"

The shopkeeper looked askance at them both, but nodded. "For you, Miss Darrow, certainly. If you will follow me, I have a small, private parlor in back."

Through the rabbit warren of bolts of cloth and half-made dresses, they followed the dressmaker until they emerged at the entrance to a small room. It was windowless, but decorated with light colors and well-lit by gas lamps and strategically placed mirrors that amplified the light. A settee and armchair richly upholstered in the palest shade of pink occupied the space along with small, delicate wooden tables.

"It's quite lovely," Effie said.

"Thank you, Miss Darrow. I do enjoy having lovely things and I am very lucky that my business has grown enough that I can now indulge myself. This is my refuge here at the shop when I need to rest. Now, please, do tell me to what I owe the pleasure of your visit."

Effie didn't hesitate, but simply dove in. "There was a young woman in here yesterday morning... she had two young girls with her, wards of their uncle, the Earl of Montgomery."

"Yes," Madame de Beauchamps exclaimed. "I remember her because she seemed so terribly familiar to me, yet I could not place her. As I get older, my memory gets worse by the day!"

Effie nodded and then looked back at Highcliff who was watching the exchange with a false air of boredom. "Well, perhaps when I utter this name, your confusion on the matter will clear up... Mademoiselle Veronique Delaine."

Madame de Beauchamps gasped. One hand flew to her mouth and the other to her heart as she stared at them wide-eyed. "Oh, I can't believe I did not see it! But the young woman... not that she wasn't lovely—of a certain, she was!—she did not make as much of her beauty. She dressed so modestly and attempted to disguise her prettiness, I think! But the resemblance is there and now... well, I cannot believe I was so blind."

"Do not take on so, Madame," Effie said. "Miss St. James does make every effort to minimize her rather striking appearance. It is something that I have cautioned all of my students to do when they begin working."

"St. James? Is she not Averston's child then? Veronique was so wildly in love with him, I cannot imagine that she would have ever betrayed him and had a child with another!" the dressmaker cried in dismay.

Highcliff coughed behind her.

Effie looked back at him and all pretense of boredom was gone. His gaze was hard and his posture was that of a man ready to do battle.

"Did you say Averston?" he demanded.

"Yes," Madame de Beauchamps replied. "Veronique came here from France at his urging... it was just before all the troubles began, you see. They were so very much in love. He wanted to marry her, you know? But she refused him. She was terrified that the scandal would embitter him toward her! It was only when she became with child that she even considered it... but she still would not agree until closer to time for the child to be born in case aught were to go wrong. There had been other babes, you see, that she had lost. She said that she didn't wish him to be saddled with a scandalous wife who would never be able to bear him children."

"How do you know all of this?" Highcliff asked.

"I was her dresser... one of them, at any rate. But she spoke freely with all of us. There were no secrets in the theater, my lord," Madame de Beauchamps answered. "As to my failure to recognize Miss St. James, well, I had assumed the child was dead. Veronique would have fought the devil himself to save her child after losing so many before her."

"You said she wouldn't marry him until closer to time for her child to be born... did they actually wed?" Effie asked.

"But, of course! By special license at St. Clement Danes. It was a secret, of course. He insisted upon it... he was terrified that whatever his mother's response would be might be too much of a strain on Veronique," Madame de Beauchamps said. "He adored her and he was giddy at the thought of her bearing his child. I've never seen two people so happy or so deeply in love."

"Would you swear to these things in court?" Highcliff asked.

"Certainly, I would!" the dressmaker replied readily. "I feel so terrible! That poor girl has gone her entire life without knowing what a beautiful soul her mother was and how very much she was loved and wanted!"

Effie felt tears pricking her eyes. No one understood better than she did just how important, how vital such a piece of information could be to someone like Callie. Someone like herself.

"Might I have a word with you outside, Miss Darrow?" Highcliff said.

"You remain here. It is very private," Madame de Beauchamps said. "I must go out front for a moment and make sure that the shop girls have everything in hand."

The dressmaker left and Effie turned to face Highcliff. "It's very bad, isn't it?"

"I doubt it could be worse. Not even if she were the daughter of Prinny himself," Highcliff admitted gruffly. "Averston will lose everything if her identity is discovered. And there has never been a man more unsuited to poverty. Though to be honest, I'd be more concerned about the dowager duchess. That woman is a terror if ever one existed. If either of them knows of her existence, it may already be too late. The wheels could be in motion even as we speak."

Effie clasped her hands together in her lap, hating the quiet certainty she heard in his voice. If Highcliff thought the man a danger, then he was. There was nothing for it but to lay out the whole truth, ugly as it was. "Mr. Burney tried to blackmail the earl. He threatened to expose Calliope to Averston if his demands weren't met... but Montgomery claims to have handled things on that front. What do you think?"

"I think that Averston and Burney are more than business associates. There are things about their personal lives that I know which Montgomery isn't privy to I believe ... and that could change the dynamic of all of this rather dramatically."

"What sort of things?" she asked.

Highcliff shook his head. "Things I don't mean to discuss with you... I'll address it with Montgomery."

"I am four and thirty years, Highcliff," Effie said. "I'm not so easily shocked as you imagine. I am well aware that there are people in this world who feel attraction for members of their own sex. For heaven's sake, I run a school for girls. Do you think I've never encountered it before?"

His face went positively blank. He stared at her for the longest moment in utter silence.

"We're not having this conversation," he said. "We're certainly not having it in the back parlor of a dressmaker's shop. I'll go out first. I need to get to Montgomery and see what he knows about Averston and Burney. But first, I need to do some digging of my own into other matters… into Averston and the dowager duchess. I'll have a carriage out front to pick you up and see you home. This is not a game, Effie. The duke and his deceptively frail-looking grandmother are more dangerous than you know and anyone who knows Miss St. James' true identity is a threat to them."

"Surely, we are in no danger! I understand that Calliope is a threat to—"

"Not yet, we aren't," he said. "But that will change. As soon as they realize we are involved, they will set their sights on us, as well. In fact, anyone who knows the truth about this and about your Miss St. James is in the gravest of danger. Go home. See to your students… and leave this to me now."

"I most certainly will not! Callie is my responsibility!"

"And you are mine," he insisted.

Effie's temper flared at that. "I am not. I have not been nor will I ever be… you've made your feelings for me abundantly clear in the past, Lord Highcliff."

He laughed bitterly. "Clearly, I have not. Effie, if you want to see Callie safe, trust me to do this. If a situation arises where I have to choose which one of you to protect—well, you'd never forgive me for choosing you and I'd never forgive myself if I did not. Please… let me do this."

"You promise to look after her?"

"I do," he said. "I will make certain she is safe… and you will make certain that you are. I'll be sending a few men over to guard your house. They'll be inconspicuous, of course, and remain outside."

Effie felt dread welling inside her. "Do you really think that's necessary?"

His lips firmed, forming a thin, tight line. "I hope it isn't. But these people are ruthless and I won't take the risk."

Chapter Twelve

"**I** WISH WE could go to the park," Charlotte said as she stroked the silken hair of her doll.

Callie smiled sadly. "Perhaps in a day or so when I'm feeling better. Now, put your doll down and practice your letters. Afterward, we're going to have a story!"

"You're going to read to us?" The hopeful note in the little girl's voice was difficult to miss.

"No, Charlotte," Callie insisted. "You are going to read to me."

"But I can't! I don't know how."

"I'll help you," William offered, looking up from the sums he was laboring over.

"Indeed, you shall. Your reading is coming along nicely," Callie said, praising the boy. He was so very eager to learn, not for the sake of it, but because he craved praise and attention. It broke her heart a little that he would work so very hard just for a kind word.

Callie rose from the table where she'd been working on additional lessons for them and crossed to the window where she looked outside. Her senses were whirling, her mind overwhelmed with all the things that had occurred. *He* was on her mind, of course. Lord Winn Hamilton, Earl of Montgomery. He had been since their conversation in the hired hack that morning. If she were honest, she would admit that he'd been on her mind far more frequently and insistently than that. It seemed her every waking thought was either about him or reminding herself of why she should not think about him. The admission that he wished to kiss her again, that he thought of her with what she could only assume was the same frequency with which he crossed her mind was doing nothing to ease her current predicament. Then there was everything else, things that she had shied away from.

Her parents. They hadn't simply abandoned her because they didn't want her. Her mother, if what had been said was accurate, had left her there on the steps of the workhouse, anonymous and reasonably safe, while she met her own certain death. And if it was true, and if it could be proven, then she was not simply the unwanted bastard daughter of a duke, but an heiress. It would change everything.

It would render her marriageable.

The sad truth was that, as a governess trained by Effie, her standards and her expectations were at cross purposes. In comportment and education, she was a lady. She viewed herself as one. But as a governess, there were few men of a station that she could wed that would not be considered beneath her or above her. That could all change. But heiress or not, she was still a bastard. She was still a woman who had been a servant. It seemed as if it would only complicate her life further.

"You're very sad, aren't you?"

The question had come from William, his small voice tight with concern.

Callie pasted a smile on her face and turned back to him. "I'm not sad. I'm only tired," she lied. "I'm sure I'll be better company tomorrow."

He shook his head, his small face clenched with worry. "No. You're sad the way our mother was when our father was gone for a long time. You're not going to leave us, are you?"

Leaving her vantage point at the window, Callie crossed to him and crouched down so they were eye to eye. "I'm not going to leave you. I adore you... all three of you. I will be here with you for as long as I can... for as long as you need me to be."

Callie didn't have any warning. He simply launched himself at her, hurling his small frame against hers and wrapping his arms tightly around her as he pressed his face against her neck. She could feel the heat of his tears, but she didn't acknowledge them. He was a little boy, after all, embarrassed by such things and clearly trying to hide them. So she simply held him and rubbed his back. After only a brief hesitation, Charlotte came to them as well. She scooted in and pressed herself against Callie's side, clinging in her own sweet way.

Those children were broken, neglected, their little hearts and spirits crushed by the years of their parents' disregard. Whatever her very complicated feelings were for their uncle, and his for her, neither of them could afford to forget that the children had to come first.

⟫⟫⟫⟪⟪⟪

IT WAS THEIR first lesson. Claudia sat stiffly on the bench beside him, her fingers poised on the keys of the pianoforte. He noticed that they trembled slightly, as did her lower lip. Uncertain of what else to do or how else to ease her nerves, Winn placed his fingers on the keys as well, struck a few notes, then hit one very sharp, very sour note that echoed about the room. She turned her head, looking at him in surprise.

"Even the best of musicians will sometimes strike the wrong chord or stumble over a note, Claudia," he said. "It doesn't matter. You simply keep playing. No one will beat you or punish you for that. Do you understand?"

She nodded. "He was a terrible man. I don't know what he would have done had Miss St. James not been here."

Winn sighed. "Well, she was here and we are both very lucky for it."

"You like her."

He shrugged. "Of course, I like her. She's an excellent governess."

Claudia's eyes rolled at that. "No. You *like* her."

Winn stared at the very grown up expression on his young niece's face and had to accept the fact, that women, regardless of their age, had the unique ability to see straight through a man no matter how well concealed he thought his secrets were. "This is not an appropriate topic of conversation."

Her eyebrows arched upward and her lips pressed together into a disapproving line that looked shockingly familiar. She looked like a younger, feminine version of himself to be precise and it was decidedly uncomfortable to be confronted with his own mannerisms in miniature.

"Really, Uncle Winn, can't you just admit it? You like her. And I'm fairly certain she likes you!"

That piqued his curiosity. While he knew he shouldn't encourage her, he was too invested in the insight she might provide to correct her again. "How do you know?"

Claudia shrugged. "You both try entirely too hard not to look at one another when you're in the same room together. It's obvious. And whenever you leave the room, Miss St. James lets out her breath on a long sigh but it doesn't sound like relief. It sounds... wistful."

"That's a rather unexpected word choice for someone who supposedly has had a very neglected education," he pointed out.

"I can still read... and I like to. I just don't like to read the things I'm supposed to be reading," she said. "And I know you went to fetch her this morning and bring her here because you are worried for her."

Now that was more than a guess. "How would you know that, Claudia?"

"I found the note in your study... the one that was thrown through the window. Is she really the daughter of a duke?"

Winn shook his head. "First, why were you in my study?"

"I was returning a book," she said. "And I saw the note crumpled up on the floor. I picked it up, read it, and then I heard the door slam. When I looked out the window I saw you walking away and I knew you were likely doing something to protect Miss St. James."

"Or I could have been going for a morning ride," he pointed out. "It's dangerous to assume that you know what people's motivations are, Claudia."

"Well, you'd look happier than that if you were just going for a ride," she said. "And I know you'd protect her. I'm not assuming anything there."

"How do you know that?"

Another eye roll. "Because you like her!"

Winn ran a hand over his eyes. "We're talking in circles. Claudia, I need you to promise me you will say nothing to William or Charlotte about all of this."

"I wouldn't dare. William would be unbearably foolish," she said.

"So he would," Winn agreed. "And to put your mind at rest, I'm taking all the steps I can to ensure Miss St. James' safety."

"You should marry her," Claudia said.

"I'm not taking marital advice from a not quite eleven year old," he stated flatly. "Besides, how on earth would that keep her safe?"

"Because she taught me all about the peerage and I know that, as our governess, if someone hurt her and that person was a gentleman, not very much would happen to them at all. But if they hurt her and she was the wife of a peer, their social equal, then it could go very badly for them," Claudia answered. "The best way to protect her is to make the consequences of harming her more severe."

Winn stared at the girl with a mixture of shock and awe. She was uncannily brilliant. "You can read any book you like whenever you like... except for the top shelf."

"What's on the top shelf?" she asked curiously.

Ovid, for one, which she should never read. Some particularly nasty works of John Wilmott that his brother had adored. It was a treasure trove of all the things she should never, ever read. "Nothing. Or rather nothing will be on it by the time you return."

Claudia grinned at him. "You're starting to sound almost paternal."

"So I am," he said, aghast at the thought.

"Marriage—"

"Enough about that," he said firmly. Not because he thought it was a bad idea or because he'd dismissed it out of hand, but because there were other things that had to be addressed first. "Whether or not I elect to pursue Miss St. James as a bride is a matter between me and Miss St. James."

"Well, you should pursue her. I know what people look like when they aren't happily married... they look like my parents did. And I don't think you and Miss St. James ever would."

In for a penny, in for a pound, he thought. "And why not?"

"Because you're good people. You care about other people and try to take care of them. Mama and Papa didn't do that. Papa only wanted to gamble and stay gone for days and weeks on end. And Mama... she only wanted Papa."

Sobered by that, Winn stared down at the keys. "We aren't getting very far in your lessons."

"Are we getting very far in yours?"

He grinned in spite of himself. "You're very cheeky, you know?"

"Yes," Claudia agreed.

"I'll take it under advisement," Winn said firmly. "Now, do you know which keys are which?"

Claudia sighed but began to rattle off the little bit of pertinent information she had actually gleaned from her one and only music lesson. Winn listened, taking in what she was saying, but part of his mind was thoroughly engaged elsewhere.

He could marry her.

It was a foolish notion, but a strangely appealing one.

⇶⇇

AVERSTON WAS IN his club, enjoying a light lunch from his concealed vantage point while Mr. Charles Burney made the rounds. He was like a begging dog, going table to table asking for scraps. Were the man not so exceptionally handsome, Averston would have never given him a second thought. But Burney was handsome and incredibly eager. So, Averston considered what to do about his latest paramour. When Burney finally was near enough, Averting called out, "Mr. Burney, a word if you have a moment."

Burney looked startled, clearly having no notion that he'd been there all along, his table concealed by potted palms and a heavy velvet drape. Appearing less than comfortable, he approached.

"Sit," Averston said. While it was offered in a welcoming tone, they both recognized it as an order rather than an invitation.

"Your grace," Burney said. "I wasn't aware that you were going to be at the club today."

Averston smiled at that, a cold expression that didn't reach his eyes. It wasn't amusement that he felt, after all. Burney's presumption that he would be privy to his schedule hinted a greater intimacy between them than Averston would ever permit. Whatever had transpired between them in those dark hours together, he answered to no one. The young man needed to remember that. "And why would you be? I see no need to grant you access to my schedule."

Burney flushed with embarrassment. "You wished to speak with me?"

"This has to stop. Don't humiliate yourself begging for scraps at the tables of your betters," Averston said with disdain.

Burney's flush deepened, but it wasn't embarrassment now. It was anger. "My betters? Hardly. And I'm left with no choice but to beg! If I don't find investors, I'll wind up in the Marshalsea for my father's debts! And if I don't get the investors my cousin needs, he'll—"

Averston waited for a heartbeat but when no more information was forthcoming, he prodded, "He'll what?"

"It hardly matters. What could be worse than the humiliation of being carted off to prison for debts I had no part in accruing?"

"That is unfortunate but it hardly changes the fact that the stink of desperation on you will send every potential investor running for the hills," Averston replied calmly, as if the idea of Burney rotting in a debtor's prison made no matter to him. He wasn't pleased at the prospect and there might have been a twinge of sympathy, even, but he wasn't one given to such soft emotions. But, he reasoned, Burney was handsome, eager, and available. While there were others who fit those requirements well enough, and he typically viewed his paramours as expendable, he found himself reluctant to end their sordid little affair on such a sour note.

"Help me," Burney implored. "It's in your power to do so."

Averston shook his head. "The trustees would never release that amount of funds on an uncertain investment."

"Then don't invest," Burney said. "But use your influence so that others will!"

Averston meticulously cut a small bite from the beef on his plate and brought it to his lips. He ate it, chewing slowly, making no move to answer Burney's impassioned plea. After he swallowed the morsel, he took a sip of his wine. He'd help him, of course. It served his own purposes to do so, but that didn't mean he wouldn't make the younger man squirm a bit before relenting. Finally, he replied, "And why should I? Do you think our friendship entitles you to any sort of special favors? It doesn't, you know. *Boys* like you, well, they're easy enough to come by."

Burney's face paled and his expression appeared, for a moment, to be shattered. Then he squared his shoulders, firmed his jaw and showed the first hint of spine Averston had seen from him. "It's nice to know where I stand, I suppose."

Averston ignored the pang of conscience. Guilt was a wasted emotion. He couldn't let Charles Burney care for him. Caring for him would bring only heartache and misery. Their relationship would only ever be about mutual desire and gratification. Anything more than that was impossible and the sooner Burney accepted that, the lesser the likelihood of him being truly hurt. "I didn't say I wouldn't help you... only not for that reason. If I'm going to do something for you, Burney, you will be required to do something for me in return. It is the way of the world, is it not?"

"What could I possibly do for you?" Burney asked. "I have nothing."

"You have charm, of course. You talk to people, Burney. They like you. That is not true of me. I intimidate them... I scare them. They think I will gobble them up and spit them out," Averston said.

"And will you?"

Averston smiled. "Very likely. But that means you, Burney, will be privy to sensitive information. Confessions and confidences that could serve me well if you choose to share them."

The younger man shifted in his chair, obviously uncomfortable, obviously already knowing something of use that he was hesitant to reveal. Averston decided not to press him, but to wait patiently for him to disclose it. He would, of course. In due time.

"Tell me the secrets of others, Burney, and I will keep yours... and help you to save your impoverished family," Averston urged. "I will even dance attendance on your pretty young sister tonight."

Burney was silent for a long moment, his thoughts clearly jumbled. He appeared to be on the verge of speaking, then abruptly changed his mind, offering a nod instead.

"Keep your ear to the ground and let me know what you discover," Averston said and then waved his hand, dismissing the younger man. "Investments gone awry, political scandals, romantic peccadillos. All of it can be useful, if one hasn't the uncomfortable fetter of a conscience."

He noted the flash of hurt in Burney's gaze. It wasn't exactly regret that he felt. Regret wasn't something he was capable of, but there might have been a moment of longing. For the first time in his life, Averston wondered what it would be like not to simply be cold. How would it feel, he wondered, to value another person's happiness over his own? He couldn't say, but he imagined it would never create the hot, tight sensation in his gut that he was currently experiencing.

But there was a method to his madness. He couldn't afford to let Burney care for him any more than he could afford to care for Burney. Neither of them was free to do so, not in their current society and not while he was still forced to live under the thumb of a dragon with ice in her veins.

"She can't live forever," he muttered to himself before taking a sip of his wine. One day, she'd breathe her last and he'd finally get her claws out of him. *One day.*

Chapter Thirteen

THE BALL WAS a glittering affair, as all of them tended to be. It was an unusual event for Winn in that he actually liked most of the people present. Most of the guests were gentry, those with lesser titles, but the turnout was good and there were any number of eligible young bachelors there to save him from Mrs. Burney's schemes. Still, he wouldn't say that he was enjoying himself. It had been just over a day since Burney's blackmail attempt had gone awry, but since that time he'd been waiting for the proverbial other shoe to drop. It was maddening and frustrating.

Winn moved to the refreshment table and retrieved a glass of champagne for himself. He sipped it slowly and carefully surveyed the room. Burney was there, careful to avoid making any eye contact with him at all. If Mrs. Burney and Amelia were in any way aware of Burney's actions, it didn't show in the least. Amelia, sweet and pretty as ever, was dancing with a calf-eyed young man who looked at her as if she'd hung the moon in the stars.

Rather the way he looked at Miss St. James, he thought bitterly. Try as he might, he could not get her from his mind. Nor could he shake the feeling that something terrible was about to occur. Between Burney's threats and stupidity, and constantly worrying that someone might see her who had also been a guest in Averston's home and observed the portrait of Veronique Delaine, he was ready to chuck it all and pack her off to the countryside, willing or no. The fear that it might very well come to that had not escaped him.

The song ended. The young fellow Amelia had been dancing with escorted her back to her mother. He'd have his dance with her and then take his leave. Before he could cross the room to claim his dance, the butler entered, and with all the pomp the scrawny man could muster, announced the arrival of their latest guest.

"His grace, Lord Gerald Alford, Duke of Averston!"

There was a murmur from the gathered crowd. Averston wasn't one to attend such events, and he certainly wasn't one to make nice with debs. *Which meant that Averston could be there at Burney's behest.* Had the man changed his mind about Burney's investment scheme? Or was there something more sinister at play? If Burney had broken his word and shared with Averston the truth about Miss St. James, it would have disastrous and possibly deadly consequences for her.

Winn was stuck between a rock and a hard place. He was obliged to dance the next set with Amelia and if he failed to do so, she would be humiliated. But he couldn't risk Averston getting away before he had a chance to speak to the man and determine what, precisely, he knew.

The decision was taken out of his hands. Mrs. Burney waved at him happily, indicating that she was well aware the next set was his. Biting back a curse, he closed the distance and bowed to the young woman.

"Good evening, Amelia. You look lovely tonight. I believe the next dance is mine," he said.

"Indeed, my lord," Mrs. Burney gushed. "We are most honored by your presence here."

Winn didn't have to respond because the musicians struck the first chord. Instead, he offered Amelia his arm, smiled at her mother and led the girl onto the dance floor.

"Don't mind Mama," she said, utilizing the in vogue French pronunciation of the word. "She's quite determined to make a match between us despite the fact that I've told her countless times we would not suit."

Winn nodded. "Your mother is a very determined woman. She will not give up on a match between us until you're matched with someone else. Even then, I have doubts."

Amelia laughed softly. "She doesn't understand. You've been like an older brother to me as long as I've known you... and I've little doubt that you see me much as you would a younger sister. The truth of the matter is, there is a gentleman that has caught my eye."

Winn's eyebrows arched upward. "And who might that be?"

"I'm not quite ready to say... not just yet," she admitted, as she twirled to the music. When they were facing one another once more, she added, "You've been such a dear friend to us. It seems terribly demanding to ask it, but would you be so kind as to look after Charlie? I think things are not at all well with him."

Winn's expression remained placid. "What on earth would make you think such?"

"He's very secretive now, when he's never been before," she replied. "And I've caught him in the study late at night, poring over the books and drinking heavily. He looks so terribly worried at such times. I tried to convince him that I didn't need a ball like this, that the expense was too great, but he was insistent."

Winn sighed. "Amelia, you are very dear to me. And you do need this ball. If you are to impress this gentleman and make a suitable match, having a debut such as this is a necessity. I will help Charles if I can."

"Will you invest in this scheme he keeps talking about?"

"No," Winn said. "But I will make an offer to him to loan him a certain amount of money and steer him toward a suitable investment. In the meantime, you should focus on making a match. That will ease his worries considerably."

"Because I'll be one less person to support," she surmised.

"No," Winn said. "Because he cares very deeply for you and knowing that your welfare has been seen to will offer him some peace, I think."

Amelia looked away, her gaze landing on her brother where he laughed and joked with those around him. Despite his apparent gaiety, there was a tension in him that was undeniable. "Thank you, my lord, for being such a good friend to us. And for your generosity, but I'm very worried that Charlie may be in some sort of trouble beyond simply financial woes. It isn't the sort of thing that just a loan will cover."

Winn nodded. "I fear you may be right, Amelia. But tonight, you should worry for nothing. Enjoy your debut. Dance, laugh, flirt. Do all the things that young girls are supposed to do before they take society by storm... and I'll—I'll speak to Burney. And I'll do what I can to help."

"Thank you. I can't tell you how much I appreciate that," she said, smiling sweetly.

"It's the least I can do. Our families have been friends for ages, after all. Tell me, Amelia, are you acquainted with the Duke of Averston?"

She was all wide-eyed innocence as she answered, "I've never met him, I think. I know Charlie wanted to have him invest in his latest venture, but I've no notion beyond that of why he's here. In truth, I wasn't even aware that he'd been invited."

"Just as well," Winn said. "He's not the sort for you. Avoid him please."

Amelia looked toward Averston where he stood there watching the festivities. "I agree. I don't think I'd have much in common with him, at all. He seems rather cold, I think."

"I think that you are a remarkably good judge of character, dear girl."

When the dance ended, he escorted her back to her mother. Walking away from the pair, he scanned the room for Averston. Finally, he spotted the man leaning nonchalantly against a column, half-hidden behind a potted palm. Noting the intensity of the man's gaze, Winn followed it and found that Averston was staring at Burney as he twirled some empty-headed, giggling chit about the dance floor.

Approaching him, Winn stated bluntly, "I'm surprised to see you here, Averston. I didn't think these events merited a spot on your already overflowing social calendar."

Averston's expression firmed, but there was a hint of amusement in his gaze. "Shall I submit my schedule to you for approval?"

Winn didn't take the bait. "What are you doing here really, Averston? The Burney family is hardly part of your social sphere. And we both know you do nothing unless there is profit or power in it. You've already rejected Burney's investment proposition."

"You're smarter than I gave you credit for being, Montgomery. You may relax in the knowledge that I am here at the request of Mr. Charles Burney... the return of a favor, if you will."

Winn's blood went cold. "Burney is a good man to know. A trusted friend... most of the time."

"Most of the time?" Averston asked. "What must the young man have done to be damned by such faint praise?"

Deciding to brazen it out, Winn replied, "He's made free with a bit of information that he ought to have kept secret. It could be very damaging to someone..." *to someone I care a great deal for.* "To someone I know."

"It rather sounds as if you are in some sort of romantic entanglement. Is the lady married? Or is she promised to someone else? Tell me, what bastard have you sired that will inherit another man's title?"

"It isn't that sort of secret," Winn said. Whether it was simply wishful thinking on his part, he couldn't say. But he didn't believe that Averston knew the truth, at least not yet. "Why did you come here,

Averston?"

The duke shrugged. "Mr. Burney thought my presence might aid his sister in making a successful launch into society. I'll even dance with the girl. But I've no designs on her. It seems you might, however. Pretty little thing, though I wouldn't have pegged you for one to court children."

"I do not have designs on her," Winn replied. "Our families are of long acquaintance and I feel what one might refer to as a brotherly regard for her... and for Burney. Tell me, what sort of favor did Burney do for you?"

Averston didn't smile, but his lips did tighten in a smirk that was likely the closest he came to such an expression. "It was of a somewhat personal nature. He provided invaluable assistance in arranging a rather particular assignation for me. It's nothing you need concern yourself with. I realize I'm hardly looked upon as a humanitarian, but I'm not a monster, Montgomery. I'm here to settle a debt. Nothing more."

Winn considered the other man's response carefully. He couldn't challenge him further on the matter without arousing suspicion. But he had to wonder what Averston hoped to gain from an association with Burney, and what cost it might have for the young man he'd long considered a friend, despite their recent disagreement. "He's a boy... trusting, gullible and easily led astray. If you've a mind to mentor him, Averston, I pray you offer him some guidance on how to conduct himself in business."

"Is that what I am to be? His mentor?"

"It's what you could be," Winn offered. "It's not a terrible thing to look after another person... to consider someone else's well-being above one's own."

"Ah... this is about your little crew of orphans, isn't it? They've made you a changed man, have they?"

Winn stiffened. "They're children who've lost everything that mattered to them in this world and have been placed at the mercy of a stranger. Surely even you would not jest about that."

Averston's expression tightened for just a moment, then he gave a curt nod. "Quite right. Some things should never be a source of amusement. I've no nefarious intentions for your young friend, Montgomery. You have my word on that."

Winn nodded. "Then I bid you good night."

Turning on his heel, Winn left the ballroom immediately. He retrieved his coat, instructed the butler to have his carriage sent home and then set out on foot. The exchange with Averston had left him too tense to simply stand around waiting for the carriage to make it to him. The walk, he decided, would clear his head.

But by the time Winn reached his own home, he realized that the short distance had done little to help him. He was still puzzling over Averston, puzzling over what sort of trouble Charles Burney might actually be in to prompt him to behave in a manner so out of character as to resort to blackmail and he was still working out the best ways to keep Miss Calliope St. James safe from even the hint of a threat.

Entering his home, Foster greeted him and aided him with his coat. "Are the children settled for the night?"

"I suspect they are, my lord. Miss St. James went up with them some time ago, but I haven't seen her come down."

Winn glanced at the case clock. It was after ten. She should have been long gone by that point. "Foster, send to the stables so that when the coach arrives it isn't unhitched. Miss St. James will go home that way. It's too late for her to walk."

Foster nodded, "Aye, my lord. I'll see to it."

Winn took the stairs swiftly, making his way to the children's quarters. Outside the door to the bedchamber Claudia and Charlotte shared, he heard whispered voices, and one of them belonged to William. Fearing that plots were afoot, Winn opened the door and peered inside. "The lot of you should be asleep."

Claudia shushed him and pointed toward Charlotte's bed. "Miss St. James was telling us a story for bedtime."

Winn looked and immediately wished he hadn't. Miss St. James was lying on Charlotte's bed, snuggled up with precocious child and both were fast asleep. Part of him was tempted to simply let her stay there, but she'd been so adamant that staying overnight in his home was unacceptable. If he breeched her trust by not waking her and sending her home, it would be an unpardonable sin in her eyes.

"Wake her, Claudia, but gently and as quietly as possible. I will see her home," he instructed. "And you, William, come with me. You need to be in your own bed."

The little boy rose and reluctantly followed him out, heading to his assigned chamber that was just across the hall from his sisters'. As they walked, Winn ruffled his hair. "What sort of story was Miss St. James telling you? Princesses in castles?"

"No. Dragons," he said. "And pirate treasure."

"Well, she certainly knows her audience," Winn mused. He followed William to the bed and tucked the boy in.

"I wish she was here all the time," William said.

"I know you do," Winn agreed. "But that's not the arrangement we made. For her to be your governess, she must return to her own home in the evenings."

William's lower lip turned outward in a pout. "Then she shouldn't be our governess. She should just live here with us... you could marry her!"

"It's a bit more complicated than that." Winn softened the rebuke with a slight smile. "Miss St. James and I... well, we might not suit one another."

"Because she's poor?"

Winn shook his head. "No. Not because of that... I've been a bachelor for a very long time. I've grown very used to living by my own rules. Wives have a tendency to change that."

"So do children. Will you send us away?"

"No," Winn replied emphatically. "You and your sisters are family. And family should always stay together."

William seemed to consider that for a long moment, then with a sly look, he suggested, "If you marry Miss St. James then she would be family, too."

Winn could do nothing but laugh. "You're a sly thing, I'll give you that. Go to sleep, William. I'll see you in the morning."

Winn rose from the boy's bedside and made for the door. He'd just reached it when he heard the boy call out softly.

"Uncle Winn?"

"Yes?"

William was silent for a heartbeat, clearly hesitant. Then he murmured softly, "Good night, Uncle Winn. I love you."

It hit him like a punch in the gut. Winn's throat constricted and it was all he could do to choke out his own reply, "I love you, too, William. Good night."

Easing from the room and into the corridor, he found himself face to face with Miss St. James. She was beaming, her eyes damp with tears.

"I didn't mean to eavesdrop. He's such a dear boy."

Winn felt his own cheeks heating. "He's a terrible scamp... and a dear one," he admitted. "I've called for the coach to see you home. You should not have stayed so late."

She gave him a watery chuckle. "I didn't mean to," she admitted. "I brought them up and tucked them in after their dinner then fell asleep while telling them a story. I suppose I didn't sleep very well last night. Not since you informed us of your theory."

"I'm sorry for that... not that I told you because I think it bears knowing," he stated, as he offered her his arm to escort her toward the stairs. "But because it has distressed you. If there was a way to keep you safe that would allow for blissful ignorance—"

"Absolutely not! I prefer the truth, my lord... always. No matter how unpleasant it may be," she said firmly.

"I thought we had agreed that in private you would call me by my given name."

She glanced at him from under her lashes. "I think we're skirting propriety enough. And I heard William. I hardly think we should encourage him in thinking there is any possibility that you and I might be anything more than employer and employee. We both know it can never happen."

"Never is a word I dislike, Calliope." Winn stopped just as they'd reached the top of the stairs. Once they descended, there would be footmen and a nosy butler to contend with, but standing on the landing, they had a rare moment of privacy in a house that was generally filled with chaos and many, many ears. "You overheard my conversation with William... all of it. Didn't you?"

Her gaze dropped to the floor and her shoulders inched backward, her pride obviously wounded by what she thought of as his dismissal of the notion. "I did. And I know what he said... about marriage. I also know very precisely how you replied."

He shook his head. For a woman of incredible intelligence, she was being a damned fool at the moment. "You know only what I said to a child. Should I have gone into detail and explained to him our different social positions and the kind of gossip that would ensue? Should I have told him that for a man to marry a woman who'd been in his employ, people would likely count the days between our wedding and the birth of our first child in the hopes of uncovering some hint of misdeeds? This is a complicated situation with complex solutions beyond his years. I also don't want him hoping for something that might not come to pass. He's suffered enough disappointment."

"And those are only a handful of the reasons why it would never work," she said. "Not that I would presume to think you might propose. I'd never be so forward. But the simple fact is, it doesn't even bear considering. Not when at the drop of a hat, a dozen reasons can easily be listed."

"And there are a dozen reasons that can be just as easily listed in favor of the notion," he protested. "The children love you. They need you. A permanent arrangement between us would give them a sense of security that they desperately need. And you love them, Calliope. I know that your heart breaks at the very notion of ever having to leave them. I must marry. I cannot bring up two young women and introduce them into society without a wife at my side. We both know that. And while you may be a governess, we both know that you have been trained in all the ways and all the things that a lady should know. Then there are other very personal reasons. Would you like to know what they are?"

"I'm assuming you are referring to the kiss we shared? That's hardly the basis for a marriage!"

Winn laughed. "They've been based on far less, I assure you. I'm not proposing to you, Miss St. James... not yet. But don't assume that I will not. Certainly not on the basis of what I said to a very impressionable young boy. There are pressing issues to resolve first. When that is done, I assure you, we will revisit the topic."

She shook her head. "It would ruin you."

"It would raise eyebrows," he countered. "When you have both a title and a fortune, very little can actually ruin you, Miss St. James."

Winn knew it was foolish, knew that he was pressing her when perhaps he should not. But as she stared up at him, her expression tense and somewhat pinched, he simply couldn't leave things as they were. He moved away from the stairs, pulling her with him until they reached the door of a small unused sitting room on that floor. Inside, the room was dark but for a bit of moonlight filtering between the curtains. The furniture was all draped with holland cloths and it was quite possibly the least romantic setting ever. But they were alone with no chance of prying eyes of servants or well-meaning, interfering children.

"What are you doing?" she demanded.

"I told you that I meant to kiss you again... and often," he said. "There's no better time like the present."

MAYBE IT WAS the darkness of the room that emboldened her, maybe it was the way her heart had ached when she'd heard him utter that denial to William or perhaps it was the unwise hope that had flared within her when they'd spoken in the corridor only a moment earlier. Whatever it was, Callie found herself not waiting to be kissed by him. Instead, she pressed her hands against his chest, her fingers sliding over the fine fabric of his elegantly tailored coat and they slid up to his shoulders and around his neck. As she did so, she had to rise on her toes and tug his head down so that their lips could meet.

It didn't matter that she had very little experience in kissing. Nothing mattered but that she got to have that brief moment of mindlessness, where the world simply fell away and her reality consisted of only his arms around her and his mouth on hers.

As she'd hoped, while she might have initiated the contact, he quickly took over. His lips played over hers, his tongue and his teeth coaxing her pulse to a fevered beat as she felt that now familiar heat begin to blossom inside her. It started at her center and spread outward, radiating through her body. While she'd never have been able to describe desire before, she wasn't so foolish that she couldn't recognize it when it occurred.

A stolen kiss in his study, another in a carriage in the middle of the day on a busy street—those were one thing. But alone in a darkened room, the house almost completely quiet with many of the servants already in their own beds and the children tucked into theirs? It was something else altogether. There was an element of recklessness and danger to that setting. She was courting ruin, after all, and she was finding it difficult to care, at least with his arms wrapped tightly about her and his hands caressing the curve of her waist, sliding to the flare of her hips.

His lips left hers, but any sound of protest was lost on a soft gasp as his teeth scraped over the tender flesh of her neck, nipping there just below her ear. The shock of that less than gentle but entirely seductive gesture had her shivering against him. And then his hands were roving over her again, sliding along her rib cage. When he touched her breast, cupping it gently, Callie was unprepared for the sensation, but even less prepared for her reaction to it. She simply sank against him, giving herself up to him entirely. As long as he was touching her, kissing her, as long as she could feel the heat and strength of him, she didn't have to think about her own precarious social position, she didn't have to think about potentially being a missing heiress or that the truths she'd been so certain of about her life and her origins were all terribly wrong. With his touch, he offered both temptation and respite.

And then just as abruptly as it all began, it stopped. He stopped.

"I can't do this... I will not do this. I brought you in here thinking I might steal a kiss. I didn't intend it to go further than that," he said.

"I don't think that was entirely up to you," she said. "I believe I instigated quite a bit of what has gone on in here."

He laughed, but it was a pained sound. "I'm putting you in a carriage and I'm sending you home, Calliope St. James... while I have the will and the strength to do so."

"I wish you didn't."

The moment the words escaped her, she knew they were a mistake. So did he. She heard his indrawn breath, and then the muffled curse that followed it.

"You will be the death of me," he murmured. "I'm not the sort of man who takes advantage of women in his employ, Calliope. And whatever is happening between us, I can't let it be that. I can't do something that is... irrevocable. Not until we know what the future holds."

"Will we ever know that? Honestly?"

He raised one hand to her face, cupping it gently. Unable to help herself, Callie leaned into that caress, savoring the touch.

"Yes," he said firmly. "We will. Now, go. The carriage is waiting for you. I can't accompany you. I can't face any further temptation tonight.... not without compromising my scruples and your virtue."

She wasn't nearly as frightened of that prospect as she should have been, which was all the proof she needed that she should do everything in her power to put distance between them and keep it that way. Stepping back, Callie nodded. "I'll see you on Monday." And in the meantime, she'd have to make some very difficult decisions.

He opened the door and slipped from the room. Callie took a deep breath and followed suit.

THE BALL WAS a success. Amelia was a success. Relieved beyond measure, Burney slipped away from the crowd. He didn't want to dampen her enjoyment of the evening, but watching bottle after bottle of champagne being opened, he was sweating profusely. The event had been financed entirely on credit. And now he had no way of paying the bills due. Slipping into the study, he made his way to the desk and sank into his chair, resting his head in his hands. There was a brace of pistols in the drawer and if not for harm it would cause his sister, he'd have put a pistol ball in his brain and ended it all.

"You're looking rather grim."

Burney startled, and sat upright. There in the shadows of the room, the dim red glow of a cheroot clutched between his fingers, was Averston. "How did you get in here?"

"I walked in. I'm a duke, Burney. I can do that," Averston replied.

"I thought you might seek your reprieve here and I wanted to see you."

Burney shook his head. "I don't have anything to tell you. I was a bit busy today so I haven't had an opportunity to snoop and play spy for you."

Averston stepped forward, closing the distance between them until he could lean casually against the edge of the desk. "That was the condition for my help, Burney, in finding your investors for you. But that isn't all that's between us, now is it?"

Burney felt his pulse begin to race. "I can't answer that question, can I? You seem to be the one with all the power in this equation."

Averston looked at him, his gaze glinting and hard even in the dim light. "Not all the power. I am here, after all. Aren't I? I danced attendance on your pretty little sister. I've been sociable, Burney, when I did not have to be. Why do you think I did that?"

"I don't know, honestly."

Averston grinned, his teeth gleaming in the darkness. "Well, it certainly wasn't for your sister. If we slip out now, we could be at the coffee house in Lincoln Fields in just a matter of minutes."

He was so tempted. Burney wanted that desperately. But he also knew that if he gave in, the power that Averston hinted that he had would be scarified. "I can't. It's impossible. We still have a house full of guests. And Amelia would be devastated if I were to simply disappear on such a night."

"But haven't you done that already?"

Burney laughed. "For a moment, yes. But not for the entire night. You really don't understand family and all the associated obligations at all, do you?"

"Why in heaven's name would I?" Averston demanded. "I've certainly never had one. It seems like a great deal of trouble, honestly."

Burney said nothing for a moment, letting that and all its implied loneliness sink in. He hovered on the brink of ruin, living half his life in secret for fear of being jailed or worse because he had the audacity to love other men. And yet, in that moment, he was overwhelmed with pity for the wealthy, haughty man in front of him. "I can't disappoint my sister… not even for you," Burney said. "But if you wished to meet tomorrow night, I could certainly make myself available."

"Don't play games with me," Averston said, his tone steely. It was obvious that he was unused to being told no or not getting what he wanted from people. "I won't be toyed with by you or anyone else. I'm not that man, Charles Burney."

"I rather thought that was what we were doing with one another… playing a game. You said yourself it can't be anything more than that," Burney replied. No matter his attraction to Averston, no matter how much he longed for the man to have some genuine affection, if not love, for him, he couldn't simply give in to his every whim. "No complicated emotions or messy tender feelings. You can't have it both ways. You said it yourself this afternoon. To get something, you have to give something."

Averston rose from his perch. "Careful, Burney. I may decide the price you ask is far too steep for the pleasure you provide."

"And I would argue that you will not see the worth of anything until it is out of your reach," Burney replied.

"Don't bother coming to the coffee house tomorrow. I won't be there."

With that, Averston walked out and Burney was once more alone in the darkness, left with the weight of the world and his family's expectations pressing in on him, along with the fear that he'd overplayed his hand yet again.

Chapter Fourteen

I T WAS MIDMORNING when the dour-faced butler showed him into the drawing room. Burney's palms were sweating and his heart raced with trepidation. What he was about to do brought him no pleasure. He was burning a bridge and ending a family connection that had lasted generations. But he was desperate. A letter had arrived just that morning from Phillip. He was threatening, as always, to expose the truth of Burney's bachelor status. It would ruin him. It would ruin Amelia. And if he couldn't get investors for Phillip, the best he could do would be to offer up enough funds himself to stay his cousin's hand.

Inside the elegantly appointed room, the curtains were drawn and the interior was very dim. She was seated on a velvet upholstered chair, holding court as if she were some despot on a throne. As he entered the room, her cold gaze settled on him. It reminded him of a snake—watchful and deadly.

"You're certainly a bold one," she said. "I'll give you that. State your business."

Burney stared at the disapproving face of the Dowager Duchess of Averston and wondered if perhaps he had not made a fundamental error in coming there. But he couldn't tell Averston—Gerald—the truth of it. Even if Averston would agree to see him again after their quarrel the night before, what Burney had to say would destroy any chance of putting things right between them. *It's the only way.* If the man discovered Burney had kept such information to himself, he'd be done with him entirely.

"Thank you, your grace, for agreeing to speak with me," Burney said, using his most ingratiating tone.

"I was curious as to what you might have to say... or rather, what you might have to say that you think could be worthy of my interest," she replied disdainfully. Even as she spoke, she was inspecting a tray of chocolates, looking for the most appealing morsel as she, for all intents and purposes, ignored his presence. There was no invitation to sit, no hint of welcome.

"Oh, never fear, your grace. I have not come to waste your time. I have come with news of your long-lost granddaughter, heir to the Averston fortunes," Burney replied smoothly. "Of course, if you feel the information unworthy of your time—"

"What do you want for this information?" The question was snapped, her tone sharp and her gaze sharper still.

"Four thousand pounds," Burney replied smoothly.

The old woman laughed. She laughed until she began to cough and wheeze, fanning herself exuberantly as she waved to her servant with her other hand. The servant rushed forward with a vial of what he could only assume was laudanum. The old woman took a small dram of it and then, after a moment, her coughing began to ease.

"I have never known any information to be worth so much," she stated blandly. "And what a specific sum to ask for, Mr. Burney. I imagine your sister's debut last night set you back a tidy sum, did it not?"

"My sister?" It sparked a fear in him like nothing else that the vicious woman was even aware of Amelia's existence.

The old woman smiled. "Indeed. Considering how closely you've become acquainted with my grandson, do you honestly think I would not make it a point to learn all I can about you? I know you inside and out, Mr. Charles Percival Burney, the third. Every dark and dirty secret... including the alarming amount of debt you're facing. I am stunned you could get anyone to give you credit to hold such a soiree as you did last night."

"My sister has nothing to do with this," he stated firmly.

"Pretty girl... I suppose she might marry well enough. Assuming your behavior doesn't cast a pall over her in the eyes of society," the dowager duchess said, her cold gaze gleaming with triumph. "Share your information, Mr. Burney, and I will decide then if it warrants payment. You'll get your four thousand pounds if I deem it so."

"I can tell you her name, where she has been reared during her absence from your eyes, and where she is currently employed," Burney stated.

"I would presume she's earning a living as her mother did... lifting her shabby skirts for anyone who will toss her a coin," the dowager duchess intoned in a manner that might have hinted at boredom if not for the quavering of her voice.

Burney saw through her. He could see the slight tremor in her hand. She feared the girl. Whatever this woman had done, she feared the identification of her granddaughter. "No, your grace. Indeed, she is quite respectable... and looks so very much like the portrait hanging in pride of place in your family home. Indeed, the resemblance is so remarkable that anyone who should ever see that portrait will not fail to recognize her."

"Her name!" the dowager duchess demanded. "I would have it from you."

"And I would have payment first," Burney replied, putting as much steel in his voice as he could muster. He would not be made a fool of by another member of this family.

The woman waved to her servant again. The girl, dressed all in black and looking like a scared rabbit, hurried away to do the dowager duchess' bidding. Moments later, she returned with a mahogany box inlaid with pearl and gold. The dowager duchess removed a key from the pocket of her gown and fitted it into the lock box where she retrieved several bank notes. A footman stood by with quill and ink. They were signed hastily, sanded and then delivered to him by the same black-clad servant girl who'd fetched the box to start with. *Four thousand pounds in hand.* Burney stared at them for the longest moment. He'd sold his soul for them, after all, but at least his mother and sister would be safe.

"She goes by the name St. James," he said. "She's currently employed as a governess for the Earl of Montgomery. But she's not in house. She resides at the Darrow School and travels to and from the earl's residence daily." It had taken little enough to get that information out of a servant. He'd found his way there this morning and smiled at a pretty maid who'd trustingly obliged his every question.

"Well, Mr. Burney, it seems you're not as worthless as I thought you would be," the dowager duchess said. She then waved her hand once more and all the servants departed, leaving them completely alone in the drawing room. "But I warn you, sir, you will stay away from my grandson."

"I believe that is up to him, your grace," Burney said.

"Oh, he thinks it is," she said. "But he'd be wrong. He's cold, you know, but not ruthless. Not really. I, on the other hand, I'd see your neck snapped like a twig and not lose a wink of sleep for it. They hang men for what you do."

Burney felt his cheeks coloring. "You can't implicate me without exposing your grandson, and we both know you won't do that."

"I can do a great many things, Mr. Burney," she warned. "You have your payment for services rendered. You may leave now. Remember what I've said, and know that I will not hesitate to see you ruined. You and your family. Your sister... pretty and so very sweet. I imagine that four thousand pounds is but a drop in the bucket of your veritable well of debts. Do you know what happens to young women like her who wind up in debtor's prison? Or worse… are left on the street to fend for themselves while their worthless male relations rot in the Marshalsea?"

Burney's fists clinched at his sides. "That will not happen. I will make certain my sister is cared for!"

The dowager duchess smiled. "Gerald needs a wife, you know? How much would thank rankle, Mr. Charles Burney? How much would you love your baby sister when she's taken your lover from you?"

"My sister has nothing to do with this!" Averston would never do that, Burney thought. No one could be that cruel. And yet, there was enough doubt there that he had to wonder.

"Not yet," the dowager duchess said. "And if you wish to keep it that way, you have only to keep your distance. Good day, Mr. Burney."

Burney turned to exit, walking away with fury bubbling inside him. He wanted to rail at her, but that was power he didn't have. Not yet.

When he was gone, the dowager duchess' servants bustled into her small drawing room once more. To her secretary, the meek-looking woman garbed in unrelieved black, she instructed, "Have Jenkins fetched and tell him to bring that other fellow with him. We've a bit of dirty work that needs to be done." The woman left to do her task.

"Shall I have them come through the servants' entrance, your grace? After the events of their last visit…" the butler trailed off, his tone clearly disapproving.

"No. Let's not do that again," she replied. The last thing they needed was some foolish maid screaming the house down. "Have them wait in the garden. I'll go to them."

"Certainly, your grace," the butler agreed before vanishing from the room to do her bidding.

Alone, the dowager duchess drummed her fingers on the arm of her chair and considered the matter of Charles Burney. He'd have to be eliminated, of course, along with this girl he'd mentioned. They both posed too great a risk to all that she'd worked so hard for over the years.

Chapter Fifteen

CALLIE WAS EXHAUSTED by the time she arrived home that evening. She'd taken her day off and walked in the park, she'd strolled amongst the shops and even attended the morning service. But she'd done it all like an automaton. Her mind was not on her surroundings much less the vicar's lengthy sermon. It was on Winn Hamilton, Earl of Montgomery, and the near seduction that had occurred. Though whether she'd been the seducer or the seduced remained in question. Yes, he'd pulled her into that room, but heaven knew, once there, she'd been bold enough in her own right.

Entering the house on Jermyn Street, she bypassed Mrs. Wheaton and made her way upstairs. She loved the housekeeper dearly, but she wasn't in the mood to be mothered. Wallowing in her misery seemed to be the safest option. She'd slept not at all the night before and all she wanted was to fall into her narrow bed and not move an inch until morning.

Removing her day dress, she eschewed dinner altogether and immediately donned her nightrail and a velvet wrapper that had been an extravagant but much beloved gift from Effie. It was the finest thing in her entire wardrobe and was not intended to be seen by anyone. She smiled at that, as she settled down into the small armchair before the window. With the candle burning on the table beside her, she reached for the book that had been discarded there. She should have taken to her embroidery instead, as she'd begun making a few items for the children, but her heart wasn't in it. No, a Gothic novel to take her mind off her own current predicament and hopefully allow her to sleep was just the thing. That the hero in the book, in her mind's eye, looked shockingly like her employer was unimportant.

A knock at her door interrupted her reading. It opened and Effie entered.

"Oh," Effie said. "I was going to suggest we have a private supper in my office as we have a great deal to discuss, but it appears you have other plans."

"I'm a bit tired," Callie said. "I didn't sleep well last night. Perhaps we could have that discussion later?"

Effie's expression shifted slightly, appearing almost melancholy for a second. "I don't think we can. It's very important. Are you certain you won't come down for dinner? I'll even break out the brandy no one is supposed to know that I have."

"I'm not very hungry, honestly," Callie admitted. "I think my mind is racing too much for such things to enter it. And if you've something that important to say, that it required the consumption of strong spirits, then perhaps you should just get it out now."

With a look of chagrin, Effie stepped deeper into the room and settled herself on the edge of Callie's narrow bed. While the rooms were small to be sure, they had been appointed comfortably. "I'm afraid I'm very obvious, aren't I?"

Callie nodded. "You rather are. It can't be that bad, can it?"

Effie clasped her hands in her lap. "I'm afraid that it can. I spoke with Madame de Beauchamps. She told me something that was rather unexpected... it seems that your parents were married in secret. Highcliff is tracking down the necessary documentation, but they were married Callie. If this is true, then you're not simply an heiress, but you're also legitimate."

That information simply refused to penetrate. Try as she might,

Callie couldn't quite grasp it. "I'm not a bastard."

"I detest the use of that word but, under the circumstances, it's certainly a forgivable lapse," Effie remarked. "I can't imagine how you must be feeling right now."

"None of it seems real," Callie stated. "It's all like a strange dream where I can't be certain what is truth and what is fiction. Everything I've known my entire life has suddenly been ripped out from under me."

"It's a great deal to take in, isn't it? Suddenly being faced with the knowledge that what you thought you knew about your origins is all wrong. But this isn't all bad, is it? To know that your parents loved one another... that they loved you?"

Callie sighed. "I always assumed that my mother was too burdened to care for me, whether because she had other children or a dozen other reasons that crossed my mind. It never occurred to me that she might have abandoned me to save my life. And now I wonder if she knew."

"Knew what, dear?"

"That I was the cause of her death... if she hadn't had me, then she would have remained content as his mistress and no one would have cared."

Effie's eyes widened. "That is not the way of it at all. I spoke with Madame de Beauchamps at length. Your mother had lost several babes already. I think she wanted nothing more than to have a child with the man she loved. And she didn't die because you were born. She died because of the greed, pride and conceit of others. It had nothing to do with you."

Callie sighed wearily. "It isn't only that... I've been so angry. For years, I've been angry at her, railed and cried and shouted my hatred for her!"

"I've never heard you do any of that!"

"I may have shouted it into my pillow," Callie admitted ruefully.

"Regardless, I felt it. Every day of my life. And to have born such ill will toward her and to now know the true circumstances, as best one can, I cannot help but feel so guilty and so ungrateful! I never even allowed for the possibility that her motives might have been anything other than selfish."

Effie rose then and walked toward her. She wrapped her arms about Callie and gave her a fierce hug. "My darling girl, you were a child who needed her mother! Of course you were resentful and angry... and yes, now that the truth has come out, you know that anger was misplaced. But it doesn't change anything from your past. You cannot take on so and hold yourself accountable for how you felt when you only knew a small portion of the story. If that were so, I'd be as much to blame as you. I wasn't a child, and even I, Callie, harbored great resentment for any woman who would be so foolish as to abandon a daughter so precious as you."

Callie felt tears threatening. She blinked at them, but a few slipped free regardless. "You're not old enough to be my mother. You never were. How could you, at the age you were, take on the raising of so many young girls alone?"

"I knew the truth of my mother, Callie. All along. I knew that she deposited me on my father's doorstep without a backward glance. I'd been the product of her attempt to trap him into marriage and elevate her own standing in the process. And when I failed to serve that purpose, she was done with me," Effie confided. "I always felt the lack... the lack of a mother's love. And any child I encounter in my life who needs that as much as I did will always have it from me. That is my purpose in this world. To mother the children of other women who cannot, will not or have been deprived of the opportunity to love them."

Callie heard the sadness in her mentor's voice. There was a longing in Effie that she hadn't ever considered, that perhaps her school and the unwanted daughters of others weren't quite enough for her.

So she hugged her back, the two of them comforting each other in the stillness of the evening as the younger girls gathered below for their dinner. After a long moment, Effie drew back.

"Now, there is another matter we must discuss... the Earl of Montgomery. I sense that there is more at play here than simply his wish to protect one of his employees," Effie said. "Is there anything you wish to tell me, Callie?"

Callie shook her head. "There is nothing to tell."

"You're certain?"

Caught, she could tell by the tone of Effie's voice, Callie capitulated. "He kissed me."

"Just a kiss?"

"Well, more than once... and perhaps a bit more than," Callie admitted. Recalling his words from the night before, she added, "Nothing that has transpired has been irrevocable."

"I see." Effie sat down on the bed again. "Did you want him to kiss you? And these other *things*, did you want them as well?"

"Well, the first time I wasn't expecting him to, but when he did, I didn't mind it. Not at all. Quite the contrary, in fact. And then the other morning, we were disagreeing about something and it just sort of happened. But last night—" Callie broke off.

"Last night?"

Callie sighed wearily, "It wasn't a matter of him kissing me as much as that I kissed him. And I would have allowed him to do infinitely more. Things halted as they did only because he is an honorable man. And William asked him if he would marry me and now it's complicated everything."

"Perhaps... perhaps not. I asked a friend of mine to check up on your charming earl," Effie said. "And by all accounts, he is a very good man. That is rarer than you think. If his intentions toward you are honorable, and based on the concern he has shown for your safety, I can only assume they would be, there will be no more kisses or there will be a proposal in your future. You must think, Callie, which of those two things you'd prefer."

"And if I don't know?" Callie asked.

Effie smiled. "Then I'd advise refraining from either until you do. I'll send up a tray with some cold meats and bread in case you get hungry later. Good night, dearest."

When Effie left, Callie continued to sit in her chair. The book lay forgotten by her side and she eventually fell into a fitful doze.

THE PUB ON the waterfront was hardly the sort of place where Winn would typically spend his evening. But he'd been in search of a man by the name of Fredrick Davis, a former magistrate who'd been involved in the inquest into the death of Mademoiselle Veronique Delaine.

"Montgomery?" the man asked as Winn approached the table in the back where he'd been told the man would be waiting.

"Yes," Winn answered. "You're Davis?"

The man grinned, showing several missing teeth. "Aye. One and only. Have a seat... a guinea per question."

He'd come prepared for just that. Winn removed one coin from his pocket and slid it across the table. "How did Veronique Delaine die?"

"Maybe I don't remember her?"

"Then I'll go now and take the rest of my coin with me," Winn stated. "I've got enough questions for you to earn a tidy sum without playing any games."

The man's gapped-tooth grin grew broader as he tapped the table. When a coin was placed at his fingertips, he slid it deftly across the table's pocked surface where it disappeared into the pocket of a tattered waistcoat stretched over his rather rotund middle. "The actress... hard to forget that one. Looked like a broken doll laying in the road, she did. Pretty thing, but someone had done her up right before tossing her out there."

"Then she wasn't struck by a carriage?" Winn asked, placing another coin on the table.

"Oh, aye. But she was dead before that happened," the man replied.

Another coin. "How?"

"The wheel cut her deep," Davis said, gesturing to his abdomen. "But weren't much blood. Smeared a bit but not gushing out the way it ought to have if she'd been alive when it happened. Seen enough corpses in my day to know that. No, Guv, she was dead before she hit the bricks, I'd say. Back of her head all smashed in though she was face down on the street. Shouldn't have injuries to both the front and back sides of her, should she?"

"Couldn't that have happened when the carriage struck her? Perhaps she was caught up under the wheels?" Another coin slid across the table to vanish.

Davis shook his head. "The carriage didn't do naught but clip her. Driver saw her laying there and tried to stop. Swerved around her and damn near upended the whole thing. Anyways, wounds on the back of her head had bled something fierce. Back of her clothes was covered in the stuff and it was almost dry… but the front? A bit of mud and some smears of blood. Still wet."

"I don't suppose you'd know who did it and how, would you?"

Davis shook his head. "No, and you don't have to pay if'n I don't give an answer. I ain't for robbing people. I reckoned at first it was a lover's quarrel. Went to the theater and they said see the duke. So I did. Thought it'd be a quick thing to pin it on him, though I knew he'd never serve a day for it much less see the noose. Men like him—and you—don't have to follow the law, now do they?"

Winn slid another coin across anyway. "You said at first. But you didn't think it was a lover's quarrel after meeting him?"

Davis took a drink from the tankard before him. "No. Telling that man she was dead near broke him. Never seen a man take on so. I ain't much for having sympathy for no man, but it was clear he was torn up about it. Kept asking for the babe. First any of us heard about it. Told him there was no babe to be found near her and she must have left it with someone."

"Did you see anyone else when you went to speak with the duke?"

"His mother was there... won't forget that old bitch," Davis said, his expression shifting into one of distaste. "She'd raise gooseflesh on the dead."

"How did she react to the news?"

Davis shook his head. "Said it was good riddance... told him to stop taking on so, that he needed to find himself a worthy bride and produce an heir that wouldn't bring shame to the family."

Winn suppressed a shiver. "You didn't much care for her, did you, Davis?"

Davis looked at him levelly. "I've seen a lot of killers in my time, my lord. Arrested men who'd taken lives as casual as taken off their hats in greeting. I've even seen some that enjoyed it. But I've never seen any person, man or woman, who could make my blood run cold the way that old bitch did. I knew... I couldn't prove it. But I knew she'd done it. Well, ordered it done. That one has a heart colder and blacker than the depths of the Thames."

"Did you find any proof?"

Davis shook his head. "I didn't waste my time looking, my lord. What good would it have done? Who'd let a duchess swing from the gallows? And I didn't want her turning that evil eye on me and mine. Not that it matters now. The wife is gone, the bloody French took my son and my daughter has gone to the north with the man she married. I'm on my own now."

Winn removed several other coins from his pocket and pushed them across the table. "And if you were ever asked to testify, not in court, but to a group of trustees of the duke's estate, would you?"

The man nodded, pocketing his coin. "I've nothing left to lose, do I? You know where to find me."

Winn rose and exited the tavern quickly. He needed to speak to Miss St. James. But she wouldn't welcome him coming to her so late at night, assuming he'd even be granted admittance. It would have to wait for the morning. Hailing a hack, he headed home. He was tired. Bone tired. But there were things that needed doing before he could seek his bed.

Entering the house only moments later, he headed for his study. As preoccupied as he'd been with what had almost occurred the night before and with his meeting with Davis, he'd almost forgotten his resolve to remove the books from the top shelf lest his too-curious niece attempt to educate herself further. Neither of them would survive it, he thought, shuddering with horror.

Stepping into the study, he reached for the tinder box to light the lamp but even as he did so, the lamp on his desk behind him flared to life. Turning toward it, he found himself facing Lord Highcliff. But this wasn't the Highcliff he'd seen swanning about society. There were no garish waistcoats, no overly coiffed hair or cravat tied with such intricate detail that half the dandies of the *ton* had done themselves injury trying to replicate it. This man, with his black hair combed back from his forehead and dressed head to toe in unrelieved black looked very much like a criminal. Which was fitting, since he apparently was one and quite gifted at it.

"Housebreaking, Highcliff?"

The other man smiled, showing even white teeth that gleamed in the dim light. "I'd thought I might rattle you a bit showing up this way. It seems you've more mettle than I anticipated, Montgomery."

"I can do a fair approximation of a fit of the vapors if you'd like. Saw my aunt have them once. Terrifying... but before I oblige, kindly tell me what the hell you're doing breaking into my bloody house!"

Winn demanded.

"Relax. I'm on your side… I have some information on your friend Burney… and on Averston. Are you aware they're lovers?"

He hadn't been. "Since when?"

"Recently, it would seem. Very recently. Were you aware that Averston has a long history of aligning himself romantically with young, desperate men who then subsequently vanish?" Highcliff asked.

Intrigued, Winn moved deeper into the room. He caught himself before he took a seat facing Highcliff from the wrong side of his own desk. "You're in my seat."

Highcliff rose then, grinning as he sketched a mock bow before he moved around the desk, vacating Winn's own chair for him.

Winn took his seat and then said, "Go on. I'm curious as to where this is leading."

Highcliff raised one finger. "Nathaniel Barber. Father lost everything when his copper mines imploded and killed dozens of workers. Became Averston's protégé if you wish to term it such, and then three months later, he was gone. No word. No sign… for weeks. Then a badly bloated corpse turned up on the banks of the Thames. Identified only by the signet ring that wouldn't come off his finger."

"It could be a coincidence. London is a dangerous city," Winn pointed out.

Highcliff raised a second finger. "Thomas Fairbourne. Bastard son of an impoverished baron, but charming enough to linger on the outskirts of society. Was suddenly everywhere Averston was. Thick as thieves. Then he, too, vanished. They found him in a ditch in Richmond. A pistol ball to his brain… all of his belongings were still accounted for."

"All right, you have my attention."

"Samuel Cavender. Father was a successful barrister, moving in polite society. Apprenticed as a clerk to Averston's lawyer and then apprenticed to Averston himself as a man of affairs. He's gone without a trace and his body has yet to be discovered." Highcliff sank into one of the chairs facing the desk. "There are a handful of others. Six in total. Missing or killed under mysterious circumstances."

"So what, he takes these foolish young men as paramours and then murders them?" Winn asked. "To what end? It might not be Averston, you know?"

"The dowager duchess?"

Winn recounted the story from Fredrick Davis. "At the time that this occurred, Averston would have been a boy of fifteen. He might have done it, but it seems more likely to be her."

"Doesn't mean they aren't both capable of murder," Highcliff answered. "And they both have motive in all of the cases mentioned. She can hardly rule society if word gets out about Averston's persuasion. The trustees in charge of the fortune that your pretty little governess might inherit are sticklers for propriety. Scandal, especially the scandal of the Duke of Averston having male lovers would effectively destroy his standing with them. They'd never approve another request for funds he puts before them. We both know that."

Winn leaned back in his chair, steepled his fingers and considered things. "And Burney is young, handsome, stupid and desperate... and will very likely die for it. He's already displayed an alarming lack of forethought. He tried to blackmail me. If he tries to blackmail either of them... I hesitate to think what the consequences might be."

"Do you really care? He has, after all, tried to blackmail you, threatened to expose Miss St. James to significant danger... perhaps it's his just desserts!"

"For having the audacity to love unwisely? For inheriting a mountain of debt from his wastrel father and trying to salvage what he can for the sake of his family? I fault his methods, Highcliff, but Burney... well, he's Burney," Winn said. The thought of the scandal this could create, the ruin it would heap on Burney's mother and on poor Amelia was terrifying. There were other men of his acquaintance who hid such affairs, who lived half their lives in secret, but Burney was not that sort. He was too impetuous by far.

"No, for having the audacity to think that his needs and wants are worth the life of someone else," Highcliff said.

A resigned sigh escaped Winn. "But he doesn't realize it. I promise you that Burney is too naive to ever realize what Averston is or the dowager duchess for that matter... he won't. Not until it's too late." And Burney, whatever he'd done and no matter how angry Winn was at him, didn't deserve whatever outcome Averston or that hateful old woman had planned for him.

"That's a very magnanimous view given that Burney was set to and possibly already has betrayed the lot of you to Averston."

"He's a grown man... an adult. But he isn't, honestly. Burney will perpetually be a rapscallion little boy like my brother was," Winn stated. "I can't let him die just because he's stupid."

Highcliff looked for a moment as if he were about to argue the point, then relented. "Fine. We'll save the idiot, too. But if he gets himself in another scrape after this one, he's on his own."

"Fair enough."

Winn rose from his desk. "Let's go, then."

"Where?"

Winn arched one eyebrow at him. "You're the one with all the information. You tell me."

"White's," Highcliff answered. "I assume you have a membership?"

"Of course!"

"Good, because I'm only a member at Boodle's." Highcliff paused as they headed out the door, "I'll have to change first."

"Yes, it wouldn't do to be seen in public wearing a waistcoat that was anything less than glaring, would it?" Winn asked. "What exactly do you do, Highcliff, that warrants such subterfuge?"

"Pray you never find out, Montgomery," Highcliff answered.

Chapter Sixteen

IT WAS FULLY dark when Callie awoke. She was overcome by a sense of unease but the source of it, in that moment of waking confusion, was unknown to her. Looking around the room, lit only by the thin sliver of moonlight that penetrated the small crack between the curtains, she saw that the tray Effie had sent up for her was untouched on the table beside the door. She must have dozed off before it arrived. The fire had died down to nothing and the room was very cold. But it wasn't hunger or cold that had awakened her. Her heart was pounding in her chest. Fear, cold and sharp, pierced her. An overwhelming sensation of dread had overtaken her senses. The house was completely quiet, all the girls having long since been put to bed. Effie was likely still awake, doing paperwork in her office, as was her habit. That was typically how the latter hours of the evening were spent. Was that what had woken her? Had Effie stumbled in the hall as she sought out her own chamber? Were the girls out of their beds and up to mischief? No. Her experience was that the more a group of girls tried to be quiet the less successful they were at it.

Whether it was instinct or simply that the earl's paranoia regarding the Duke of Averston had managed to invade the darker recesses of her mind, Callie was instantly on alert. Huddled in the chair where she'd fallen asleep earlier, Callie hunkered under the small throw that she'd covered herself with. The chair faced the window and the door was behind her. Peering around the edge of the winged back, Callie eyed that door as if it were about to grow teeth and snap at her.

But no, the truth was far worse. As she watched, the knob twisted and the door opened, just a crack at first, and then, very slowly, it swung inward. Ducking back until she was completely concealed, she made sure her feet were drawn fully into the chair and the edges of the throw concealed as well. From behind, no one would even know she was there. And if she were lucky, and they were stupid, they wouldn't think to look further than the bed for her at this time of night. Squatting there, still and silent, in the corner of the chair, she made herself as small as possible. In truth, she willed herself not to even breathe.

"Where is she?"

The voice was low and gruff, masculine, unrefined. It was the voice of a man from the streets. A hireling, no doubt.

"Don't bloody know, now do I?" the second man replied. His voice was rougher still, with a thick cockney accent, and he coughed after uttering his churlish reply.

"Bloke said she was 'ere!"

"The bloke was clearly wrong, John. Perhaps this ain't 'er room… or perhaps she slipped out and is warming someone else's bed instead!"

The clinking of crockery told her that her dinner was being raided.

"Dinner is cold and untouched," the man he'd called John stated, his words muffled as he consumed food that had been intended for her.

"It was, anyway. You bloody idiot! Now she'll now we was 'ere!"

"Don't matter no way, does it, 'enry? If we find 'er, someone will know for certain we was," John said. There was a hint of enjoyment at that, a veiled threat in those words that indicated he would have undertaken whatever task had been assigned to them with great enthusiasm.

"Bloody 'ell," Henry muttered.

"We could check the other rooms," John suggested hopefully.

"And wake up a passel of screaming girls? I won't swing cause you fancy seeing a bunch of little girls in nightclothes! No. We'll watch the 'ouse and see if she comes out in the morning!"

"What then?"

Henry let out a long-suffering sigh, as if he were beyond frustrated with his compatriot who was equal parts brutal and stupid. "Then we nab 'er on the way to 'er nabob employer's 'ouse!"

"She's gotta be 'ere somewhere," the first man insisted.

They both went utterly silent as a door closed somewhere else in the house. Whether it was one of the children going to the water closet or Effie closing everything up for the night, the men seemed very aware of their threat of discovery. When no alarm sounded and the house settled once more into the routine silence of night, the wiser of the two spoke. "We're going. Not paying us enough to swing for it, is 'e?"

"But 'e is paying us," the other man insisted. "And we needs the money!"

"The deal was, find 'er in 'er bed, slit 'er bloody throat from ear to ear before she could even scream and be gone. If she's awake, if she struggles, we'll wake the entire 'ouse. If we go 'unting for 'er, the watch'll be on us. And you 'eard 'im! Nothing is to lead back to 'im. I say better to not do it than do it wrong and get pinched. No. We wait."

The two men crept out into the corridor. She could hear their footfalls, faint on the carpet that ran down the length of the corridor until they faded into the night. Even then, she exhaled slowly, her breath coming out as the faintest whisper. It sounded like cannon fire to her ears.

Callie stayed precisely where she was. She dared not move nor even breathe deeply for fear that they might not really be gone. A dozen scenarios played in her head—they were trying to lure her out, they'd change their minds and come back, the one man who'd been so eager to see the task done would return alone. The fear was crippling in a way nothing else ever had been. It left her trembling, with silent tears sliding down her cheeks and a bone-deep cold that she feared would never go away. Even when the bright light of day began to filter into the room, she didn't move. It wasn't until Effie knocked on the door and strode inside that she even made a sound.

"Callie, what is it? What's happened?"

Slowly, Callie turned and looked back at her. "I think Mr. Burney has given us away. Two men came in the night—" She broke off, unable to finish.

Effie's face paled and she rushed forward. "Did they hurt you?"

"They didn't find me. I'd fallen asleep in the chair and I suppose they must have made a noise. I awoke before they entered and I hid myself here as best as I could. They said... they said they meant to find me asleep and slit my throat so I wouldn't have a chance to scream."

Effie hugged her tightly. "We will employ guards. You will not be alone ever... even if I must stand over you at night myself."

And what would stop them from hurting Effie? Nothing. If they grew desperate enough, would it matter that they were breaking into a house full of children? No. Men as ruthless as those, men who clearly had no qualms about doing murder, would not hesitate because their victims were young. It was a risk she would not and could not let Effie take.

"I don't think I can stay here, Effie. I can't put you in danger. I certainly can't put this house full of young women in such jeopardy. These are the kind of men who take pleasure in hurting others. They must see me leave this house and they must see that I do not mean to return to it," Callie stated firmly. "Send for the earl."

Effie shook her head. "My darling, you cannot reside in a bachelor household."

"I don't mean to," Callie replied. "He mentioned going to the country... and that's what I will do. He can send me to one of his country estates for a bit until all this is settled."

"And the children?"

Callie's lip trembled. "I'll have to leave them. I don't want to. I pray they will understand. I can't be near them and place them at risk."

Effie stared at her for a moment. "I'll send a message to the earl, but no decisions have yet been made, Callie. And I don't believe he'll send you off to fend for yourself at one of his homes in the country. He's not that sort of man."

"What other solution is there?" Callie demanded. "My presence puts everyone in danger."

Effie hugged her. "He'll come up with something, I'm sure."

⇢⇢⇠⇠

WINN HAD ONLY just returned home. It was dawn. He was exhausted. After making the circuit at the clubs, they'd haunted gaming hells and other nefarious places where they might find either Averston or Burney. That neither had been seen was cause for alarm. If Highcliff's assertion that Averston was murdering the young men he had affairs with rather than risk exposure, Burney's knowledge of the identity of the true heir to Averston's fortune meant that he would be killed for certain. Who, after all, could pose a greater threat to him? Also, Burney's willingness to dabble in blackmail made him a liability.

Exhausted, but his mind too chaotic for sleep, Winn retreated to his study once more. He'd only just taken a seat at his desk when his new butler, Foster, entered. "My lord, an urgent message has arrived regarding Miss St. James."

Winn rose and took the missive from the silver salver it had been delivered upon. He broke the wax seal and read it. Then to be certain, he read it again. "Foster, have the maids start packing. Everything the children have and any items from the school room. And have my valet pack for me, as well. We'll be leaving the city."

"When, my lord? You can't mean today!"

"I certainly do," Winn answered. "We haven't time to waste, unfortunately. I shall return in an hour or so... I want everything in readiness. Children will be up and dressed and bags will be loaded into the carriages and carts for the journey... and your aunt, Mrs. Marler, will accompany us for the sake of propriety as Miss St. James shall be with us, as well."

Foster frowned and looked very concerned. "Yes, my lord. I'll see it done."

Winn nodded and then immediately left the house, heading once more for the Darrow School. Fear, anger, fury at what might have happened, indignation that Burney had ignored his warnings—all of that was driving him. Long strides ate up the distance and early as it was, there was little traffic on foot or otherwise to impede his progress. He reached the school in record time. He didn't have to battle his way in either. Miss Euphemia Darrow opened the door herself and ushered him inside, leading him to a small drawing room he'd not previously entered.

"Where is she?"

"She is upstairs, Lord Montgomery," Miss Darrow replied. "Before you see her, you must know that she means to ask for sanctuary at one of your country houses... without you or the children. Callie feels her presence is a danger to you all and she's determined to be foolishly noble about the whole thing."

"What happened, precisely?" Winn asked.

Miss Darrow moved to the settee and sank down heavily upon it. "Two men broke into the house last night. Callie had been upset and had fallen asleep in her chair in her room and awoke when they entered. Thankfully, she was well concealed from them there. Had she actually been in her bed, they would have—she overheard them say they meant to slit her throat from ear to ear while she slept, so that no sound would be made and no one would be alerted to their crime."

His heart stuttered in his chest, the beat going erratic for a moment. When he could form the words, he asked, "How did they get in?"

Effie sighed. "A door in the dining room, it faced the back garden. It was found unlocked this morning. They must have cut through the mews and made their way in through the garden gate."

"Highcliff needs to be told," Winn said firmly. "I won't ask what your relationship with the man is. It isn't my place, but it's clear he's invested in your well-being and this... this cannot stand. What the Duke of Averston, or the dowager duchess, have put in motion will not simply stop because Callie is no longer present. Any hint that you or anyone else is aware of their actions could place you in harm's way."

Winn said nothing further as the door opened and Callie entered. Her face was pale and he could see violet shadows beneath her eyes, a testament to the fact that she'd not slept at all the night before.

"Have your bags packed," Winn stated. "We'll be leaving London within the hour."

"Effie will provide another governess for the children so that their education does not suffer while I am away," Callie offered.

"That is entirely unnecessary as the children are going with you... as am I," Winn replied. "You are not simply going to one of my country estates to take your chances on your own. I will not simply leave you to whatever fate the Averstons have in store for you."

Her lips pressed together in a firm line that displayed her disapproval of his response quite clearly. "I won't endanger them—"

"They are in danger already. As am I. Do you think they will stop at eliminating only you, Calliope?" Winn demanded. "You may be the primary target at the moment, but we will all feel their wrath eventually."

"Then what good will running do?" she asked.

"It will give us time. And an opportunity to summon the trustees of the family fortune to meet you and decide for themselves if you are the true heir," Winn replied. "Our only option is to take the power from him and from his dragon of a grandmother."

"There's more, Lord Montgomery," Miss Darrow said. "I spoke with Madame de Beauchamps. According to Madame de Beauchamps, Callie was not illegitimate at all. The former Duke of Averston and her mother married in secret at St. Clement Danes. While you and Lord Montgomery are safe in the countryside, Highcliff will help to procure the necessary proof of that... it will prevent anyone from challenging their decision once it is made."

"Effie," Callie said imploringly, "Explain to him why this cannot happen! I must think of the children!"

Miss Darrow rose and walked toward Callie, embracing her. "I cannot. There are many ways to hurt those children... and your absence is one of them. Trust Lord Montgomery to keep you safe and trust that Highcliff and I will do what is necessary here to end this threat once and for all. Please, Callie? Please!"

Chapter Seventeen

HIGHCLIFF STARED AT the body laid out on bank of the lake in St. James' Park. He hadn't known Charles Burney well, but he'd certainly known him well enough to recognize the man. Burney's skin carried the grayish cast of a person who had been dead for some time, though having been in the water, Highcliff would be hard-pressed to say how long. But given that they hadn't located Burney or Averston at any of the typical haunts for men of their standing and persuasion, it would require a bit of investigative work to pin down the man's time of death.

"How did he die?" Highcliff asked.

The man standing beside him, rough-looking and wearing a dark coat, answered in a voice that still held a hint of cockney to it. "Strangled with his own neckcloth, he was."

"How can you be certain it was his?"

"His is missing... found one discarded in the bushes down by the bridge. Stands to reason if we've got a corpse and with no neckcloth and a neckcloth with no owner, they'd likely go together, wouldn't they?"

Highcliff rolled his eyes. "Ettinger, I've been up all bloody night long. How can you be certain the neckcloth was the murder weapon?"

"Wrinkles in the fabric... not an exact science. But I've never seen a neckcloth wrinkled in that fashion just from being tied. Looks as if it was wound about a man's fists." The Bow Street Runner held his closed fists out in front of him, about ten inches apart. "Not quite sure how a young strapping lad like that was overpowered by just one bloke though."

"Drink," Highcliff said. "If I had to guess, I'd say the victim had imbibed quite a bit of brandy or some other potent spirit." *Possibly laced with something else to further incapacitate him.*

"You think he was drinking with the one what killed him?" Ettinger asked. "Maybe more than just drinking?"

"I'd say they were intimately acquainted," Highcliff replied. "But let's not bandy that about."

"Just like the others, then?" Ettinger guessed. "Same man. Same untouchable fucking gent who gets away with murder just cause of his title?"

Highcliff rose. "It'll be the last one. That I can swear to you. But let's handle this discreetly, Ettinger. This young man has a mother and a sister who are still in society. In fact, the sister had her debut just the night before last. Extravagant affair. Financially, they'll be ruined by it. But for a moment, she was the bell of the proverbial ball. Now this. Terrible, but not insurmountable. If any hint of the truth about the nature of his relationship with his murderer was to come out—"

"It won't," Ettinger stated. "I'll see to it. But if there's another one, Lord Highcliff, I don't much care who asks me to keep my mouth shut. It has to end."

Highcliff nodded in agreement. Ettinger was a good man with a good heart. He also had hammer-like fists and somewhat flexible methods. Even as a runner, he was often on the wrong side of the law but always for the right reasons. "I can promise you, Ettinger, there are changes coming... changes that the perpetrator of this crime will not be able to halt, nor will he be able to avoid them."

"Fine. Then I'll quash any rumors or whispers that might cause trouble," the runner said. "But I'll be letting the true powers that be in on all of this."

The Hound. Ettinger served two masters and had for a very long time. "How long can you keep this up? One day he'll ask you to do something at cross purposes to your employer's," Highcliff stated.

"Ask. He will ask, my lord, and I will refuse. Wouldn't be the first time. We have an understanding, the Hound and I," Ettinger said. "And I could ask the same of you... when will you give it all up and just be an idle gentleman as the world believes?"

"When I am as dead as our unfortunate friend here," Highcliff replied. "Send word to his family... and send someone who will be kind to them, will you?"

"I'll go myself. It's on my way," Ettinger replied.

Highcliff rose from where he'd crouched next to the corpse of Charles Burney. "Check in on the Darrow School. Since it appears you're off to Jermyn Street, that is."

"I'm not your errand boy, my lord."

Highcliff grinned. "It's related, I assure you. Ask if anything untoward has occurred."

"And if it has?"

"Send for me," Highcliff said. "At once. In the meantime, I'll be running my own errands."

IT HADN'T TAKEN her very long to pack. While she did have some very nice things, they were small in number. Primarily because she refused to allow Effie to spend ridiculous sums of money on her. With all of her belongings packed into two valises, Callie paused to look around the room. It had been her home, her sanctuary. It had been the first place that had ever truly been hers and the first place where she'd felt safe. Even if they did manage to neutralize the threat from Averston, that feeling of security was gone forever. It wasn't simply the room that had been violated, but her. For the rest of her life, she'd hear their menacing words as they discussed what they had planned to do to her. And all for something as low as money.

"Are you ready?"

Callie jumped. It wasn't that she'd been lost in her thoughts, but her nerves were so jangled that everything seemed to set her off. Turning to face Effie who stood in the doorway, she replied, "No. I'm not. I'll never be ready to leave here. What if I don't come back?"

Effie stepped into the room an took Callie's hand in hers. "My dear, the Earl of Montgomery will see you safe. Trust him to do so... I know that I do."

"These people... the Duke of Averston and the dowager duchess... I've never even met them. And yet, I know they are completely evil. Their wickedness threatens everything and everyone I hold dear," Callie mused. "How does a person become so terrible and heartless?"

"Some people are born that way, I think. The piece of ourselves that allows us to love one another, to have empathy for one another, it's missing in some people, I think."

"I think perhaps it was better not knowing who my family was," Callie said.

"My dear, they are not your family. They are people to whom you happen to be related. It is not the same at all," Effie said with a smile. "We are your family. And we always shall be."

Callie could have cried with the gratitude she felt at that moment. It seemed that Effie always knew just what to say to her.

"Now," Effie continued, "go to the country with your employer and the children."

"I'll be ruined, afterward. Rendered unmarriageable and unemployable."

"But still alive," Effie pointed. "Death is an irreversible state. The rest, we can manage."

Well, there was no denying the logic of that statement. "You're quite right. Priorities!"

"Not to mention that the fortune you may inherit will be more than ample inducement for most gentlemen to overlook any questions of virtue," Effie added pragmatically.

Since the maids were helping in the dining room with Effie's absence, the two of them carried Callie's bags down to the foyer. Effie's words regarding her fortune and her reputation were still ringing in Callie's ears.

Winn was waiting for them at the foot of the stairs and took both cases. "The carriage is here," he said. "It arrived only moments ago."

"Are the children inside?" Callie asked.

"No. They are in the dining room with the other students enjoying a hearty breakfast. Mrs. Wheaton was kind enough to extend the hospitality to them and to Mrs. Marler who is with them," he answered.

"Oh... do they know what's happening? They aren't frightened are they?" Callie asked. She couldn't bear it if they were afraid. That was the last thing she wanted, to bring more fear and uncertainty into their lives when they had already been through so much.

"They do not. They think we are retreating to the countryside because of a problem at the estate and a desire to get them out of the city with its terrible air," Winn replied. "In short, I lied."

"But for a very good reason," Callie said. "Do you think the villains will follow?"

"I think they will send minions to do their bidding," Winn stated. "But it will take some time to figure out where we've gone. And in that time, I'll be preparing for every eventuality. I will keep you safe. I swear it."

If anyone could make such a promise and keep it, it would be him, she thought. He was a man of honor, who lived and breathed it. "Thank you."

No more was said as Mrs. Wheaton entered then carrying a hamper of food. "Some cold meats, bread and cheese. There are some apples in there, as well. The children will enjoy them on the journey, I think."

"Thank you, Mrs. Wheaton," Effie said. "That was very thoughtful of you. I'm sure everyone will be very grateful for the nourishment later."

Callie remained quiet, still uncertain whether or not it was a good idea for them to all be together. If something happened to one of the children because of her, she'd never be able to forgive herself.

"It will be fine," Winn said. "It will be. Have faith, Miss St. James."

Faith was in short supply for her. Unable to say anything else, she simply nodded and offered a weak excuse of a smile. "Goodbye, Effie."

"Only for a time,' Effie replied. "Have hope, my dear."

꘡꘡꘡

SHE SEEMED UTTERLY defeated. Whether it was the fright she'd had or the resulting exhaustion from it, it appeared as if the experience had simply deflated her. Winn watched her cautiously as they exited the Darrow School to the waiting carriage. He scanned the street for any potential dangers as they were leaving and, seeing none, assisted her inside. To the coachman, he said, "To the St. James Workhouse."

Other than a raised eyebrow, the coachman showed no qualms about the order. He gave a jerky nod. "Aye, m'lord."

Inside the carriage, Callie was seated next to him with Claudia beside them. Mrs. Marler sat on the opposite seat with William and Charlotte. He felt Callie's gaze on him and turned to meet her questioning stare. It was clear from her expression that she'd heard his instructions to the driver. So he whispered his explanation as softly as possible. "We're going to the workhouse first to ask if anyone there might have any information about the day you were found. I realize the chances are slim, but we cannot afford to squander any opportunity."

"I don't want the children to see that place," Callie said.

"But I want to see it!" Charlotte protested, clearly having heard every word they'd said. "It's from the story you told us!"

"That was a very prettied up version of events, Charlotte," Callie explained. "There's nothing about the workhouse in real life that you would enjoy."

"It will be good for them to see it," Winn stated. "They need to understand that there are people living in this country significantly less fortunate than they are. Perhaps by not shielding them from such things, they may be inspired as they grow to attempt to alter them. But perhaps not today… we have a long journey ahead of us and do not have time for an adequate tour." The last part of his statement was directed at Charlotte and at William.

Callie shook her head. "Very well. You all will wait in the carriage with Mrs. Marler and we shall find another time for you to visit the workhouse and develop, what I hope, will be a sense of charity."

Winn watched her, the way she met the children's gazes, the way she touched their shoulders or their hair when she was speaking to them so that they could easily know her statement was directed at them without her needing to shout. It had been less than a week and yet the changes she'd wrought in them already were beyond measure. As were the changes she'd wrought in him, he thought.

He was thankful when the carriage halted, when they reached the workhouse. Inside the close confines of the carriage with her, he could smell her perfume, he could see the various shades of her hair as the sun streamed through the window and lit the varying hues. It was too much. In less than a week, she had infiltrated every crevice of what he'd thought was a reasonably hardened heart.

Heart. Winn sat up straighter in his seat. Was he in love with her? Surely not. Surely he had not fallen so quickly! But then he looked at her once more. Was it so very unreasonable? She was beautiful, kind, generous with her time and with her obviously very tender heart. Three children who had been little better than hellions were transforming right before his eyes with her gentle guidance. How could he not love a woman such as her?

"Is something wrong?"

Her gentle prompt made him realize that the carriage had halted entirely and he was just sitting there. "Just collecting my thoughts," he lied. "Children wait here with Mrs. Marler... also, please don't do anything to make her wish to leave us."

"But we want to go!" Charlotte said.

Winn looked at her sternly. "I know you do, poppet. And another time, I will take you so that you may see it and so that you may offer some sweets or some other gifts to the children there. But today, we must hurry, so you will wait here. All right?"

She popped her thumb into her mouth, but nodded. "You pwomise?"

"I better than promise," he said. "I swear it on my honor."

Charlotte nodded and settled back onto the seat once more. She clutched her doll and leaned against her brother who tolerated the contact reasonably well. It would likely not last in such a manner though the whole of the journey, but at least for the moment, they were not at one another's throats.

Winn hopped down from the carriage and then reached in to help Miss St. James disembark. His hands closed over the narrow span of her waist. When her feet touched the pavement, he didn't release her immediately. Instead, he stood there for just a moment, looking into her eyes. "We will get this sorted out," he said. "One way or another."

She looked up at him, her eyes clouded with worry. "Don't make promises you can't keep."

"Then this promise is one I'll make to you right now, Calliope St. James. I will do whatever it takes to see you safe." *And to make you mine.* The latter part he didn't dare utter. Not yet. She wasn't ready to hear such things and she was far too vulnerable to be bombarded with such. It was also a vow to himself as much as it was to her. For a man who'd lived his life not believing in love at all and thinking marriage was fine for other people, he'd certainly done an abrupt about-face on the subject. "Now, let's get inside."

They walked toward the heavy wooden gate set with iron bars and manned by two guards. It looked more like a prison than a place for the poor, he thought. Beside him, he felt her tense, felt the heavy weight of her past settling over her. Uncaring of who might see or what anyone might think, he reached for her hand. Taking it in his, he held it, feeling the coldness of her skin even through her gloves. He also noted the slight tremor.

"I swore I'd never return here," she said.

"This will be the last time," he vowed.

The small door in the gate opened and a man's face appeared behind the iron bars there. "What you want?"

"We need to speak to the superintendent of this place," Winn stated.

"Oh, well, he ain't got time for that!"

"I am the Earl of Montgomery, sir, and he will make time," Winn replied, his tone brooking no argument. "And you will keep a civil tongue in your head or be seeking a new situation before the clock strikes noon."

The man, apparently chastened, closed the small door and the gate groaned as it opened. Stepping inside, into the yard, Winn was struck with how very crowded it was. People were everywhere. Young children, women, all of them stooped over needlework.

"You get paid per the piece but only if it's good quality," Calliope explained. "And working outside, even in the cold, you get better light to make sure your stitches are even. But if you're not careful, someone will steal your completed work."

He allowed his gaze to follow where she pointed, to a woman who was reaching down into a basket at another woman's feet and pilfering her work. "Should we not warn her?"

"The last thing you do in a place like this is draw attention to yourself, my lord," Calliope answered. "The two of them will sort it out in the dormitories later when there are no guards about. If they fight in the yard here, they'll be out on the street."

"This way, m'lord," the sour-faced man from the gate said, and led them toward the imposing brick building. They didn't enter through the main doors, but were led to a staircase off to one side that carried them up to the second level. The guard knocked. "A gentleman to see you, sir. The Earl of Montgomery!"

Several locks and bolts could be heard disengaging inside and then the door opened to reveal a slight man with a tuft of white hair and spectacles perched on the end of his nose. Beside him, Winn felt Callie draw back as if she'd been struck. Clearly, she recognized him.

"May I help you?" he asked.

"We have some questions regarding a child left in your care," Winn stated.

"I'm afraid I have nothing to say on the matt—"

Callie lifted her chin. "You do have something to say on the matter. I was the child in question and I will not be put off. Now, you may invite us into your office to speak or we stand here in the open where all your inmates can get a good look at you."

The man's face paled. Immediately, he stepped back. It was more out of shock than invitation, but Winn was willing to take any advantage they could get. Pushing into the office, past the stick figure of a man, he kept his hand tight on Callie's and drew her inside, as well.

After blustering for a moment, the man quickly closed the door and began setting all the locks and bolts. "It pays to be cautious," he said by way of explanation. "After what the peasants did in France, well... I'm cautious of rioting."

"Perhaps if you offered more than a thimbleful of gruel and a sliver of moldy bread, their full bellies would do what all the locks in England will not," Callie stated coolly.

The man stiffened, his spine going poker straight. "We provide as we are able, Miss."

"St. James," she said softly. "How sad it is the only name I have is the one granted me by this abominable place."

"What is it that you want?" he asked, moving toward his desk.

Winn noted there was a tray on his desk, laden with meat and cheese, bread, a pot of tea. There was more food on it than most of the poor souls in that yard had seen in a week. It was little wonder he kept his door locked and barred. "This woman was left at the workhouse as an infant and given into the care of a vicar—"

"Vicar Albertson. He placed me with a foster family, Chambers," Callie filled in. "And when they died, the vicar returned me here."

"Yes, Miss St. James," the superintendent said. "I'm aware of who you are."

"Good," Winn said. "We need to know everything about the day she came here."

"Well, certainly she can tell you all of that," the man said dismissively.

"Not when she was returned here... when she was left here the first time as a babe," Winn stated. He was fairly certain the man knew precisely what they had meant. He was simply stalling and that meant he knew something of import.

"I couldn't possibly remember so long ago."

Winn walked over to the door and carefully flipped back one bolt. "For every minute you delay answering, I will unlock one more. And when the last one is freed, I will personally hold this door open while every person in that yard is invited to come up here and help themselves to what remains of your meal. I imagine that when those poor souls see how you are dining versus what is served to them—"

"We found her in a basket outside the gate," the man said in a rush, the words tumbling one over another. "Don't unlock that door! Please! I beg of you!"

"What else?" Winn demanded, his hand hovering over the next lock. The little man had no hope of overpowering him. It was a fact everyone in that room was aware of.

"There was a note in the basket. We were asked to take the child to the Lampton Theater at Drury Lane and give her into the care of a woman named Eliza. That is all. I swear to you! That is all."

"But you didn't do that, did you?" Callie asked.

"The vicar said a couple would take the child on! It was his sister and her husband! He said it would be a better life for a child than some loose woman who trod the boards," the superintendent said, all but wailing.

"My father was alive then. That loose woman at the theater would have taken me to my father," Callie whispered. "My life might have been entirely different but for selfish, judgmental hypocrites such as you and the *good* vicar!"

The superintendent found some courage then and shouted back at her, "He'd have tossed you out in the street like every other bastard and you'd have been back here… assuming you lived long enough!"

Winn was away from the door in an instant, lifting the odious little man by his waistcoat and slamming him against the wall. "You'll mind how you speak to her or you'll not have a tongue to speak with at all! Is that understood?"

The man nodded, sobbing in fear by this point. Winn dropped him and he sank to the floor, still sniveling. Winn looked at the man's dinner once more and, with one swipe of his hand, sent the tray flying. Crockery and cutlery clattered about him and the majority of it wound up on his clothes. "I should force you to eat every bite until you choke on it."

"He isn't worth having it on your conscience," Callie said. "Let's just leave this place. Let's leave it and leave him to live and die with his many sins."

Looking back at her, Winn noted that there was a steeliness about her he had not seen since she'd stood toe to toe with him, yelling at him in his library. It was good to see the color back in her cheeks, but nothing could disguise how exhausted she was. Taking her arm, he strode toward the door. After undoing every single lock, they stepped out onto the small landing at the top of the rickety stairs. As they were making their way to the bottom, Winn asked a question that he dreaded the answer to. "What did he do to you?"

"He was as fond of the cane as Monsieur Dumont," she answered evenly. "But I think his enjoyment of the punishment might have been more licentious in nature."

"Did he—"

"No," she said, the word emphatic and sharp. "He did not. For him, beating little children was all that he required for his pleasure. And the guards were more interested in girls who were slightly older than I was, those just in the first bloom of womanhood, as it were. I was still very much a skinny, sickly child. I suppose I can be grateful that the near starvation I endured left me wholly unattractive to every man here."

Euphemia Darrow deserved to be recognized as a saint, he thought. "Let's leave this place. You'll never return here... but I will. And if it's the last thing I do, I will see that man removed from power. I will see this place being run fairly, with proper food and shelter for those who reside here."

She frowned at him. "Why would you do that?"

Winn reached out and cupped her face gently. He didn't kiss her. Not in that hellish place, but he said, "For reasons you are not yet ready to hear."

"I don't want to leave London," she said.

"It's too dangerous to stay. I can't protect you and the children unless we are all under one roof."

"Then we shall be. I shall simply move into your home on Piccadilly and we'll deal with the consequences of that when we must. All the answers are here. In London. We can't stop this problem by running from it—from them."

Winn met her steady gaze. This wasn't the hollow-eyed and terrorized girl he'd seen that morning. Somehow, bringing her back to the horrors of her childhood had helped her rediscover just how remarkably strong she was. "If that's what you want, then we'll stay here. I'll send a note round to Effie and to Highcliff. We'll convene at the house tonight and discuss our course of action."

Calliope looked around at the women and children laboring over needlework in the yard. "How terrified my mother must have been to depend on a place such as this for aid."

Winn ushered her down the stairs and they left the St. James Workhouse behind. But even as they exited the gate, he recognized one indisputable fact. They might leave it, but it would never leave her. For better or worse, the place had marked her to her soul.

Chapter Eighteen

BUNDLED INTO THE carriage once more, they made their way back to the house on Piccadilly. Callie looked at the children's faces and prayed she was making the right choice. The very last thing she wanted was to put them in more danger. But surely, traveling the countryside and being isolated at an estate far from town and far from anyone who might provide assistance would only increase the danger to all of them, she reasoned.

As if reading her thoughts, Claudia said, "I'm glad we're not going to the country. We've only just arrived here, after all. And there's so much about London to enjoy. And Uncle Winn's library. It's very grand."

"It is grand," Callie agreed. "And today, we'll go there and make a list of the books available in it that you should read."

Claudia's expression soured quickly. "Are they boring?"

"Some of them may be, but many of them are quite enjoyable," Callie replied. "I would advise using the exciting books as a way of rewarding yourself for making progress on the one's you are not quite so fond of."

Claudia's only response was a baleful stare.

"I want to read all the books," Charlotte pronounced. "I'll read them to my doll and she'll be very smart, too!"

"Dolls can't be smart, silly," William corrected her. "They don't have brains! Just empty heads!"

"They do, too!" Charlotte shouted at him. She would have stamped her little foot if it actually reached the floor of the coach.

"Don't yell at her, William," Claudia said. "She's only a baby. She doesn't understand!"

"I'm not a baby! I'm six!" Charlotte said, again gesturing angrily.

"You're four," William and Claudia both corrected in unison.

Winn intervened at that point, before mayhem could ensue further. "That is enough. Not a word from any of you until we are home."

All of the children clammed up entirely, William and Charlotte sulking. But it was Claudia who held Callie's attention. The girl glanced between Winn and herself, eyeing them both speculatively and with more than a little concern etched on her features. Mrs. Marler had remained silent through the whole exchange. But she did ruffle William's hair a bit, and Callie was fairly certain that he would be getting a sweet or two when they returned home. The boy was impossible not to spoil, but then, so was sweet little Charlotte with her cherubic face and big, blue eyes.

With the children quiet, Winn looked at Callie and uttered one phrase that made her stomach roll and her breath hitch with fear. "I think we should send a letter to the trustees of the Averston estate. The sooner we contact them, the sooner all of this can simply go away."

"Do you think that will make it worse or better?" she asked.

"Worse to start with, but better in the long run," he answered honestly. "Their only real power lies in secrecy and if we out the whole ugly lot of it, then we take that power from them."

She shivered with fear, but nodded. "Fine."

When they finally reached the house, the mood of the occupants was notably subdued. The children disembarked first, then Mrs. Marler was aided by one of the footmen. Winn exited the carriage next, hopping down easily. As always, he moved with a kind of innate grace and power that made Callie feel clumsy in comparison. When he turned back to her, Callie accepted his outstretched hand and allowed him to assist her from the carriage. The children were already being ushered inside by the warm and efficient housekeeper.

As her feet settled more firmly on the paving stones, Callie realized how close she stood to Winn, how very little distance separated their bodies. Immediately, her mind conjured the sensation of his kiss, the memory so full and real it was almost as if she could feel it all over again.

"Do not look at me that way," he warned softly.

"What way?"

"As if you wish me to repeat my inappropriate behavior from the library, and the hack... and that damnable room upstairs," he said.

She wanted to say something sassy or flirty, something that would make her seem far more worldly and sophisticated than she was. But nothing would come to mind. Instead, she stood there looking as utterly poleaxed by him as she was.

Then the carriage simply exploded next to her head. Bits of wood and leather flew everywhere, stinging her skin. Then they were tumbling to the hard stones of the walk, his large body covering hers, shielding her from whatever it was that had occurred. Another loud bang resonated and another bit of the carriage simply disintegrated before her eyes as she peered over his shoulder.

Someone was shooting at them.

"We've got seconds while they reload," he said, tugging her to her feet. "Stay behind me and stay low. The shots are coming from above and to the left."

The entire time he'd been speaking, he'd been pushing her into position and making for the steps that were only a few feet away. It was only when they reached the top of them, just a few feet from the door that Callie heard another shot ring out. He faltered and she could feel something warm and wet under her hand where it pressed against his side. Then they were in the house, the door slamming closed behind them.

"You and the children to the library," he said. "Keep the curtains drawn. Foster, I want bolts on the windows in there."

"Certainly, my lord," the butler said, springing into motion almost instantly.

"You're hurt," Callie said, noting the spreading red stain on Winn's waistcoat. "You've been shot."

"It's but a graze," he insisted. "Take care of the children!"

"Where are you going?" she asked.

"To the roof," he replied. "It's the best chance of catching the bas—brigands."

Callie didn't even have time to protest. She was too stunned by it all. Then William was whooping with excitement.

"I want to go with Uncle Winn!"

That brought Callie crashing back to reality. "Absolutely not. You will march directly to the library and while we are there, you shall practice writing your letters and being quiet."

His little face fell. "I want to chase the bad men."

Callie sighed. "When you are older, you may chase all the bad men away... but right now, you are still too little. And I cannot bear the thought of your being hurt. So come to the library with us and spare my mind anymore worry."

Ushering the children ahead of her, Callie followed behind them. But her gaze was fixed on the last point on the stairs where she'd seen Winn. *Please let him be well,* she prayed. Even as she battled back the panic that erupted at the thought of him getting hurt, she put on a calm face for the children and tried to soothe their fears. And the best antidote for fear was to stay busy.

With William settled at the desk working on his letters and Claudia ensconced before the fireplace, flipping through a book about exotic animals, Callie seated herself near the door to wait.

Claudia approached her then, carrying the book she'd selected to read. Softly, she asked, "Is this about the note?"

Callie met the girl's too-wise and knowing gaze. "Yes. I believe that it is."

Claudia sighed. "I don't want anything to happen to Uncle Winn. I like him. I really do."

"And he likes you," Callie replied reassuringly.

"But what will happen to us if something happens to him?" Claudia asked, biting her lip worriedly as she glanced at her brother and sister.

Callie reached out for the girl, pulling her close and hugging her tightly. "Your uncle will be fine. Even if something unthinkable happened, he will have made provisions for you. It's simply the way he is. When he returns, you may ask him about them so that you never have to wonder."

⟫⟫⟫⟪⟪⟪

WINN EASED HIMSELF out onto the ledge through the attic windows. He ignored the twinge in his side where the bullet had grazed his flesh. It wasn't terribly painful, but he was sweating and it burned like the devil. Climbing up onto the slate tiles, he stayed low and looked at the rooflines. Three houses away, he caught sight of movement. Looking back at the footmen who'd followed him out, he said, "Get some men on the ground in the back of the mews. They're unlikely to climb down the front of the houses where they'd be seen."

"Aye, m'lord."

The servants moved away, and Winn moved forward. He clambered over the roof and managed to leap down to the lower roof of the house next door. There, concealed form sight, he ran, closing the distance between him and the gunman. Hoisting himself up onto the roof of the next house, he used the many chimneys and the ornate cupola to provide shelter. The fourth house, he was jumping down once more. As he landed in a crouch, another pistol ball whizzed past him, imbedding itself into the brick of the house behind him. The man raised a second pistol. As he fired, Winn threw himself onto the tiled roof. The pain in his side exploded until he literally saw stars dancing before his eyes. Still, he forced himself back up to standing and charged toward the man before he could get the brace of pistols reloaded. He reached him just as the man raised the pistol once more. The shot went wide as Winn rushed him, taking him down to the tiles. They rolled toward the edge, and only Winn's boots catching against the lip of the gutter kept them both from going over.

"Why were you trying to kill her?" Winn demanded.

"Money! Why else?" the man snapped. "Let me go."

"Tell me who hired you!"

"Don't know his name. Didn't ask. He said she paid him to pay us and we was to see the bitch dead!"

Winn didn't have a chance to ask any further questions. The gutter gave then, separating from the house entirely. The pair of them slid toward edge, the burlier man going over first. Winn managed to snag the cornice of the building where the gutter had attached. He hung there, the other man clinging to him. They were three stories up. Not so very high, but certainly high enough that the fall would do damage and possibly result in death.

"Don't let me fall," the man said. "I can get word to her. I can send for him and he'll lead you right to her!"

Winn moved one booted foot toward the building, finding a toe-hold there on the intricate masonry that wrapped the upper floor of the house, while the man who'd tried to kill Calliope only moments earlier still clung to his leg. With one foot perched there, one arm hooked around the heavy stone cornice, he reached one hand down to the man, "Give me your hand!"

The man wouldn't let go. At that point, he'd closed his eyes and was simply praying incoherently. And then Winn felt the man slipping.

"Give me your hand! Now, man!"

There was no response. The man's grip began to fail. And then he was simply gone, sailing silently to the stones below without ever opening his eyes.

Winn heard the thud as he hit, saw the spreading crimson stain on the stones below. And then his footmen were there. One ran through the garden gate of the house and into the kitchens. Within seconds, servants were rushing about inside, opening windows all along the upper floor. With a decided lack of grace, a pair of maids and a sturdy kitchen girl helped him into the house through the window just below him.

He collapsed on the floor, sweating, bleeding, breathless... but alive. Very much alive, unlike the man who'd attempted to take Calliope St. James' life. And one thing that man had said stood out to Winn. The man had been hired by an intermediary to be sure, but the mastermind of the whole plot had been referred to as *she*. The Dowager Duchess of Averston.

Chapter Nineteen

C ALLIE WAS BESIDE herself. Winn had returned home, assisted in by some footmen. Following them up the stairs, she entered his chamber just as his valet began removing his soiled coat and waistcoat. The man clucked over the damaged and stained fabrics as though they were priceless artifacts, even as he left his injured employer to struggle out of his ruined shirt on his own.

"They're clothes!" she snapped. "I would think you'd be more concerned about the man who'd been wearing them!"

Chastened, the valet took the garments and fled. Footmen were helping Winn onto the bed and he was waving them away. "I'm not so gravely injured as I appear, Miss St. James. I'm simply too old for hand to hand combat and trying to hold the added and considerable weight of a grown and somewhat stocky fellow as we dangled off the edge of a house three stories up."

Her throat went dry and she felt her heart stutter in her chest. While she'd been aware that he was disrobing, being confronted with the reality of his bare chest was not something she'd been prepared for. Forcing herself to deal with only the most pressing matters at hand and not her own maidenly sensibilities, Callie focused her gaze on the ugly wound in his side. There was a great deal of blood, some of it already dried, making it impossible to determine the severity of the wound at a glance. "You were hanging over the edge of the roof?"

He flexed his hands, the scrapes and bruises on them obvious even from a distance. "From the gutter to be precise, but yes."

"And where is this man now?"

He looked up at her then, his expression stoic but still quite revealing. "He's dead, Calliope. I tried to save him... I offered him my hand, but he wouldn't take it."

Dead. Which meant that Winn had been terribly close to the same fate himself. "What if you'd fallen as well?"

"But I didn't," he said firmly. "I've lost a bit of flesh and a small amount of blood—"

"A small amount? This is hardly insignificant!" She gestured toward blood smeared on his side.

"Well, it's hardly life threatening either," he said, and even as he said it, he placed one hand over the wound as if to show that it didn't hurt. The gesture was wasted as he winced with pain. "It's ugly and inconvenient. The pistol ball took a bit of hide. Nothing more."

"It's more than simply ugly and inconvenient! You could have been killed and it would have been my fault. You need a physician! Why has no one sent for one?" She was practically yelling as the few lingering servants looked on as if she'd become a madwoman.

He shook his head. "Because it's little more than a scratch. It's almost stopped bleeding even," he said, holding up his hand as proof.

Callie's fists were clenched at her sides to keep them from shaking. "He shot at us with the children mere feet away. What if one of them had been struck? I couldn't live with myself if something happened to one of them. I know I've only been here for two weeks, but I love those children dearly. If the unthinkable happened to any one of you because of my presence—"

"You couldn't bear it if something happened to the children because you love them. Tell me the truth, Calliope. Why couldn't you bear it if something happened to me?"

At that softly voiced question, everyone in the room went utterly silent. The servants didn't even dare breathe and as Callie looked at him, her eyes wide with shock and fear, she was terrified to utter the answer.

"Out," Winn said. "Everyone out of this room... except for you, Calliope."

The servants scattered, leaving them alone entirely. And she simply stood there and looked at him, unable to form the words.

"Why would it be unbearable to you if something were to happen to me?" he demanded again. "Because I can tell you right now, I'd throw myself in front of a hundred pistol balls for you and it's not because, excellent as you may be at it, you're the damned governess!"

And that set her heart to stuttering in her chest all over again. It seemed to lose its rhythm for just a moment before regaining it, only to beat faster and faster. So much so that she felt dizzy from it and sank down onto the nearest surface which just happened to be the edge of the very same bed he was sitting upon. "Why would you do that?" she finally managed to ask.

"Because improbable as it may sound, I have fallen hopelessly in love with you," he stated, sounding none too pleased about the fact. "As if those heathen children hadn't upended my well-ordered bachelor life enough, Calliope, you had to come along with your sweet, winsome smile and your alabaster skin and remind me that a solitary life is not necessarily a satisfying one."

Callie's hands folded in her lap. "You love me? I don't know what that means in the scope of all this."

"Ideally, it means that I would ask you to be my wife and you would agree to it."

"But I'm a governess," she said, sounding utterly bewildered by it all. "And I may be illegitimate... or at the very least it will be very difficult to prove I am not. I may or may not be an heiress and everything is so very complicated. I find it very difficult to believe I'd be worth all the trouble, regardless."

"I don't care if you're illegitimate. I don't care if you're a governess, if you're an heiress or even if you're the Queen of bloody Sheba.
I care that you are you... and that you are mine," Winn whispered
softly. "So say it, Calliope. Say that you'll be mine."

"It's a terrible idea," she said.

"I thought that... for a while. And then I was dangling off a roof a
few moments ago. I realized the only terrible idea I've ever had is to
let unimportant and trivial details keep me from being with the
woman I love. What could be worse than denying myself something
so magnificent for reasons that are stupid and not even my own?"

Could such a thing really be happening? Could the girl no one had
ever wanted really be faced with the prospect of such a wonderful man
proposing to her? He was intelligent and funny and terribly sarcastic.
He was also kind and caring and protective of those he loved. He was
so terribly hard on himself and expected so much of himself while
being generous and forgiving to others. How could she ever say no?
Because it would ruin him. "I just never thought you'd ask... or rather,
I only ever allowed myself to imagine all the reasons you wouldn't.
We'd be breaking all the rules. You know it's impossible. Or it ought
to be."

"It won't be pretty, you know?" He rose from the bed as he spoke,
putting some distance between them which allowed both of them to
breathe easier. "Society is founded on rules... you're very right about
that. But high society is a different beast altogether. It's driven
fundamentally by seeking approval of those who, by luck, birth or
circumstance, have managed to garner the most popularity or power.
I've never especially played their games. But because I'm not naturally
the sort to rebel against something for the sake of it, I've always been
accepted." He wasn't saying it to talk her out of that. Rather, he was
simply stating matter of factly what the reactions would be.

"That's hardly a persuasive argument," she pointed out. "Those
are, in fact, the very reasons I ought to refuse you."

"I don't care about any of it. They can all hang... the whole bloody world can hang," he said with a half-smile.

It was the smile, she thought, that did her in. Standing there, shirtless, covered in blood, and yet he looked like he hadn't a care in the world. In that moment, he could very well have been the sort of rogue she'd always been warned about by Effie. "It'll be difficult for the children... when it's time for them to go into society as they get older, people will hold it against them—that I am what I am."

He nodded. "They will. And what of our children, Callie? We already have a houseful, but I can assure you, if you become my wife... it will not be a chaste union. I will have you in my bed at every opportunity."

"You're very certain of yourself!"

He grinned then. Bare chested, with blood still seeping from the wound on his side as he casually poured himself a glass of brandy from the decanter on the table—he might have never been a rake or a rogue by society's standards, but he more than looked the part. "I'm very certain of us. And Claudia tells me that you like me. That you *like* me. She placed extra emphasis on the word and I can't imagine she's wrong about such things. Women rarely are."

"She's not a woman. Not yet."

"Certainly closer to it than I'm comfortable with," he added. "It makes my heart race and my palms sweat when I think of all the horrible young men out there who will be after her fortune... or her virtue."

"But it's perfectly all right for you to be after mine? Virtue, that is, as I currently have no fortune to speak of," Callie added the last with a self-deprecating laugh.

He drained the glass in one long swallow, his breath hissing out after. "Yes, but my long-term goals are entirely honorable."

Callie's breath hitched. There was something in the way he emphasized long-term goals that told her he was planning something more immediately that might be slightly less honorable. And a part of her was terribly excited by the prospect. "I'm more concerned about your short-term goals."

"You should be," he said, and then strode toward her, closing the distance with long decisive strides.

⇶⇷

As he crossed the room toward her, seated on the edge of his bed with her hands folded primly in her lap, there was nothing quiet and demure about her expression. Her eyes widened, her pupils dilated, and her soft, lush lips parted on a soft gasp—she looked like a woman who was perfectly willing to be compromised. And while he had no intention of allowing things to go too far, he also knew that if Calliope was given the opportunity to think clearly, she'd allow herself to be swayed by reason, by the innumerable list of perfectly valid points that made a union between them seem both scandalous and somewhat foolish. And he couldn't let that happen.

He stepped closer, until his knees were bracketing hers, and then he leaned forward, so much so that she had to lean back. She was now reclining on his bed, her weight resting on her elbows, and he was looming over her. And there wasn't a hint of fear in her expression. Challenge? Yes. Excitement? Certainly. Curiosity? It was there in spades. There was also heat. He could see his own desire reflected back at him.

"Is this how you mean to convince me?" she demanded. "Bully tactics and intimidation?"

"Is that what this is?" he asked, his lips quirking in a smile. "I thought it was just a kiss."

"If I've learned one thing from you thus far, it's that there is no such thing as just a kiss," she said. Her cheeks were flushed with excitement and her breath had quickened.

"Having enjoyed such a limited quantity, Calliope, you're hardly an expert yet," he replied smoothly. As he smoothed one errant tendril of her lovely hair from her face, the tips of his fingers skated over the soft, tender skin just below her jaw.

"And you are?"

And with that challenge, she'd effectively sprung the trap. "I can demonstrate if you like."

But he didn't have to. Because she lifted herself up, looping one hand around his neck. Her fingers threaded into his hair and she pressed her lips to his. It was a bold move and a brash one, though not entirely unexpected. His Calliope was no shrinking violet. She was a passionate creature and a woman of incomparable bravery and strength.

Winn took control of the kiss, gentling it, easing her into things that were unfamiliar and more than likely unexpected. It was the most natural thing in the world to raise one knee to the mattress, to climb onto the bed and pull her up with him until they were both lying across it. Mindful of his injury and that getting blood on her dress would likely not endear him to her, he shifted to his side. It had the added benefit of giving his hand freedom to roam over her lush curves even as he coaxed her lips apart and slid his tongue between them. She stiffened against him, more from shock than protest, and after a second's hesitation, settled once more. It took only the span of a few heartbeats until she was returning his kiss just as ardently, mimicking, exploring, and God help him, seducing him with every breath.

The pins slipped from her hair, letting the mass fall free of its loose chignon to fan out over the pillow. The taste of her, the softness of her lips, the sweet and slightly breathless sounds she made—it was far headier than the brandy he'd just consumed. And so much more addictive. He craved her. He wanted her the way he'd never wanted another woman in his entire life. But it wasn't just the need to have her physically, to know every intimate secret of her body. It was the need to hear her voice, to see the soft smile that tugged at her lips when William was being incorrigible, or the way her face softened and her eyes lit when she looked at Charlotte. Then there was her quiet patience with Claudia, her innate understanding of what a girl poised between two phases of her life might need. It seemed that everything she did was thoughtful, measured, and imbued with wisdom... until it came to him. Then she was just as reckless and foolish as he was. It was that which gave him hope for them both.

In a very short time, she'd become all-consuming for him. It ought to have terrified him. And were it not for the fact that he knew firsthand what danger she faced, it might have. But the very real prospect of losing her so surpassed any inconsequential fear of commitment that it became an insignificant thing entirely. He'd faced that fear and come out the other side of it determined to take what happiness he could with her and damn the consequences.

Pulling his lips from hers, he kissed a trail along her cheek to her ear, and then down her neck. His lips skated over the delicate and lovely arc of her collarbone. And even as plied her with kisses, he was tugging at her gown until it slipped lower, freeing her perfect breasts. She still wore her stays and chemise, but they offered little impediment. Each garment was tugged aside with ruthless efficiency until he could see the rosy peaks of her breasts and he could place his mouth over one taut nipple.

A sound escaped her that was half-gasp and half-pleasured moan. Her hand tightened on his hair, not to push him away but to hold him even closer. Her other hand was at his back, her nails scoring his skin. And then he became aware of another sound—an insistent knocking upon the door that could only mean one thing. Trouble.

Pulling back from her, Winn tugged her clothes back in place and helped her to sit up. She stared at him, her eyes glazed and her parted lips still swollen from his kiss.

"You were quite right, Calliope. There is no such thing as just a kiss," he said, his gaze sweeping over her.

She scrambled off the bed. "You should answer the door... after I've hidden in your dressing room."

Winn said nothing. He simply watched her as she scampered toward the doorway and disappeared beyond it. Cursing her, cursing his own foolishness in thinking that kiss would only impact her ability to think clearly, he sat up and yelled, "Enter!"

The door opened and William, Claudia and Charlotte appeared, their little faces etched with concern. That would effectively wilt any man.

"You're hurt," Charlotte said and immediately popped her thumb into her mouth.

"It's not very bad," he said. "Just a scratch. I'm quite all right."

"You're certain?" Claudia demanded. "You're not simply saying that because men have to pretend that nothing hurts and they're completely invincible?"

His brows furrowed as he frowned at her. "You sound remarkably like Miss St. James." It felt strange to call her that, to speak so formally of her when just moments before she'd been laid out before him and he'd been—well, it was best not to think of what he'd been doing.

"Where is Miss St. James?" William said sharply. "She said she was coming up here."

"She's in the dressing room," Winn answered honestly.

Claudia was suddenly wearing a frown to match his own. "Why is she in your dressing room?"

Calliope emerged then. Her hair tidied and pinned back up somehow. She carried a stack of cloth that looked suspiciously like one of his shirts. "I was getting bandages, Claudia. Your uncle's wound isn't very serious, but it still needs tending. If you'd like to help, why don't you run down to the kitchen and tell Cook we need some hot water and whatever herbal salves she might have to ease the pain and prevent the wound from becoming putrid."

"I'll stay," Claudia said pointedly. "It wouldn't be proper, after all, for the two of you to be alone. But William and Charlotte can go. You remember what you are to ask for, William?"

"I'm not stupid," he groused. "Hot water and salve."

"Go with him, Charlotte," Callie said. "Neither of you is to carry the hot water, but you may carry any medicines that Cook sends up."

The little girl and her brother ran from the room and Claudia stepped deeper into it. She settled herself on the one chair in the room, a wing chair before the fire and looked at both of them with far more sophistication than a girl of ten or eleven should ever have. "To borrow William's words, I'm not stupid either. What was really going on in here?"

Winn smiled. Calliope might be able to fight him, but she wouldn't fight them both. "You should know, Claudia, that I have honorable intentions. I've asked Miss St. James to be my wife."

Callie gasped. Claudia clapped her hands and squealed in delight, much the way a child actually should.

"That's wonderful news!" Claudia exclaimed, a bright smile lighting her face.

"Well, not precisely," Winn said. "Miss St. James has not yet accepted my offer. She's worried that because of her position as a governess and the fact that her parents may not have been married, that people will not look favorably upon our union."

"No one who matters would think anything of it, other than that you belong together and should be very happy with one another," Claudia said. "And if they do think otherwise, they're not someone you should wish to know anyway."

Out of the mouths of babes. He turned to look at Callie and noted that she appeared utterly at a loss. "Those are very wise words, indeed, Claudia."

"It isn't that simple," Callie said, looking at him. "We both know that. And it's terribly unfair of you to bring Claudia into this. You mustn't say anything to your brother and sister, Claudia. I don't want any of you disappointed."

"I won't. But it's perfect, you know?" she said. "William is terrified that you'll leave us one day. So is Charlotte, though she won't say anything. She changed the name of her doll to Calliope. She said it was so she could keep you always. If you marry Uncle Winn, then you'll be our aunt. And no one could ever make you leave us."

And that was the moment Winn saw her crumble.

CALLIE'S SHOULDERS BEGAN to shake. The sobs started before the tears. She didn't even really understand what she was crying for. Yes, there had been two attempts on her life in the past twenty-four hours. Yes, she'd confronted the very man who'd abused her so horribly as a child, the same man she now knew had failed to honor what must have been her mother's dying wish, thus altering the course of her life forever. And the man she adored, the man she'd fallen in love with probably from the first moment she'd laid eyes upon him, had asked her to marry him and all she could do was count the dozens of reasons why such an action would be doomed.

Winn rose from the bed and moved toward her but Claudia rushed to her first. The little girl wrapped her arms around Callie and squeezed her tightly. "I'm fine." The words were broken by her sobs and sounded completely unconvincing.

"It's all right," Claudia said. "When you're so used to things going wrong, it's very scary when they suddenly go right."

Callie laughed through her tears. "You're a very bright girl. Do you know that, Claudia?"

"I might have an inkling," she said. "There aren't many people in this world that I would ever consider trusting. Everything my father said to me, I doubted. Everything my mother said... well, she said it with good intentions but could never follow through on any of it. But I trust you. And I trust Uncle Winn. And if I can trust you both, don't you think you really ought to trust one another?"

Callie wrapped her arms around the young girl and placed a kiss to the top of her head. "Very, very wise. I imagine that when I am your aunt, you will lead both your uncle and me on a merry chase."

"When not if?" Winn said.

"When," Callie replied, nodding her head. "When. And we should make it sooner rather than later, I think."

"I'll get a special license. We'll marry tomorrow," he said.

Claudia began spinning in circles, laughing and dancing around Callie. She was still doing so when her siblings returned. And then the squeals and laughter of all three of them nearly brought the roof down.

Chapter Twenty

I T WAS LATE afternoon when Highcliff sauntered up the steps to the Piccadilly residence of the Earl of Montgomery. He'd been summoned, and considering that Effie had told him just that morning that the earl, his nanny and his brood were to make for the country, he could only assume that there had been a not insignificant event which had inspired the change of plans.

The butler, a surprisingly young fellow for the position, opened the door and showed him in. "His lordship is in the library, Lord Highcliff. If you'll follow me—"

"No need, young man. I know the way," Highcliff said, grinning as he breezed past the startled servant. Entering Montgomery's library, he found the man pacing, his fingers steepled under his chin and a pensive look on his face. "This doesn't bode well."

Montgomery looked up. "Good. You're here. I need a special license."

Of course he did. Highcliff stepped deeper into the room, moved past Montgomery and made directly for the brandy decanter perched on a table in the corner and poured himself a healthy measure into one of the ready glasses. "Naturally. Everyone in bloody London needs a bloody special license because they all want to bloody well get married. What happened to men wanting to avoid the parson's mouse trap? Hmm? I've never in all of my life known so many men who wanted to go skipping down the aisle to a lifetime of being harangued by one woman for the remainder of their days!"

"Calliope does not harangue, Highcliff."

"Yet," he replied, and drank deeply from his glass.

"We went to the St. James Workhouse this morning."

Highcliff lowered his glass. "That's a bit of hell on earth. Did you discover anything?"

"Apparently there was a note in the basket with her when she was left there. Those in charge at the workhouse were supposed to contact a woman named Eliza at the Lampton Theater in Drury Lane."

"Which they didn't do obviously," Highcliff grimaced. "To what end?"

"It's not unheard of for childless couples to pay for an adoption... but in this case, I imagine there was a debt or favor owed. The vicar had a sister who wanted a child and the weasel who was in charge of the workhouse had a baby in his possession that would fill the bill."

"He'll be dealt with," Highcliff said.

"I'd be obliged on that score. You aren't the only one who can call in favors, but I imagine yours are less about simply removing his livelihood," Winn said. He'd sent letters to several very prominent members of Parliament following the chaotic events of the morning, but it didn't feel like punishment enough for the man's sins. "I've made arrangements to have him removed from his little kingdom. I've also sent a letter to the trustees of the Averston estate. No doubt, they've already convened to discuss matters. Another reason for the urgency of my marriage to Calliope. It's one thing to murder a lowly governess. It's another to kill the Countess of Montgomery in cold blood."

Those were all excellent points that Highcliff had no counter for. He drained his glass and refilled it. "Fine. You want a special license, I'll get you one. But you're not marrying her for such noble reasons, Montgomery. You're marrying her because you want to marry her.

Why?"

"Because I love her," Montgomery replied without hesitation. "If the opportunity presented itself, would you not marry the woman you love?"

Highcliff shrugged. "There is no woman I love."

Montgomery's brow arched. "You've evaded the truth often, Highcliff, with misdirection and humor. But I believe that might be the first time I've ever known you to lie outright. By the way, she's here. Effie, as she has asked that I call her, is upstairs with Callie now. We have things to discuss, all of us together."

"Drawing room," Highcliff said, his tone surly and his expression chilled as he turned and strode toward the door of the library. He made his way unerringly to the drawing room and waited.

In the library, Winn shook his head. Highcliff was a man of mystery, a man of contradiction, and he strongly suspected, a man who was quite tortured under his urbane and fashionable exterior. Stepping out into the corridor, he noted Foster looking at Lord Highcliff in confusion.

"I've worked here seven years, my lord. I've never seen that man in this house, and yet he seems to know it like the back of his hand," the butler mused.

"Sometimes, Foster, it's best just not to question things," Winn said. "Send a maid to fetch Miss St. James and Miss Darrow, please. And I suppose tea or something of that nature would be appropriate."

"It would indeed, Lord Montgomery."

Winn paused. "Have I really had so few visitors to this house in recent years that I've actually forgotten what to do with them?"

"Yes, my lord," Foster said. "I believe you preferred to be entertained elsewhere or to meet with friends at your clubs though that had lessened of late, as well."

Winn considered it and shook his head at that unfortunate truth. He'd been on the verge of becoming a recluse. "See to the refreshments, Foster."

"Certainly, my lord."

Entering the drawing room, he crossed immediately to the fireplace and waited there for the ladies to arrive. Highcliff was still sipping his brandy, heedless of social edicts that prohibited such spirits so early in the day and in mixed company. Winn imagined that Miss Effie Darrow had something to do with that.

A few moments later, Calliope entered along with Miss Darrow. Winn noted that the tension in the room was a palpable thing upon her entrance. She and Highcliff stared at one another like fighters before a match. Miss Darrow looked disapprovingly at Highcliff's brandy. Highcliff, in turn, arched his eyebrow in challenge as he raised the glass to his lips once more.

"Well, I'll start," Highcliff said. "Charles Burney is dead."

"What?" Callie gasped.

Winn's expression hardened. "When did you discover this?"

"Early this morning. His body was pulled from the canal at St. James' Park."

Winn recalled his previous conversation with Highcliff about the fate of Averston's lovers. It would seem Burney had fared no better.

"Was it an accident?" Miss Darrow asked. "Please say that it was."

Highcliff shook his head. "He was dead before he even touched the water. Strangled with his own neckcloth it would seem... or at least that's what Ettinger—from Bow Street—thinks."

"We need to confront Averston," Winn stated. "We need to corner him and demand the truth from him... and offer him the option to deal with the dowager duchess on his own."

"We've no proof," Highcliff responded.

"There was an incident this morning," Winn admitted. "A man with a pistol was taking shots at us as we got out of the carriage... after visiting the workhouse. When I caught up with him on the roof of a neighboring house, he inadvertently confessed something in the struggle. He referred to the person who hired him as 'she'. I'm past thinking that Averston himself is the issue. I'd lay money on it being her all along—the dowager duchess. But without confronting him, we'll never know for certain."

"You didn't tell me that!" Callie said.

"Well, to be fair, we were rather preoccupied with other matters," Winn replied. "I've asked Highcliff to procure a special license and he has agreed. The sooner we are married, the sooner the stakes for taking your life will be raised dramatically. We can't afford to wait."

"He's right, Callie," Effie said. "I know that isn't why you've agreed to marry. But taking a hastier route to the altar is for the best under the current circumstances."

"Right," Highcliff said. "Let's go speak to Averston and then I'll set about procuring another special license. I no longer have any favors to call in with the archbishop. They've all been spent. Hopefully, he's simply feeling magnanimous."

"We need someone here guarding the house," Winn replied.

"Ettinger has been keeping an eye on Effie. He followed her here," Highcliff admitted.

Effie let out a startled sound. "You've had someone watching me? Spying on me?"

Highcliff whirled on her then, marching toward her in such an obvious fury that Winn was on the verge of intervening. But the other man halted just a foot from Miss Darrow. Still, when Highcliff spoke, his words were harsh and his tone clipped. "I had someone protecting you. And any time I feel that you are in danger, I will have someone protecting you. Do not try me, Euphemia. Do not try me. Do not. Not today."

"I think it's excellent that someone is watching the house," Callie spoke up. "After all, the safety of the children must be our first priority! Don't you agree, Effie?"

And with that, Effie was painted into a corner. "Certainly. I am in full agreement with that, Callie. You're quite right. It's a good idea... no matter the source."

Highcliff smirked. "No worries, Effie, darling. My ego will survive the beating. As for Ettinger, he'll be watching everything outside along with his trusted men. There are others still stationed near the school. Everyone should be right as rain."

"Then we should go before it gets any later," Callie stated.

"We?" Winn and Highcliff demanded in unison.

"I'm going with you," Callie stated.

"That's impossible," Winn replied, the denial automatic. "It cannot and will not happen."

"Why? Clearly secrecy is not an option. If it is his grandmother, the Dowager Duchess of Averston, and not Averston, perhaps my presence will provide enough of a shock that he will be caught off guard and may answer questions more honestly."

"She isn't wrong, Montgomery," Highcliff interjected. "It might make a difference."

"Well, I'm hardly staying here alone," Effie said.

"You're not alone," Highcliff snapped. "Ettinger will keep you and the children company inside the house."

"Need I remind you, Lord Highcliff, that I am not someone to be ordered about by you or by any other man!" Miss Darrow's words and tone were cool, but her eyes were snapping with temper.

"Actually, Effie, it would make me feel so much better if you stayed with the children. I don't want them to be afraid," Callie said.

Effie's lips pressed into a firm line. "Very well. I shall wait here with them. But all three of you will return to this house when the task is done."

Highcliff sketched a bow that could only be called mocking. "As you command, Miss Darrow."

Effie's glare was positively glacial. "I'm going up to monitor the children. I shall see you when you return."

Highcliff let out a world-weary sigh and scrubbed a hand over his face. "I'm going to collect Ettinger and set him to guard duty."

Winn was now alone with Callie. The two of them looked at one another. "What has gotten into them?" Callie asked.

Winn had his theories, but they were hardly appropriate to discuss at that time. Sexual tension. Thwarted desires. He would bet money that both were on edge not because of what had happened but because of something that had almost occurred. "Get your pelisse," he instructed her. "It's chilly outside. As for Highcliff and Miss Darrow, let's just leave them to work things out themselves. We certainly did."

Callie's eyes widened. "You don't think... really? They are in love? They act like they cannot abide one another."

"I don't know that I would call it love. I think perhaps they are attracted to one another and fighting it bitterly enough that they are now fighting one another just as bitterly. But leave it be, Calliope. That is not a situation we can fix and any meddling might only make it worse."

"I won't meddle," she agreed. "Does it constitute meddling to find out what might have occurred?"

Winn couldn't bite back the grin that her mischievous tone teased from him. "It depends on the amount of fishing you have to do for that information... and if you should discover something, you are bound by the rules of betrothal to share it with me."

Callie's lips quirked in return. "The rules of betrothal? I wasn't aware of any such thing. Were those rules discussed at length prior to my acceptance of your proposal? If not, I can hardly be bound by them."

Winn reached for her hand, tugging her forward until she stood close enough that he could wrap his arms about her and steal only the most innocent of kisses. Even though it was barely a brush of their lips, he felt the heat coiling inside him. Lust was a familiar sensation to him, but not the incessant, clawing need that she seemed to evoke in him.

"What spell have you put me under, Calliope St. James?"

Her reply was uttered on a breathless laugh. "I think perhaps we have bespelled one another."

The sound of a throat being cleared quite loudly and with little patience prompted them to break apart. Highcliff stood in the doorway looking rather nonplussed by their display of affection. "Ettinger is on his way up to the nursery. A note has been sent round to the Hound of Whitehall."

That pronouncement hit Winn like a punch to the gut. "The Hound of Whitehall? Why on earth are you in communication with him?"

"Several girls that are students of Miss Darrow have come to be in her care as a result of the Hound rescuing them from... undesirable situations. I thought he'd prefer to have men of his own looking after the school," Highcliff responded. "And suffice it to say, he and I have an understanding about things that occur within the city of London which he has a vested interest in. This would be one of them."

"Why?" Winn asked. "What possible interest could he have in all of this?"

Highcliff smiled. "Let's just say he's got his own reasons for disliking the Duke of Averston. Now, my carriage awaits."

Chapter Twenty-One

A VERSTON MET HIS grandmother's steely gaze as she entered his study. As a rule, they resided in separate households and had as little to do with one another as possible. He was in a foul mood having sent a note round to Burney that morning and not receiving a reply. It hadn't been an apology per se, but he had accepted that he'd spoken more harshly to the man than he should have and that their disagreement was trifling in nature. It wasn't love. He didn't love, as a rule. But it was more than lust, enough so that it bothered him that the young man had not replied. Now, to have his grandmother to deal with on top of that, it was enough to make him want to crawl head first into a bottle of brandy and never come up.

"I'm in no mood for a scolding," he remarked as she walked in.

"You appear to be quite out of sorts, Gerald."

"Don't call me that," he snapped. "You know I prefer to be called Averston."

"And I'd prefer for you to be married to a respectable young woman with an heir and a spare rattling about in that monstrous nursery upstairs. We shall both have to accustom ourselves to disappointment it seems. Someone has contacted the trustees claiming to be the missing heiress," she said frostily.

He laughed. "For the twentieth time. Many claims have been made over the years and all have failed to provide any legitimate proof of their claims."

She stepped deeper into the room, settling herself on one of the chairs facing his desk. "This one may be more problematic than the others. But I've taken steps to ensure that it is handled."

Averston frowned. "You've never bothered to involve yourself in these matters before. Which makes me question why this one is different. Do you think there's a possibility this claimant is the genuine article?"

His grandmother leaned forward, her eyes glittering like shards of broken glass. "It doesn't matter. Genuine or not, she's entitled to nothing. Or do you wish to give all this up to the misbegotten by-blow of a French whore?"

"What have you done?" he asked, a sense of dread filling him. "We have acted, for decades now, on the presumption that the child died. But if the child survived, contrary to what my wishes might be, we cannot intercede!"

"Can we not?" she laughed. "I've been interceding in events that might bring shame to this family since before you drew your first breath! And if you don't curb your wickedness and your own licentious behavior, no doubt I'll be doing so after you have gone. Though there shall be no one left to leave any of it to!"

He'd said it many times, but mostly in ill-received jest. But now, looking into ice-cold gaze of the woman before him, he wondered if perhaps his joke didn't hold a spark of truth. "Did you kill her?" he asked.

"Who?"

"Veronique Delaine. I know it's been whispered, but I only ever half-believed it. I thought perhaps it was just rumor and innuendo metamorphosing into legend."

She reached out, gripping his arm with a strength that shocked him. Her talon-like nails scored his skin and she hissed at him, "I did then as I will do now... what is required. *Whatever* is required."

Averston looked at her then, seeing her for perhaps the first time. He'd thought her a controlling, managing old woman. But the truth was so much worse. She was actually a monster. "Oh my God. You did do it... you murdered that woman and left her child to whatever miserable fate might await her." He was more stunned by the realization than he ought to have been.

"Don't act so missish," she said. "Had I not done so, you'd have been a pauper all along. Your worthless uncle would have left every penny to her to be squandered on whatever husband he managed to purchase for his illegitimate spawn. I saved you from that fate, Gerald, by being ruthless and by being willing to take risks. You must be prepared to take them, too, or it will all be for naught."

There was a knock on the door and the butler entered immediately after. The man's normally stoic face was pale and white. "Forgive me, your grace, but there are... well, there is a group of people in the entry hall who are requesting an audience."

"Who the devil is it?"

"The Earl of Montgomery, Lord Highcliff, and there is a young woman, your grace... a Miss St. James."

"Show them in," the dowager duchess said. When the butler gave a stiff bow and retreated to do just that, she glared at him again. "You will have to dirty your hands now... or leave me to handle things as I see fit."

Averston had no notion of what she meant, but he was fairly certain he was about to find out and that things were going to take a turn none of them could be prepared for.

Moments later, the door opened once more and the aforementioned trio entered. Highcliff looked slightly worse for wear, as if the man had possibly had a rough and overindulgent night. Montgomery, as always, appeared quite put together. But it was the woman who held his attention. Even at a distance, he could see her face quite clearly. He could see the uncanny resemblance to the portrait hanging in the hall beyond. And with every step, that resemblance grew more pronounced. If she'd been wearing a robe à la française and had her hair powdered and piled high in the fashion of the past century, she could well have been Veronique.

"I see I am about to be usurped," he said coolly. It was the strangest thing. He almost felt relief. The thing he'd dreaded for so long, that had hung over his head for almost all of his life, had finally occurred. And all he felt was free. Free of the limitations and free of the grasp of the vicious woman who stood beside him.

"You are," Highcliff replied. "But that isn't why we're here. Are you aware that Charles Burney is dead?"

Averston felt the floor shift beneath his feet. Handsome, full of life, desperate to please and desperate to save his nearly destitute family—Burney couldn't possibly be dead. "You must be mistaken. I saw him Saturday night at his sister's debut. He was hale, hearty and perfectly fine!"

"No mistake," Highcliff said. "He was murdered. Strangled with his own neckcloth and dumped in the canal at St. James' Park. He was found floating face down in the water near Birdcage Walk. An area that I believe you are familiar with."

Averston paled then. "Are you here to blackmail me, Highcliff? You know I haven't more than a tuppence of my own... and the woman with you will likely take that, as well."

"We're not here for you," Montgomery stated. "We're here for her. She's the one who ordered the threat on Miss St. James' life, she's the one who ordered Burney to be murdered, and your previous... associates, as well. Nathaniel Barber, Thomas Fairbourne, Samuel Cavender... and others."

Averston sank into his chair, staring at them in horror as the weight of their accusations sank in. He'd known about Nathaniel. Not about her involvement, but he'd thought it was just thieves and a terrible stroke of luck. He turned to his grandmother, saw her haughty glare. But more than that, he saw the note of triumph in her gaze. It was true. She'd said it herself. That she would do whatever was necessary. "You really are the most vile, wretched creature to ever live. You'd do anything to preserve the appearance of our upright name... even doing murder for the sake of it."

The dowager duchess sneered at him. "Of course, I would. I killed her worthless whore of a mother years ago. She begged and pleaded, you know?" The old woman smirked at the young woman as she said it. "She promised to take you and run away, to disappear and never see my son ever again. But I knew that he would never allow that. He'd follow her to the ends of the earth. The only way to stop it was to see her dead, to give him a corpse to mourn. To my dismay, you proved much harder to eliminate. She hid you well."

CALLIE LISTENED TO the words of the wicked, evil woman before her with a dawning horror. By circumventing her mother's instructions, the woman's dying wish, her life had most likely been spared. The theater would have been the first place her father—and the dowager duchess—would have looked. "You have no remorse for anything you've done. Not even for murder."

"And why should I?" the dowager duchess snapped. "I've protected this family. I've provided for Gerald here, ensuring that the trustees would allow him access to the family fortune as he needed it. You think your pretty face and that portrait in the hall will be all that's required to sway them? Think again!"

"The sworn testimony of people who worked in the theater with Veronique Delaine might help with that. As well as documentation from the church where the former Duke of Averston married his mistress prior to the birth of their child will no doubt carry some weight, as well," Highcliff informed her imperiously.

"I don't want the money," Callie said. "I've managed my whole life without it. I certainly don't need it now."

Highcliff blinked at that. "Don't be so hasty, dear girl. Your future husband might wish to have some say in the matter."

Callie looked at Winn. "I don't want it. I really don't. Do we need it?"

Winn stared back at her. "No. We don't. You and I shall be fine without it."

The dowager duchess laughed then. "Oh, my! You are certainly like your mother... in far more than looks it would seem! You've snagged an earl, no less. She managed a duke, but then I suppose she was a bit more alluring than you, and certainly no stranger to seducing men to her will. Pity, Montgomery, I had thought you were smarter than all of this."

Callie ignored her. Instead, she walked toward the desk where the Duke of Averston was seated. "I'm sorry that you've been hurt by all of this, and that you've lost people you cared for. But you needn't worry about the money. I really could not care less. I don't wish to be acknowledged. I don't wish to be recognized as a member of this family. I only want the chance to live peacefully with my betrothed and his wards without worrying that we might be attacked at any moment."

The duke looked up at her. "You can't possibly be serious. No one would simply walk away from that amount of money."

"What would I do with it?" Callie said. "I'm a governess. That's what I do. That's how I even came into this world where my past was finally discovered. If the earl states we do not require it, then we do not require it. But if you wish to have it, in truth, without any hindrances placed upon you, then you will have to support us when we go before the trustees. And something will have to be done with her... an asylum perhaps. It's not the hanging she so richly deserves, but it will at least prevent her from being able to do damage to anyone else."

"I'll see to her," Averston stated. "That I swear to you. And no one will be making any further threats upon your person. I may be cold-hearted, but I'm not a monster. No matter how often she tried to make one of me."

Callie nodded. "I am sorry. I know that you cared for Mr. Burney."

Averston shook his head. "I didn't. Not really. But I could have, given time and opportunity. It will be handled, Miss. St. James. You and your earl, and whatever Highcliff is in all of this, may depend upon it."

Looking at him, Callie realized that the outward persona he pre-sented, the cold and distant facade, was just that. He was a lonely man, made lonelier by the burden of keeping up appearances to suit the Machiavellian woman next to them. Sparing a look at the woman who was, by blood at least, her grandmother, Callie addressed her directly. "There are no words for what you are and what you have done. But there is a hell waiting for you when you die... one that will burn hotter and brighter and longer than any other hell before it. Because you, Madam, have earned the lord's wrath and the devil's attentions with every breath you've taken."

The dowager duchess smiled coldly, her blue eyes pale and hard, glinting like the crystal of the chandelier that hung above them. "My dear girl, you are foolish to think it matters. There is nothing beyond this earth. I've watched enough people die, gasping their last breaths, to know that when a life ends, that's all it does. It just ends. There is no soul, no eternal part of us. There's what we leave on this earth when we are gone and whatever manages to grow in the ground above our rotting flesh. Keep your talk of hell and the devil. Even if he existed, it is not I who should fear him."

Callie's own gaze hardened and she said with all the ice she herself could muster, "Then at least when you breathe your last, you will leave no lingering presence to taint the rest of us."

The old woman laughed. "You aren't just like your mother. There's a bit of me in there, too. Watch that you don't let it spread like a cancer and turn you into what you most despise. Though there would certainly be some poetic justice in that."

"I could never be like you... because I don't see people as a commodity to be bartered and sold and used. I'm capable of actually loving someone. I don't think you ever were." With those final words, Callie turned and walked away from both Averston and the dowager duchess. She marched toward Winn and kept her gaze on him, lest she look back at the horror of what she'd actually come from. As she reached him, she asked, "Will you show me the portrait of my mother? Let me see her."

"Come along," Winn said and offered her his arm.

Callie accepted it and let him lead her out into the corridor. Halfway down, he stopped and they turned toward the portrait of Mademoiselle Veronique Delaine. Callie gasped as she saw it. "She was stunning. She was so beautiful."

"She certainly was," Winn agreed. "And you are just as beautiful... more so to me, because I can see beyond your pretty face. What that horrid woman said to you—you're nothing like her, Callie. You never will be. Your heart is too kind and your soul too filled with compassion for others."

"I don't feel very compassionate right now. I feel angry and even a bit mean. I hate her, Winn. I've been angry before, I've been wounded and hurt and afraid of others... but I've never hated. Not until now," Callie said as she looked up at the portrait of her mother once more. She'd never know her, never know her father, and all of that was because of that awful woman.

"She took so much from you. It's only natural," he offered.

"We don't have to marry so quickly now," she said. "I think, despite what we might have initially believed of him, that the Duke of Averston is not our enemy."

"We're getting married tomorrow... and if you think my decision to marry you and my desire to do so with the utmost haste can be laid solely at the door of those people, then I have done a very poor job of expressing my feelings to you. I want to be your husband. I want you to be my wife. And I'm too impatient to wait."

"Is it really over? Can it really be that simple?" she asked.

Winn looked past her to the door of Averston's study. Highcliff was still inside. "It may be for us. I daresay what's taking place in there at this moment is simple for no one."

⟫⟫⟪⟪

Highcliff approached the desk and stared down at the Dowager Duchess of Averston, who'd seated herself there. "You won't just stop because you've been discovered and told to do so. Those two in the corridor might be naive enough to believe that... but the three of us know better, don't we?"

"What are you suggesting?" Averston asked, never bothering to look at his grandmother.

Highcliff removed a small vial from the inner pocket of his coat. It was something he'd carried for emergencies since his days in France. Being a spy was a terrible way to live. But a captured spy? He'd always vowed to end his own life rather than betray his country. So that small vial of poison had been often replaced and never used, not by him. But it would finally have its day.

"Colorless, odorless, undetectable... and, I'm told, painless," he said, placing the vial on Averston's desk.

"You wish for me to poison my own grandmother?" the duke demanded. "I can't do that... no matter what she deserves."

"Relax, puppy," the dowager duchess said. "He never intended that you should do it. You're offering me the coward's way out, Highcliff?"

"I'm offering you a chance to spare your family more scandal and degradation. After all, who would question a woman of your age passing peacefully in her sleep?"

The dowager duchess picked up the vial. "The sooner the better, no doubt... at least for the lot of you!"

"If you wish to avoid scandal, certainly. Naturally, you will need time to get your affairs in order," Highcliff replied.

"Young man, my affairs have never been out of order," she snapped. "And you may keep your poison. If I do this, it will be on my own terms, by my own means and in my own time." With that, the woman rose.

"You're not leaving here," Averston stated. "Whatever you decide to do, it will occur in this house. I cannot trust you to leave it and do no harm to others."

"I'm to be your prisoner, then?"

"My guest," he corrected. "Since you are so very concerned about scandal, we can hardly call it what it really is. I'll send for you things and have one of the servants show you up."

"As I know the way, that's hardly necessary. You mean to set them to guard me."

"Yes," Averston said. "I do. He didn't deserve to die like that. He was a boy. Young, impetuous, foolish perhaps... but he loved his family and was trying to secure a solid future for them. His mother and sister will be impoverished. Heaven knows what will become of them, and all of it for the sake of your pride and vanity."

Highcliff cleared his throat. "I believe that's my cue to leave. You have only to send word, Averston, if you require further assistance in this matter."

With that, Highcliff sketched a quick bow and then left the room to join Montgomery and Miss St. James in the corridor. "Time to go," he said. "Our work here is more than done. Much, much more."

"And the dowager duchess?" Montgomery asked.

"Averston has it in hand. Trust me," he said.

Montgomery shook his head. "Against all probability, Lord High-cliff, I do. Rather implicitly." To Miss St. James, he added, "Let's go home, Callie."

Chapter Twenty-Two

"**W**HAT HAS OCCURRED between you and Lord Highcliff?"

Callie had asked the question softly. She was very aware of Effie's strange mood. Her friend and mentor had been quiet, but not in that thoughtful way she normally was. Callie could feel the sadness emanating from the other woman.

Effie looked up from straightening the folds of Callie's gown. She appeared startled by the question. "Nothing has occurred between us." The denial was hot and quick. It was also completely untrue.

Callie glanced at her reflection, noting the perfection of the gown Effie had gifted her for her wedding. The lilac silk fit her to perfection. "This was never your gown, was it?"

"It was," Effie said. "But I might have sent it to Madame de Beauchamps for alterations… rather speedy ones. It turned out perfectly."

"He's been your friend for many years," Callie said, switching seamlessly to the previous subject. "But I've often suspected that you feel much more for him than friendship. Is that it?"

Effie sighed. "Our feelings for one another are friendship… and many other things besides. They are so complicated now that I think the words do not exist to express it fully. But complicated or not, we've said and done things to hurt one another, Calliope, and I do not think Highcliff and I can recover from."

"You love him," Callie said. It wasn't a question. It was obvious and perhaps it was only because she'd managed to fall in love herself that she finally understood the truth of Effie's feelings for Highcliff.

"I love him, I hate him, I adore and revile him," Effie stated with a bitter laugh. "We've too much history between us to ever have a future. It is long past time that I face that and perhaps sever ties for good."

Callie took Effie's hands in hers. "Do not make rash decisions that you will have to regret for many years to come. This past week has been impossibly difficult. It's been fraught with danger and uncertainty on so many fronts. Now is not the time for irrevocable actions."

"If not now, when?"

Callie smiled. "You always told me to act prudently, to consider the consequences of any action before taking it. Is it terrible of me to offer that advice back to you?"

Effie moved to the small settee where she'd placed her pelisse and reticule. From within the little velvet pouch, she retrieved a pretty hair ornament of silver and pearls. "You'll need something borrowed," she said. "And no it isn't terrible. You're very wise to throw my own words back at me. I can't refute them without looking like a fool. I shall not make any decisions for a while. Not until things have settled a bit between Highcliff and me."

Callie didn't let out her sigh of relief. Instead, she did a slow and measured exhale. She had not given up hope of a happy ending for Effie and Highcliff. It was obvious that they were terribly in love with one another, once she'd opened her eyes to the possibility of it. It was equally obvious that they were both terribly lost in their own ways.

"If we do not hurry, you are going to be late for your own wedding," Effie pointed out.

She'd insisted that Callie return to the Darrow School for the night, but she hadn't stayed in her old room. Instead, she'd shared a room with one of the other older girls and was now getting ready in their shared chamber. "Winn is supposed to send the carriage."

"It's already arrived," Effie said. "I believe his household is as eager to see him married to you as he is. Are the children really that incorrigible?"

"No... well, perhaps William," Callie admitted with a smile. "But he's very sweet and wants so desperately to love and be loved. He's just full of life and mischief."

Effie smiled, albeit a somewhat watered down version of her normally sunny expression. "He reminds me very much of a little girl I once knew."

Together, they descended the stairs and exited to the waiting carriage beyond. It was a short distance to the church. They'd elected to get married at St. James' Church, Piccadilly as it was the parish church for both of them, though they'd never encountered one another at services there.

After only a few moments, the carriage rolled to a halt and a footman climbed down from the perch on the back of the carriage to help them down. Walking toward the doors of the church, Callie stopped short. The Duke of Averston stood there. What on earth was he doing there? Surely, after everything that had transpired, he hadn't come there to halt the ceremony?

"I've not come to cause problems," he offered, as if sensing her discomfiture.

"Then why have you come?" she asked.

He was silent for a moment. When he finally spoke, he held his hands out in a gesture that could almost be interpreted as pleading. "For good or ill, we are the only family... the only blood... that either of us has. Barring our grandmother, of course, but she's rather a sore subject at the moment."

"I'm going inside now," Effie said. "This seems very much like a conversation that requires a bit of privacy."

When Effie had disappeared inside, Callie turned back to him. "So you wish to... what? Attend my wedding as if we are bosom companions?" she demanded.

He smirked, his lips quirking in a sardonic way. "No. The past is gone, after all, and cannot be reclaimed. But someone whom I... admired... recently expressed an abundance of sympathy for me due to my lack of relations. I find myself wondering if perhaps he was not correct in pitying me so."

"You are here because you wish to be a family?" Callie queried. She couldn't quite fathom it. He'd seemed so cold and distant, so disdainful of any softer emotions or sentimental connections.

"I had hoped we might lay the foundation for a future where we can at least be civil to one another," he said. "But perhaps there is too much muddy water under this particular bridge."

As he began to walk away, Callie wavered. Uncertainty prompted her to call out, "Wait!"

He turned back to her. "Yes?"

"I've never had anyone beyond Effie... even my foster parents when I was a small child—well, they could hardly be classified as kind. They were certainly not what one could consider family. I'm not entirely certain how we should proceed with this."

"I wish I could offer more guidance in the matter. I think, in this instance, we are the blind leading the blind... but I had thought it would be appropriate to attend your wedding. That is what cousins do, isn't it?"

She smiled. "Then perhaps we should go in before my betrothed thinks I have run away."

He shook his head as a soft laugh escaped him. It was a rusty sound, as if it were something he hadn't done very often. "We can't have that. But before we go inside, I wanted to tell you that I have written to the trustees and informed them that I have complete faith in your claim to be the missing child of my uncle and the woman he secretly married, Mademoiselle Veronique Delaine. In short, Miss St. James, I am here to provide my support, little as it may mean to you."

Callie was silent, not really knowing how to respond. Finally, she managed, "I'm sorry."

He frowned, seeming to be suddenly unsure. "You don't want me here?"

"No," she said. "Well, yes. I mean… you're certainly welcome to be here and I'm glad of it. I'm sorry that we've never had an opportunity to be family. I hope, going forward, we will have a chance to rectify that. And I'm sorry that you're losing everything that ought to be yours."

He smiled, though it was but a cautious quirk of his lips. "Not everything. I might not be the wealthiest duke, but I am still a duke. Even poor, I'm still a catch."

She laughed. "I suppose you are."

"If you'd permit me to escort you in? I believe you have a very eager bridegroom awaiting you."

Callie looked at his proffered arm and felt the strangest sense of connection. It was something that had been so terribly absent from her life all along. Placing her hand on his arm, she willed away the tremors that overtook her and allowed him to lead her into the church. Winn waited for her at the altar. Effie stood close by, as did Lord Highcliff. The children were there, as well, having been corralled into behaving by Mrs. Marler who had likely bribed them with the promise of cake.

In all, the ceremony was impossibly brief. They recited the words as the vicar instructed them. They bowed their heads, prayed when told to do so, and simply followed instructions the man knew by rote. At the end of it, they signed the church register and then it was all done. Callie looked up at Winn, at her husband. How could such a momentous event be over so quickly?

"There's a lovely wedding breakfast prepared at the house," Mrs. Marler said and the children all bustled out with her. Highcliff escorted Effie and Averston followed them.

Alone in the church, Winn took her hands. "It's a bit anticlimactic, isn't it?"

Callie smiled. "I don't think it's that. I think… I was honestly too nervous to take it all in. I'm not even certain what we said to one another just now."

Winn laughed. "I'll remind you later. Are you ready to go to your new home? To our home?"

And with those simple words, the reality of it settled in on her entirely. Tears threatened, but they were happy tears. Callie simply felt overwhelmed by the joy she felt in that moment. "I am." She placed her hand in his and let him lead her from the church, ready to embark on a life together.

→≫≫◄◄◄←

THE RETURN TRIP to the house on Piccadilly was a boisterous one. There was much laughter in the crowded coach. Highcliff had produced a bottle of champagne and glasses. The cork released with a loud pop that had them all giggling and then he poured the bubbling liquid, spilling as much on the upholstery as he got into the glasses that he passed around. "I only brought four," he said, passing the last one off to Averston. "That means I drink from the bottle."

"Not for the first time," Effie quipped primly.

"It certainly is not," Highcliff agreed.

Winn noted that the pair seemed to have achieved an unsteady truce despite their recent discord. There was still a noticeable coolness in their interactions, however. It wasn't the temper of the day before. This was something far worse. Still, they were both putting on pleasant faces and attempting to be festive. Averston was stiff, his presence a complete surprise, but not an unwelcome one. He hoped, for Calliope's sake, that she might come to have some sort of relationship with someone she shared blood with.

When they arrived, the smaller carriage bearing the housekeeper and the children had already unloaded and she was bustling the children into the house. The servants were lined up in the entryway, happily cheering as they entered. In the dining room, the wedding breakfast, complete with a cake far too massive for such a small party, had been laid out.

The children were shrieking with glee and William's eyes had glazed over the moment he saw the cake. They'd grabbed Callie's arm and dragged her into the dining room, pointing to every treat with absolute delight.

"Don't worry. They're all going back to the Darrow School with me."

Winn turned to Effie who'd snuck up beside him. "Pardon?"

"My wedding gift to you," she said with a smile. "I'm taking the children with me and they will be returned to you safe, sound and hopefully better behaved by tomorrow."

Winn uttered a silent prayer of thanks. "Miss Darrow, were I not a married man, I would kiss you for that."

"Save your kisses for your bride. Now, eat quickly and make your escape."

With that, Winn made for the dining room and let the festivities begin while anticipating their ending and the wondrous things that would follow.

Making his way to Callie, he pried her hand from William's. "If you want a piece of cake, you'll need to let her go so she might actually cut it."

"No cake. Not yet," Callie replied. "You've eaten nothing of any substance and I won't have you all getting ill." To Winn she added, "You help Charlotte with hers. Claudia, William and I will prepare plates for them and for us."

Winn watched her go, leading the older children. He felt a tug on his hand and looked down at little Charlotte. As always, his heart melted a bit when he did so. Leaning down, he hoisted her up into his arms. "Let's get you some breakfast, shall we?"

"Will you and Aunt Calliope have babies now?" she asked.

His heart thundered in his chest. "At some point, I'm certain we shall."

"Will you still love us if you do?" The question was voiced softly and then her thumb popped immediately into her mouth.

Winn felt his chest tighten. Gently, he pulled her hand away from her mouth and pressed a kiss to her cheek. "Charlotte, my sweet, I can promise you that Calliope and I will always love you... just as we will always love William and Claudia. The three of you brought us together, after all."

Charlotte laid her head on his shoulder. "I love you, Uncle Winn."

Holding the little girl close, Winn looked around the room and realized just how full his life had become. It was chaotic, certainly. But the alternative was something he'd never wish to return to. How alone he'd been, without ever realizing it!

Callie approached him then, carrying two plates while William and Claudia each held their own. "What are you thinking so pensively about?"

"That a little chaos is a small price to pay for this much happiness. Now, let me feed this child before she starts chewing on the furniture," he said, prompting a giggle from Charlotte. Impulsively, Winn leaned forward and kissed Callie softly on the lips.

"What was that for?" she asked.

"Because I can. Prepare yourself, Wife. I mean to do that every opportunity I get," he warned.

"Kissing is disgusting!" William said, making a face from the table where he'd already dug into his breakfast.

Highcliff clapped the boy on the shoulder. "I'll be expecting a revised opinion in a few years."

Laughter was still bubbling around the room as they were all seated around the table together. It was the first opportunity he'd had to ask her about the most curious part of the day thus far. "Averston?"

Callie glanced over at him, all wide-eyed innocence. "What?"

"Do not say what as if you aren't perfectly aware it was unexpected. Did you ask him to come?"

She ducked her head. "No, I didn't. It was rather a surprise for me, as well. But I think it was a nice gesture, don't you?"

"That depends on what will come of it, I suppose."

And she smiled once more, beaming at him in a way that literally stopped his heart. "Family, of course."

He continued to stare at her, simply swept away by how beautiful she was and by how much he simply adored her. Even as the laughter and low hum of conversation filled the room as everyone enjoyed their meal and the celebration of a newly formed family, Winn felt as if they were the only people in the world.

***

THE DOWAGER DUCHESS finished the last letter and placed it on the table. They weren't sentimental goodbyes. She certainly didn't believe in such things. Instead, they were written in the same vein with which she might have conversed with the recipients. Some were snide. Some were belittling. Others still were bossy and manipulative. Those letters represented the last opportunity for her to manage people as she had been doing throughout her life.

Getting to her feet, she draped her shawl about her shoulders and rang for the maid. When the servant entered, not her own lady's maid as Gerald had decided that the woman could not be trusted, but a maid from his own household, she glowered at the girl. "See that those go out in today's post. I'm going out into the garden."

The maid bobbed a curtsy. "Yes, your grace."

Once the girl was gone with the letters, she waited for a few moments and then stepped out into the corridor. The girl would likely have informed the two footmen stationed at the bottom of the stairs to prevent her from leaving the house. If she did go out to the garden, they'd follow her and hover until she could do nothing.

Gerald had left Highcliff's vial of poison in her room lest she change her mind and make use of it. But that was the coward's way out. She'd not lie in a bed, covered in her own vomit when she died. No. She'd die with the same decisiveness and violence with which she had lived. Rather than going down the stairs, she climbed upwards to the next level.

There was a long gallery that looked down onto the ornate marble floor of the entryway. It was lined with the portraits of family members past, those who'd acquitted themselves with honor and duty and a few who had done nothing worthy of the family name other than to die and spare it more indignity. Walking along that narrow hall, she glanced at each portrait as she passed it, until she reached the portrait of her late husband. She'd never loved him, but she'd certainly seen his worth. It was why she'd consented to the match, after all. Being a slightly well-heeled duchess was much preferred to being the wife of even the wealthiest merchant, after all.

Turning away from the portrait, she looked over the railing to the foyer below. From that point, a height of at least three stories, and with her age and blasted infirmities, there was little doubt the fall would kill her. Placing her hands on the banister, she leaned out. A fraction of an inch more, leaning out further and further by the second, until she finally felt the pull of it, the slight dizziness that took her, and then she let herself fall, tumbling over the wooden banister. She never uttered a sound. But the servants shrieked as she hit the floor. There was but a split second of awareness, a brief flash of pain and then nothing. Blackness drew in around her as all the sounds seemed to blur into a distant hum that grew fainter until it, too, was simply gone.

Chapter Twenty-Three

I T WAS STILL early, not quite noon, but Effie and the children were gone. Highcliff and Averston had left as well. The servants had all but vanished, it seemed. Looking around the room, Callie realized that she and Winn were entirely alone.

"Oh," Callie said in surprise. "Well, it certainly cleared out very quickly, didn't it?"

"I think everyone is very discreetly giving us the opportunity to retire upstairs without being observed," Winn offered with a wicked grin.

"Oh... you mean now? During the day?" She was both scandalized and intrigued at the notion.

Winn's lips turned up at the corners as he bit back a smile. "It was the middle of the morning when I had you in my bed yesterday, before we were... interrupted."

Callie felt a blush stealing over her cheeks, one that was not entirely from embarrassment. "So it was. I found it was all so much easier when I didn't have time to think about it... and feel awkward and uncertain... and, well, a bit ignorant."

"You're not awkward. You are graceful and beautiful. Everything about you is perfect," he said, stepping closer to her. In a voice pitched low, slightly rougher than his normal voice and yet strangely seductive, he added, "You may be uncertain but that, and your ignorance which has hampered you not at all thus far, can be rectified easily enough. Come upstairs with me, Callie, away from any prying eyes. Let me hold you again and kiss you... until neither one of us can think at all."

Callie felt the breath rush out of her. "You say such wicked things."

"If you give me half a chance, I'll do wicked things, as well. And I promise you, Callie, you'll love every bit of it. Take my hand," he urged.

She simply didn't have the will to resist him, nor did she particularly have the desire to do so. Placing her hand in his, Callie let him lead her to the expansive staircase and then up the stairs to the suite of rooms they would now share. Before she could even enter the room, he'd lifted her in his arms and was carrying her over the threshold. "What are you doing?"

"It's tradition." he replied.

"You're going to hurt yourself!"

His eyebrows furrowed as he glowered at her. "Are you suggesting, Lady Montgomery, that I am too old or perhaps infirmed to do my duties as a bridegroom?"

"I'm suggesting that you were wounded yesterday morning and I don't wish to see you exacerbate your injuries," she answered primly.

"Ah," he said, crossing the room with long, sure strides until they stood beside the bed. There, he dropped her so unceremoniously that she bounced on the soft surface, a surprised laugh escaping her.

"That was hardly romantic!" she protested as she sat up to give him a mock glare.

"Perhaps not. But was it fun?" he teased.

"Maybe," Callie admitted, her lips pursing as she tried to not grin.

Winn reached for her feet, removing her slippers and tossing them over his shoulders. One struck the door, the other landed atop a table, sending items scattering. And he never even glanced in their direction.

His gaze remained focused on her, and while a smile played about his lips, there was no mistaking that he was quite serious and that his focus on her was intense and unbreakable. Then he was shrugging out of his coat, his waistcoat and cravat following. She'd seen him in less, of course. Only the day before, she'd seen him shirtless. There had been ample opportunity for her to reflect on it, to conjure in her mind's eye the image of him with his firm muscles and sun-darkened skin, along with the dark hair that curled over his chest and narrowed to a thin line as it bisected his abdomen. Recalling that now, along with the incredible sensation of having his body pressed to hers, of his hot kisses as they'd feathered over her neck, she found herself impatient with her own clothing. She felt constricted, restrained by the many layers she wore.

As if he'd read her thoughts, he placed one knee on the bed, levering himself onto it so that he was seated behind her. She could feel the heat of his fingers brushing against her skin as he deftly released the buttons at the back of her gown. When the buttons were freed, the garment fell loose about her shoulders, but he didn't remove it from her. Instead, he slipped his hands inside the silk and began kneading her neck and shoulders. And wherever his hands traveled, his lips followed. Long, soothing strokes of his firm hands to soothe and soft, feathery kisses to seduce.

Callie could do nothing but give herself over to those sensations, her head lolling to one side, baring her neck to him. Then his mouth was there, trailing kisses along that tender flesh that were not at all feathery. They were hot, open-mouthed, punctuated with nips of his teeth and the sensual glide of his tongue over her skin until a breathless moan shuddered from her parted lips.

By the time he had finished, she was utterly boneless, her body limp against his and her head resting against his shoulder as she struggled for some sense of self-control and restraint. "I'm not entirely certain but I think I might be a wanton."

He pressed a soft kiss against the skin just below her ear. "A man can hope," he said, his soft laughter fluttering against her ear.

Callie shivered against him. It was instinct more than anything that had her turning her head, seeking his lips with her own. The kiss was, for lack of a better word, incendiary. She clung to him, even as his arms enfolded her completely. Pressed into the warmth of his body, into the firmness and strength of him, she felt sheltered and protected, cared or in ways that she never had. And even when he shifted them so that she was laid back on the bed and he was stretched out next to her, all without breaking the kiss, she found herself clinging to him. Her arms wound about his neck of their own volition. There was no conscious thought at all. Layers of clothing simply vanished. She was lying beneath him, clad only in her shift and stays, her petticoats and gown having long since been discarded. It was then that doubt reared its head once more.

"You're remarkably skilled at removing women's clothing," she remarked breathlessly as he placed a series of tender kisses along her collarbone.

He lifted his head and met her questioning gaze. "Calliope?"

"Yes?"

"Stop talking. We've no distractions or interruptions this time. There are no hellion children to come barging in the door. Let us enjoy it while we can." He punctuated that statement by pressing a kiss to the arc of her collarbone that left her shivering.

Callie's hands had slipped inside the open neck of his shirt. She was startled by how hot his skin felt, how smooth it was over the firmness of the muscles that rippled beneath her touch. And then there was the tantalizing contrast of the crisp hair that adorned his chest. The contradicting sensations fascinated her. "You could remove your shirt... that was certainly sufficient inducement yesterday."

"Are you trying to seduce me, Lady Montgomery?" he asked with a grin, but he was shrugging out of his shirt, tugging it over his head. It hadn't even landed in a heap on the floor when he tugged the straps of her stays from her shoulders and, within seconds, that garment was sailing to the floor as well.

Callie had no time to think, no time to even survey what was surely masculine perfection. His lips descended on hers once more as his hands drifted over her body, his fingertips brushing her skin through the thin layer of her chemise. Those touches, the drag of the fabric over sensitive flesh, were both soothing and impossibly arousing at the same time. But none of that compared to the moment that his hand cupped her breast, his fingers gently kneading the soft mound even as his thumb brushed over the taut peak. A gasp escaped her and she shivered against him.

Then his mouth was there, his lips closing over that hardened bud of her nipple. While his touch was gentle, her response to it was anything but. She felt as if her entire body had been consumed by heat. It exploded within her, leaving her heart pounding and her blood racing in her veins as she arched against him, helpless to do anything but surrender.

WINN STRUGGLED FOR some semblance of control, for some hidden reserve of control. He wasn't brutish enough to give in to his own pleasure without seeing to hers first. But the sweet abandon with which she responded was more temptation than any man could stand. With every inch of her skin that was bared to him, his need rose, hot and insistent. Stroking his hands over her silken limbs and the softness of her breasts, he savored every shudder and moan from her. Each soft gasp, every time she shivered and arched against him, was precious to him.

And then he slipped the delicate chemise she wore from her entirely, shoving the garment down over her hips until he could tug it free and toss the crumpled linen to the floor. Then she was naked in his bed, her normally alabaster complexion flushed with desire. Winn kissed her again, even as one hand stroked the supple flesh of her thighs, soothing, coaxing, until they parted for him and he could touch her intimately. The heat of her was the sweetest kind of torment, but he endured it as he explored her body, learning the ways to please her. He noted which touches made her gasp, which made her moan, those that made her arch and strain against him. And then he noted those that made her tremble and cling to him as the pleasure built inside her. But it was the sound of his name on her lips as she came for him that would be forever emblazoned on his memory.

He couldn't wait any longer. Moving between her parted thighs, he hitched her knees high on his hips until he was nudging inside her. Slowly, carefully, he eased his way until he could feel the fragile barrier of her innocence. He kissed her, claiming her mouth just as he claimed her body.

When it was done, he went still immediately, struggling to breathe, struggling to cling to the last vestiges of his willpower. And then, slowly, she began to relax again, her hands which had been fisted against his back slowly eased until he felt the splay of her fingers along his sides.

"That wasn't exactly what I anticipated," she said.

Winn smiled then, kissing her again. When he drew back, he replied, "We aren't quite finished yet... and it only gets better from here."

And then he showed her. With slow, rhythmic strokes, he built that perfect tension once more, until she was clinging to him, her back arched and her head thrown back in beautiful abandon. With more patience than he knew he possessed, he held his own pleasure at bay until she crested that peak again. Then he followed her over the edge, thrusting deep, holding her to him as her soft cries echoed around them.

Eventually, the room grew quiet, even their ragged breaths settling until they were just soft whispers of sound. Rolling to his side, Winn pulled her with him. He found himself unwilling to let go of her, even for a moment. And luckily for him, she was content enough to rest easily in the circle of his arms, her head on his chest and one of her hands clasped in his.

Neither of them spoke, but then again, they didn't need to. They'd already expressed the depths of their feelings for one another. There was something almost sacred in that silence as they lay there together, as if to speak would break the fragile spell that held them cocooned together away from the world and all the ugliness it could hold. Eventually, they fell into a deep sleep just that way, entwined together, wrapped in the tangled bedding and one another.

Chapter Twenty-Four

AVERSTON WAS IN his study. Seated in the chair across from his desk was a woman he should have resented, a woman he should, based on everything that had been drilled into him since childhood, despise. And yet, he found himself glad of her presence, glad to have her there in the home where he'd welcomed so very few visitors. In the weeks since his newfound cousin had been married to the Earl of Montgomery, they'd been frequent visitors to his home and had welcomed him on numerous occasions into theirs. It was a strange feeling to find himself suddenly welcomed into a loving family when he'd never known such a thing truly existed before.

That wasn't true, of course. He'd known that people could love and be loved by their families. Charles Burney had shown him that. Thoughts of the young man he'd shared such a brief romantic interlude with often crossed his mind and brought with them a pang of sadness and a wealth of regret. After all, if he hadn't sought to further his association with Burney, then his grandmother would never have begun plotting against him. He'd all but painted a target on Burney with his attention. It was a bitter pill to swallow.

"Are you well?"

Averston looked up, noting the worried expression on Calliope, Lady Montgomery's, pretty face. "Quite well, Cousin. Thank you."

Forcing his attention back to the document before him, he went over it again and again. Yet no matter how many times he read it, he still could not make sense of it.

"You're mad. They'll lock you in Bedlam for this," he said.

"Who would do it?" Calliope asked. "Not my husband. I have his wholehearted approval on the terms. And why on earth would you take such steps when they are so favorable to you?"

He laughed, a rusty sound that he was entirely unused to producing. "This isn't favorable. It's madness. You're giving away the entire fortune."

"No. I'm giving away a large portion of the fortune. There are numerous charities that will get hefty donations, as well as the Darrow School. The mother and sister of Mr. Charles Burney shall be well taken care of... and so shall you. After all, it was your investments and your business acumen which helped to amass that fortune, was it not?" Callie pointed out. "What fairness is there in turning it over to me? Winn has all he can to do to keep up with his own properties and estates. I certainly have no head for business!"

"Yes, but you will have children one day and they should have some access to this fortune."

"Then when my children are born you may include them in your will if you choose," she replied firmly.

Averston looked back at the document once more. "And the trustees agreed to this?"

"The trustees no longer have a say. Once it was determined beyond any doubt that I was the daughter of the 10th Duke of Averston and his wife, they had to release the funds to my husband. And this was undertaken with Winn's full knowledge and approval," Callie explained. "We really do not need the money. And it isn't right that you should have to manage family estates on a sliver of a budget just because my late father was trying to punish his mother."

"Which she deserved," Averston said, his gaze flicking to the black velvet band around his upper arm.

"She did," Callie agreed. "Sign the papers, Cousin. Sign the papers and have all that is dear to you free and clear. There is only one thing I would ask you for."

"And what is that?" Averston asked. He'd give it to her, of course. How could he not when she'd placed the proverbial keys to the kingdom in his hands?

"I would like the portrait of my mother, and I'd like to hire someone to paint a duplicate of the portrait of my father so that I might have both in my own home," she said. "It seems silly to want portraits of people I've never known, doesn't it?"

"No. It doesn't. It's a connection to them that has been denied you for far too long. You've every right to the portraits. Both of them. I'll have them delivered to your home. Not a copy either. The original is yours. I doubt he'd mind it hanging in Hamilton's gallery rather than this one. Heaven knows he shouldn't have to share wall space with the dowager duchess!"

Callie grimaced. "You make an excellent point. Are you well, truly?"

"I am," he said. "I don't expect you to understand the nature of my relationship with Mr. Burney."

"But I do," she said. "You cared for him. And you were deprived of the opportunity to find out if it could have been something more than that. There is nothing so bitter as regret and missed opportunities."

He drew in a sharp breath. "And you do not revile me for it."

"It is not for me to dictate where, how, when or who you love, Cousin," she replied. "I understand the world holds such relationships in contempt, but the world is wrong about many, many things."

Averston signed the documents, sanded them and when they were dry, folded them before passing them back across the expanse of the desk to her. "Thank you for that."

"For what?"

"For accepting me," he said. "I truly had no notion such a thing could exist in my life."

Her kind eyes were filled with sadness and sympathy. "She took so much from me but, in the end, I was spared her influence on me. I didn't have to live under her thumb or being twisted by her to serve her purposes. I think in that way I was very lucky. And I think you underestimate what a truly remarkable person you are to have withstood her influence for as long as you did without caving to it."

"I'm not good, Calliope. I am not kind nor am I warm and loving. I don't possess those traits. I am grateful for your friendship, for your acceptance of me. But that doesn't make me a good man," Averston warned.

She smiled then, rising to her feet. "Oh, Cousin... I don't offer you my friendship. I offer you my love. We are family, after all. And acceptance is simply part of that. As to your character, well, time will tell. But there's something remarkable that happens to us all, Averston, when someone loves us unconditionally. It makes us better, whether we wish it to not."

Averston had no notion of what she was doing as she walked around the desk. By the time he realized that she meant to embrace him, to hug and comfort him as if he were some sort of wounded child, it was too late to stop her. "Sweet heavens, woman! Get hold of yourself!"

She went on hugging him as if she hadn't heard a word he said. It was, in spite of his protests, strangely comforting to him. When at last, she stepped back, she smiled up at him in a manner that could only be described as beatific. "For better or worse, Gerald, we are the only blood relations either of us shall have. At least for a time. I won't stand on ceremony and allow you to be hurt and alone... not when I can help it."

"I'm not one of your charges. You don't get to governess me," he said.

"You'll come to dinner on Friday?" she asked.

"Will you promise not to hug me?"

"I shall promise to refrain from hugging you unless I feel you need to be hugged," she said, still smiling. "It is the best I can do."

He sighed. "Fine. I'll see you at dinner. But I'm having a talk with your husband. You can't just go around hugging men! Good lord. How have you survived this long?"

"But you're my cousin," she protested, even as she picked up her reticule and made for the door. "I will see you on Friday."

She exited the library and Averston was alone again. Alone, but perhaps for the first time in a very long time, he did not feel lonely. And for that, he had Calliope to thank. And Montgomery, Highcliff and Effie Darrow for that matter. Regardless of what they knew about him and his lifestyle, they'd welcomed him openly into their little circle. He wasn't foolish enough to think the entire world would be so understanding, but he was beginning to see that perhaps his grand-mother had used that against him, as well, mocking him and making him believe that no one would ever tolerate him.

Opening the top drawer of the desk, Averston moved several items until he found the letter buried underneath. He'd hidden it there, tucked it away so that he wouldn't have to look at it. So that he wouldn't have to face what had occurred.

Before he could talk himself out of it, he broke the seal and read the neatly penned note.

Your grace,

I do hope this letter finds you well. I wanted to tell you that, following the tragedy of my brother's death, I found some entries in his journal that made particular reference to you. I've hidden these away. It would be a lie to say that I was shocked by these things. The truth is, my brother thought he was hiding things from everyone. But he could never hide things from me. Regardless, there is nothing that my brother could ever have done that would damage my deep and abiding affection for him.

My mother, however, would be quite scandalized by them. But I did want you to know that Charles held you in very high regard. I didn't need his journals to tell me that. I could see it in the way he looked at you. I daresay that his feelings for you were quite beyond what you might have expected. I've no wish to make assumptions, but I thought perhaps you might wish to have these books. They could be damaging in the wrong hands and I can't keep them here for fear my mother would find them. Please send word and I shall have them delivered to you.

Also, I must thank you for attending the ball. It meant the world to my brother and to me.

Sincerely,
Miss Amelia Burney

Averston sighed, folded the letter and tucked it once more into the drawer. It was too late to call on her. But the following day, he'd go to see Miss Amelia Burney. He owed the memory of her brother that.

CALLIOPE STEPPED OUTSIDE the residence of the Duke of Averston and smiled. Directly across the street, she could see her husband walking in the park with Claudia, Charlotte clinging to his neck like a monkey and William running wildly about them, swinging a stick like it was a sword.

How she loved him! How she loved them all. The children had invaded her heart from the very first moment. But she'd been more cautious with him, as any woman should. Crossing the street, she joined them near the gates.

"Now can we go to Gunners?"

"Gunter's," Winn corrected Charlotte with a grin. "And yes, now we may go to Gunter's."

"You spoil them shamelessly," Callie said, smiling as he leaned forward and kissed her cheek.

Winn set Charlotte down. "Go chase your brother down and tell him we're going for ices." With Charlotte gone, he leaned in once more, and this time, he didn't kiss her cheek. He kissed that delicate and so very tender spot just below her ear which made her shiver. Then he whispered, "When we get home, I'm going to spoil you, too."

Callie spared a glance for Claudia who was watching Charlotte closely as she chased down William. "I believe that's called despoiling," she whispered back. "Now behave."

He grinned at her. "It's only called that if we're not married. Being married, it's referred to as being an attentive and thorough husband."

There was no chance for her to reply. William and Charlotte returned then, running at them like wild things. "I want a coconut ice!" Charlotte said.

"And I want lemon!" William cried.

"You shall all have the flavor of ice that you desire so long as the shop has it," Callie offered smoothly. Claudia held Charlotte's hand. William skipped ahead of them and she and Winn were left to walk behind.

"It's all rather remarkable, isn't it?"

"What?" Callie asked, looking up at Winn, noting his somewhat bemused expression.

"You were mere yards away from me. Growing up at the Darrow School, you were yards away from me, from Averston, from the place that should have been your home."

Callie shrugged. "There was more than distance separating me from all those things. Class can be an unreachable barrier. I was a servant... beneath notice. Or at the very least that is what I was being reared for."

"Hardly that," he said. "You could never be beneath notice. But whatever strange stroke of fate brought you into my world when it did, I am grateful for it," he said, his tone heartfelt and weighted with

About the Author

Chasity Bowlin lives in central Kentucky with her husband and their menagerie of animals. She loves writing, loves traveling and enjoys incorporating tidbits of her actual vacations into her books. She is an avid Anglophile, loving all things British, but specifically all things Regency.

Growing up in Tennessee, spending as much time as possible with her doting grandparents, soap operas were a part of her daily existence, followed by back to back episodes of Scooby Doo. Her path to becoming a romance novelist was set when, rather than simply have her Barbie dolls cruise around in a pink convertible, they time traveled, hosted lavish dinner parties and one even had an evil twin locked in the attic.

Website: www.chasitybowlin.com

Printed in Great Britain
by Amazon